Sweat glistened on her waxy face.

Then her expression changed, her eyes filling with acceptance—the same resignation Parker had seen on his father's face before he'd committed suicide.

Denial rose inside him. Desperation screamed through his skull. He had to do something. He had to stop her somehow. But the slightest move, and Brynn would die.

Her trigger finger moved. Knowing it was hopeless, Parker dived off the bed toward Brynn, flinging himself toward her with all his strength. But she was too far away.

The gun went off, the suppressor silencing all but a quiet pop.

Buried Secrets: Three murder witnesses, one deadly conspiracy

Dear Reader,

Desperate people do desperate things. Sadly, for millions of troubled teenagers, this often means running away from home. But life on the streets can be brutal, exposing these vulnerable children to dangers they never expected, making it difficult to stay alive.

That's the premise for my Buried Secrets trilogy. Fifteen years ago three desperate girls left their homes for different reasons, then banded together for protection on Baltimore's treacherous streets. But their lives grew even more precarious when they witnessed a murder committed by a powerful man—who saw them watching. Terrified, they hid the evidence, changed their identities and went on the run to survive.

Now fifteen years later, a chance photograph in the newspaper exposes their identities, blowing the lid off their secret past—and sending each on a journey more dangerous than they'd ever dreamed.

I hope you enjoy their stories as they face down their pasts, confront enemies determined to silence them permanently and finally find the love they deserve.

Happy reading!

Gail Barrett

GAIL BARRETT

Fatal Exposure

To Brynn —
Thank you for
inspiring my
heroine's name! :)

Gail Barrett

HARLEQUIN® ROMANTIC SUSPENSE

Recycling programs
for this product may
not exist in your area.

ISBN-13: 978-0-373-27827-5

FATAL EXPOSURE

Copyright © 2013 by Gail Ellen Barrett

This edition published by arrangement with Harlequin Books S.A.

For questions and comments about the quality of this book,
please contact us at CustomerService@Harlequin.com.

Printed in U.S.A.

GAIL BARRETT

always knew she'd be a writer. Who else would spend her childhood grinding sparkling rocks into fairy dust and convincing her friends it was real? Or daydream her way through elementary school, spend high school reading philosophy and playing the bagpipes, then head off to Spain during college to live the writer's life? After four years she straggled back home—broke, but fluent in Spanish. She became a teacher, earned a master's degree in linguistics, married a Coast Guard officer and had two sons.

But she never lost the desire to write. Then one day she discovered a Silhouette Intimate Moments novel in a bookstore—and knew she was destined to write romance. Her books have won numerous awards, including a National Readers' Choice Award and Romance Writers of America's prestigious Golden Heart.

Gail currently lives in western Maryland. Readers can contact her through her website, www.gailbarrett.com.

To Binnie Syril Braunstein,
a woman with a generous heart.

ACKNOWLEDGMENTS

I'd like to thank the following people for making this story possible: Tom Beck, Chief Curator and Head of Special Collections at the University of Maryland, Baltimore County, for answering my questions about photography; Lesley Gourley of Photohunter, whose phenomenal talent is matched only by her kindness; Wesley Wilson, Chief of the Enoch Pratt Free Library, for taking time out of his busy schedule to give me a personal tour of the library and helping me find a place to hide the film; Loni Glover, Karen Alerie and Mary Jo Archer for their invaluable input and support; and last—but definitely not least—an enormous and heartfelt thanks to Officer Robert Carusone of the Baltimore Police Department for not only answering my endless questions, but letting me tag along with him on patrol. Rob, you're the best! Any mistakes are definitely my own!

Chapter 1

Cold case detective Parker McCall tightened his grip on the newspaper, his gaze riveted on the photo of the woman splashed across the *Baltimore Sun*'s front page. She could have been any affluent shopper strolling out of the pricey art gallery—her long, glossy hair tumbling over her shoulders, the collar of her woolen coat turned up against the brisk November wind.

Except for her wary eyes.

The eyes of his brother's murderer.

The eyes that had eluded him for fifteen years.

He lowered the newspaper to his cluttered desk, the laughter and banter of the detectives beyond his cubicle receding to a distant buzz. Then, hardly breathing, he tugged his wallet from the back pocket of his jeans. Working as carefully as a scientist handling nuclear material, he extracted a worn, faded photo and placed it alongside the page.

For several excruciating seconds his gaze lingered on the image of his younger brother, his heart making its usual lurch of guilt and remorse. Sixteen years old, his cheeks badly hollowed, his body wasted by his addictions, Tommy leaned against a graffiti-sprayed wall near Baltimore's Inner Harbor, one emaciated arm slung over the waiflike girl at his side.

The girl Parker had failed to find.

Until now.

He shifted his scrutiny to the girl, taking in her sparrow-thin legs, the baggy sweatshirt dwarfing her scrawny frame, her unruly mop of auburn curls. Then he homed in on her eyes—bleak, world-weary eyes aged far beyond her years.

He sliced his gaze back to the woman in the newspaper. She was still petite, still thin and older than the adolescent slouching against the wall beside his brother, but he'd stake his life they were the same.

A punch of adrenaline making his heart sprint, he skimmed the article accompanying the front-page spread. Amazingly, the woman appeared to be B. K. Elliot, the world-renowned photojournalist whose exhibit had opened in the gallery that week—a photographer so reclusive that no one had known what she looked like until now. But rumors about her abounded, claiming she was everything from a traumatized war vet to a homeless woman disfigured in a fire.

Regardless of her identity, B. K. Elliot's photos had caused a worldwide furor in recent years, winning both the Pulitzer for Feature Photography and the prestigious Hasselblad Award. Even Parker, who didn't know squat about photography, could recognize the power in her unsettling work. Her photos chronicled the poverty and violence of street life with brutal, disturbing honesty.

A perspective only a former runaway could know.

The exhibit's grand opening had been mobbed, bringing the bigwigs out in droves. Parker's boss, Colonel Hugh Hoffman—head of the Baltimore Police Department's Criminal Investigation Division—had attended, along with his political mentor, Senator Alfred Riggs. Helping teen runaways was one of the Colonel's signature projects, as was this cold case squad.

Parker switched his attention back to his brother's photo, dead sure now that the women were the same. But he needed expert verification, something more concrete to go on before he charged off to find her, half-cocked.

Rising, he scooped up the paper and photo, then strode past the cubicles lined up like jail cells, the stained industrial carpet muffling his steps. Too late he spotted his supervisor, Sergeant Enrique Delgado, manning the coffee machine near the exit. Unable to avoid him, Parker slowed.

"Packing it in already?" Delgado asked, his shrewd gaze taking in the newspaper tucked under Parker's arm. "Another exhausting day at the desk?"

Parker tamped back a spurt of dislike. Nicknamed "Iglesias" for his slick Latin looks and equally slick reputation with women, Enrique Delgado had transferred in from the gang unit when his cover got blown and a shoot-out nearly claimed his life. But Delgado considered this assignment in the cold case squad beneath him—an opinion he voiced freely, not earning him any friends. Even worse, the Colonel had put Delgado in a supervisory position over far more seasoned homicide detectives, like him.

Brownnosing and office politics at their worst.

Parker leveled him a glance. "Yeah, I threw my back out opening a drawer."

"Whoa, you should put in for hazard pay."

Ignoring Delgado's mocking laughter, Parker shouldered open the door to the hall and strode out. Still scowling, he bypassed the snail-paced elevator and made a beeline for the stairwell, then started up the scuffed steps. Technically, he should have informed Delgado about what he'd found. Like it or not, the man was his supervisor—and with Parker's dubious family background, he couldn't afford to buck the rules. But there wasn't a chance in hell Delgado would let him investigate his brother's death. And Parker had worked for too many years to forfeit his chance at the killer now.

Silencing his protesting conscience, he exited the stairwell two floors later and veered to the nearest desk. "Is Sudhir in?" he asked the secretary, who was speaking into her headset. She nodded and waved him past, her silver rings glinting in the fluorescent light. Seconds later, Parker knocked on the police artist's door.

"Come in," Sudhir called out, and Parker strode inside. Balding, his paunch encased in a purple-and-black Baltimore Ravens T-shirt, Sudhir Singh had been a fixture in the precinct for years, long enough to warrant an actual office, albeit with a Dumpster view. He worked a variety of jobs, from sketch artist, interpreter and polygraph test administrator to unofficial coordinator of the underground football pool.

"Hey, Sudhir. You going to the game this weekend?" Parker asked by way of greeting.

"You bet." Parker waited, muzzling his impatience until Sudhir wound down his tirade over the team's most recent trade.

"So whatcha got?" he finally asked.

Parker handed him the old photo. "This girl. I need you to age her fifteen years. I think I've found a match."

His attention instantly snagged, Sudhir swiveled toward his equipment, motioning absently in the direction of an empty chair. "Have a seat."

Parker pulled up the chair and sat. Leaning forward, he locked his gaze on the monitor as Sudhir scanned the photo in. Several seconds later his brother and the runaway girl appeared on the computer screen.

Parker's belly went taut, the sight of his drugged-out brother prompting the usual litany of self-reproach. He should have done more to save him. He should have found a way to keep him in rehab until he'd stopped destroying his life. He should have fired that useless counselor and searched for someone better, someone who could have found a way to reach him and convince him to stay off drugs.

And he definitely should have anticipated the effect their father's arrest and suicide would have on Tommy, who'd idolized the man.

But Parker had failed. Only twenty-two himself when his father had died, he'd been too busy salvaging his budding career, trying to prove that he wasn't corrupt. And his brother had paid the price, running away from home, embarking on a downward spiral of drugs and crime that had ended with his senseless death.

But the day he'd lowered Tommy into the ground, Parker had made a vow. He wouldn't fail his little brother again. He would bring Tommy's killer to justice, no matter how many years it took.

His jaw clenched, his gaze still trained on the monitor, Parker watched intently as Sudhir cropped his brother from the photo and zoomed in on the runaway girl. Several keystrokes later, her face filled the screen, those big, bleak eyes a sucker punch to his gut. She didn't look like a killer; he'd give her that much. She looked too young, too fragile, too harmless. But the most innocent face could hide the blackest heart.

"She looks about twelve, maybe thirteen, in this photo," Sudhir said, tapping on his keyboard. "So her current age would be what, late twenties?"

"Yeah, that sounds about right."

Switching to his mouse, Sudhir began using his age progression software to manipulate her face. "What kind of lifestyle does she lead? Does she smoke? Drink? Do drugs?"

"Drugs, probably." Tommy had only hung out with other addicts toward the end.

"Any other factors that might affect her appearance, like wind or sun damage to her skin?"

Parker frowned. As a runaway, she would have been exposed to the elements. But if this woman really was B. K. Elliot, her photos sold for thousands of dollars a pop—meaning her impoverished days were long gone.

"Let's say she was homeless during her teen years," he decided. "Then she straightened herself out and led a comfortable life after that."

Sudhir added a trace of squint lines around her eyes. "Weight gain?"

Remembering the photo in the newspaper, Parker shook his head. "No, keep her thin."

"How about her hair?"

He studied the image taking shape on the screen. "Longer, just past her shoulders. And not so curly, just kind of wavy and thick."

Sudhir continued to work, slowly transforming the scrawny adolescent into a young woman. A hauntingly beautiful woman with a small, feminine nose, elegantly sculpted cheekbones and an intriguingly sensual mouth.

His heart picked up its beat.

But what held him captive were her eyes. Her eyes were wounded, poignant, raw, as vulnerable as those of the children in B. K. Elliot's photos. They drew him in, sparking a sense of awareness, an oddly tumultuous feeling that went beyond the usual pull of attraction for a pretty face.

Something he had no damned right to feel for a woman involved in his brother's death.

With effort, he shrugged off the erotic tug.

A moment later, Sudhir released the mouse and sat back, his chair creaking under his weight. He tilted his head to the side. "So what do you think?"

His heart beating triple time, Parker unfolded the newspaper and held it beside the monitor. Sudhir's low whistle echoed his thoughts. She was a dead ringer for the woman in the paper.

"I think I found a killer."

Now he just had to track her down.

Unable to shake the weariness dogging her steps, Brynn Elliot pushed open the door of her Alexandria, Virginia, row house and trudged inside, the blast of heat enveloping her like a caress. God, she was tired. A week spent scouring the streets of New York City in near-freezing temperatures had done her in—and not just physically. It was the suffering that got to her, the violence inflicted on those defenseless kids. And with every passing year the runaways looked younger, more cynical, their wounded eyes filled with more despair.

A feeling she'd once known well.

Knowing better than to go down that depressing track, she deposited an armload of newspapers and junk mail on the kitchen table, then shrugged off her backpack and coat. She couldn't change her past. And neither could she rescue the world. She simply tried to reveal the truth, to force the hypocrites in high society to face the hell of these children's lives—lives *they* had betrayed and destroyed.

Really not wanting to revisit those old ghosts, she glanced at her kitchen phone, its voice mail indicator light flashing like a squad car at a crime scene, then crossed the kitchen to the pantry and rummaged for a can of soup. The messages would be from Haley, a perpetual worrier, needing to make sure she was safe. Brynn had missed her weekly call-in thanks to the punks who'd stolen her cell phone in New York. She was just glad they hadn't noticed her camera. The photos she'd taken of the child prostitutes on Rockaway Boulevard were her most poignant work to date.

Impatient to upload the photos to her computer and get to work, she dumped the soup into a bowl and stuck it into the microwave to heat. Then she called up her voice mail, set the phone to speaker and started disposing of her junk mail so she could clear a space to eat.

"Brynn, are you there? Pick up the phone," Haley's voice called out. Smiling at her friend's predictability, Brynn tossed several pieces of junk mail into the bin.

"Brynn, it's important. Call me right away," her next message said.

"I will," Brynn promised. "Just give me a minute to eat."

"Why haven't you called me back?" Haley demanded in her third call, desperation straining her voice. "Where are you?"

"In New York, fighting off a couple of punks." Punks she could have evaded in her younger days. Making a mental note to buy another disposable cell phone, she threw another batch of junk mail away.

"For God's sake, Brynn, why haven't you called me? Have you seen the newspapers? I need to talk to you right away."

The papers? Brynn paused, unable to ignore the urgency in Haley's tone. Had there been something about Haley's shelter in the newspaper, something that might have exposed her friend's identity—a danger they all had to avoid?

Worried now, she dumped the rest of the advertisements in the trash, then started flipping through various newspapers, not sure what she was supposed to find. But whatever it was had to be important. Haley wasn't the type to panic. She dealt with high drama daily in her shelter for runaway, pregnant teens. And if she was worried enough to call…

Her sense of anxiety growing, Brynn riffled quickly through the papers, scanning political columns and crime reports to no avail. Then a front-page photo caught her attention, and everything inside her froze.

It was a photo of *her*.

The room swayed. She gripped the table for balance, a dull roar battering her ears. Someone had photographed her leaving the art gallery—and splashed it across the front page. *But how had they figured out who she was?* She hadn't spoken to a soul. She hadn't even greeted the clerk. She'd simply strolled through the exhibit, discreetly checking the status of the photos, then left.

Praying she was somehow mistaken, she unfolded the newspaper, but there wasn't any doubt. The headline screamed "Mystery solved!"

Reeling, she sank into a chair. How could this have happened? She'd been so blasted careful. She'd lived off the grid for years—always on the move, constantly changing her identity with her friends' help. Even later, when her career had taken off, her agent had stepped in, doing all the promotional work, accepting awards on her behalf, never revealing what she looked like or where she lived. Now a momentary lapse—a quick visit to the gallery to estimate her earnings—had destroyed everything. And all because she'd needed to upgrade the plumbing in Haley's shelter before she left on her New York trip.

Staggered by the scope of the disaster, she pressed her fingers to her forehead and tried to think. A reporter had connected her to her work. Exactly how he'd done that, she didn't have a clue. But the media would come out in droves. Her stepfather would hunt her down. So would Tommy's killer, assuming he was still around.

Panic bubbled inside her. She was in danger. Terrible danger. So were Haley and Nadine.

No, Nadine would be all right. She'd called a few weeks back to let Brynn know she was heading to Peru, journeying to the remote mountain villages to do her charity medical work. No one would find her there.

But Haley… She was in D.C., running her shelter for pregnant teens—an open target for their enemies.

If she wasn't already dead.

Horrified, Brynn leaped to her feet, knocking over her chair as she lunged across the kitchen and grabbed the phone. Punching in Haley's number, she prayed that she'd pick up.

The doorbell buzzed.

Her heart slammed to a halt. She snapped her gaze to the door. The microwave dinged, but she didn't move, didn't breathe, her attention riveted on the front door.

She'd never met her neighbors. No one knew she lived here except for her agent and two close friends. And the media couldn't have found her this fast. She'd bought the historic row house under a fictitious name.

The doorbell sounded again.

She silently disconnected the phone. All her senses hyperalert, she tiptoed across the kitchen to the door, careful not to make any noise. She stopped and held her breath, afraid that even the tiniest hitch would give her away. Then she put her eye to the peephole and peeked out.

A man scowled back. She took in his black, slashing brows, the harsh angles of his chiseled face, the dark beard scruff shadowing his jaw. He was tall, in his late thirties with a strong neck roped with tendons, shoulders as thick as planks. His midnight hair was short, his mouth drawn flat. Authority radiated from him in waves.

A siren went off in her head. *A cop.* After a lifetime spent on the streets, she could detect one from a mile away. And even wearing a leather jacket and jeans, everything about this man screamed *police*.

Her thoughts whirling wildly, she backed away from the door. He must have seen her come home. He'd probably staked out her house and lain in wait. It was too late to pretend she wasn't here.

Struggling not to succumb to panic, she fled back into the kitchen, jerked her coat off the chair, and pulled it on. Then she threw her backpack over her shoulder—just as the doorbell sounded again.

"Be right there," she called out, hoping to buy some time.

Knowing she only had seconds to escape him, she sprinted into her small home office, grabbed her laptop from the desk and shoved it into her bag. Then she knelt at the fake outlet beside the bookcase and pried the cover off. She pulled out her stash of emergency cash and added it to her bag, then took out her semiautomatic handgun and slammed a magazine home. She stuck the weapon into an outside pocket of the backpack and rose.

She spared a glance at the basement but instantly ruled it out. A cop wouldn't come alone. He probably had a partner watching her backyard—including the tool shed, which hid the cellar door. But she'd prepared for this day, planning for this very emergency. She'd even bought an end-unit row house with this disaster in mind.

Moving faster now, she raced up her stairs to the guest bathroom, which faced the open side. Then she quietly pushed open the window and peered out into the night. The crisp autumn air chilled her face. The rumble of traffic from the D.C. beltway hummed its usual background noise. A car sped down the street, its headlights sweeping over the ancient oak tree growing beside the house and illuminating the edge of her fenced backyard.

No sign of a partner. Maybe the cop really had come alone.

Unwilling to take that gamble, she scrambled onto the windowsill and grabbed hold of the nearest branch, the cold bark rough on her palms. But then she paused, her throat tightening with a stab of regret. She was so damned tired of this. She'd spent more than half her life on the run, always looking over her shoulder, always terrified she'd be found. This row house was her first-ever attempt to set down roots, to lead something even remotely resembling a stable life. To have a garden, a home. To put an end to the utter loneliness that plagued her in the dead of night.

But she knew the futility of dreams. Predators ruled this brutal world, a lesson she'd learned at an early age. And unless she wanted to end up a victim, she had to go on the run again.

Jerking herself back to reality, she adjusted her grip on the tree branch and swung onto the sprawling limb. She crept to the trunk, inched over the huge, gnarled branch that stretched across the neighbor's fence, then dropped onto their patio, landing with a muffled thud. Her heart racing, she darted into the bushes and hid.

For several seconds, she didn't move. She held her breath, listening for signs that she'd been seen. But no one looked out the neighbor's window; no one raised an alarm. Praying her luck would hold—and the cop would keep ringing her doorbell instead of circling around to the back—she snuck through the shadows to the gate and pressed her ear to the wood.

Silence.

Now came the risky part.

She had to exit through the alley. There wasn't another way out. And she couldn't wait; once that cop realized she'd fled the house, he would search the entire block—including the neighbor's yard. She just hoped that if he *did* have backup, his partner would be watching her back door instead of the neighbor's gate. Her pulse quickening, she cracked it open and peeked out.

She swept her gaze down the dark alley, over hulking, tomblike cars, past trash cans looming like phantoms in the quiet night. The cold wind gusted, ruffling the bushes lining the fence, but she seemed to be alone.

Now or never.

She sucked in a breath, swung the gate open wider and stepped through.

Just as the shadows leaped.

Chapter 2

Parker lunged at the woman fleeing the alley, a hot rush of fury fueling his steps. There was no way she was going to escape him, not after all this time.

"Stop! Police!" he ordered, grabbing hold of her shoulder. But she whipped around, catching him off guard, and rammed her elbow into his head. He staggered back at the sharp jolt of pain.

Damn. The woman could fight. But she still wasn't getting away.

Shaking off the pain, he surged forward as she took off running again. His feet jackhammered the pavement. Shadows zipped past in the night. He put on a burst of speed, catching up to her in a few long strides. Then he went in low, locking his arms around her waist, and lifted her off her feet.

She twisted and thrashed like a hellcat, but he gritted

his teeth and held on. She dropped her pack, snapped her arm back in another attempt to hit his head, but he ducked and dodged the blow. Then she reached down and grabbed his leg, jerking it up hard between hers. Thrown abruptly off balance, he fell.

Hell. He'd underestimated her. *Again.*

But this time he didn't let go. He dragged her down to the pavement with him, his arms encircling her waist. She landed atop him a split second later, knocking the breath from his lungs. Grunting, he rolled over and pinned her down.

"Stop fighting," he rasped between gasps for air. "I'm not trying to hurt you. I'm a cop. I only want to talk."

But she wriggled and squirmed, managing to pin his arms to his sides with her legs before he anticipated her intent. Then she jabbed her finger beneath his ear, sending excruciating shocks sizzling through his nerves. White spots danced behind his eyes.

So she wants to fight dirty. He could accommodate that.

Furious now, he wedged his elbow around her knee and swung his leg over hers. Then he flipped her over, reversing their positions, and trapped her between *his* legs.

For a moment she went stone-still, her uneven gasps filling the night. Then she shoved against his chest, struggling to gain enough space to break free. But he bore down even harder, using his strength to make her stop.

Sweat trickled down his jaw. His breath seesawed in time to his careening pulse. After several futile attempts to get loose, she stopped.

"Let me go," she cried, her voice muffled.

"Why should I?"

"I can't breathe."

He didn't doubt it. He probably had seventy pounds of muscle on her.

"Please." She sounded desperate now. "I...can't... breathe."

Unable to dredge up any sympathy, he steeled his jaw. "You going to talk to me this time?"

"Yes."

"Somehow I'm not convinced."

"I said I would." Despite her predicament, temper flared into her voice.

"You'd better," he warned. "You try running again, and I'll hurt you for real this time."

Too ticked off to trust her, he rolled over, positioning himself on top. Then he lumbered to his feet, every sense alert in case she tried to bolt. When she didn't make a move to join him, he reached down and pulled her up. Still breathing heavily, he pulled out his badge and held it up.

"Put your hands behind your back and face the fence," he ordered, taking out his handcuffs.

"What?"

"You heard me." He wasn't taking the chance that she'd run again.

"You have no right—"

"You ran from the police. You assaulted an officer. I don't need another reason than that. Now turn around— unless you'd rather I haul you in."

Her gaze flicked to his shield again. Even in the dim light trickling from a nearby row house, he could see her jaw go tight. But she turned and held out her hands.

Wary of another trick, he slapped on the handcuffs, the delicate feel of her wrist bones causing a startling burst of heat in his blood. *Forget that she's a woman,* he reminded himself as she whirled around. She was a possible suspect in his brother's death, the last one to see him alive, not a potential date.

He picked up the backpack she'd dropped and searched it, unearthing the small, semiautomatic pistol she'd hidden inside. Still keeping one eye on her, he removed the magazine. "You have a permit for this?"

Her gaze skidded away.

"Right." *Stupid question.* He stuffed the gun in his jacket pocket and shouldered the bag.

Her eyes returned to his. "So what do you want?"

"Information."

"You always tackle people you want to question?"

"You always climb out the window when someone knocks on your door?"

Her mouth pressed into a line.

"I'm here about Tommy McCall," he added.

"Never heard of him."

He ignored that blatant lie. "I suggest you remember fast, or I'll haul you in for questioning."

"On what grounds?"

"On the grounds that you have information about his death."

"I told you. I don't—"

"Your choice." He pulled out his cell phone and punched in a number, calling her bluff.

She held his gaze. Several tense seconds ticked past. "Fine," she bit out at last. "You want to waste your time on useless questions, ask away."

He pocketed the phone with a nod. "Let's take this inside."

Her jaw dropped. "You expect me to let you into my house?"

"You expect me to believe you won't run if we stay out here?"

"How can I? You've got me in cuffs."

"I'll take them off inside."

Her lips tightened again, distrust flickering in her shadowed eyes. Then she huffed out an angry breath. "All right, but I'm telling you, you're wasting your time."

Her staccato steps rapping the pavement, she led the way up the alley and back through her garden gate. Parker hugged her heels, unwilling to give her an inch of space. He wouldn't put it past her to try to escape again, even wearing the cuffs. They crossed a tidy, fenced-in patio and entered her house through a mudroom door. Once inside, he snapped on the overhead light.

He continued trailing her into the kitchen, his gaze still glued on her rigid spine. They came to a stop, and he spared a glance around, noting the empty soup can on the granite counter, the time flashing on the microwave. A wrought iron table occupied one corner, one of its chairs overturned. A stack of newspapers covered the glass.

The top one showed the photo of her.

"All right," she said. "Undo my hands."

"You promise to answer my questions?"

"I said I would."

He tossed her backpack onto the pile of papers and pulled out the handcuff key. He reached for her wrists and unlocked the cuffs, trying to ignore the alluring fragrance of her skin and hair. Then he stepped back, his impatience mounting as he waited for her to do her part.

But she took her time, righting the chair, taking off her peacoat and draping it over her bag. At last she turned to face him, and for the first time, he got a close look at her in the light. She was even more attractive than he'd expected with her wary green eyes and delicately winged brows, that long tumble of auburn hair. Her mouth was evocative and full, her high, sculpted cheekbones tinged with pink. A smattering of freckles dusted her small nose.

He raked his gaze down the rest of her—over her small, high breasts and slender waist, slim hips clad in low-slung jeans—and his heart began to thud. She looked amazingly like the computerized image, but softer, far sexier. More vulnerable.

Vulnerable? He stifled a snort. He wouldn't make that mistake again.

He returned his gaze to hers. And without warning, a sense of awareness arrowed between them, a deep tug of sexual attraction that caught him unprepared. His belly went taut, a rush of adrenaline accelerating his pulse.

He bit back hard on a curse. Wrong time. Wrong place. Definitely the wrong woman, considering she was a potential suspect in his brother's death. And her reaction didn't help—her eyes going wide and dark, her breath catching on a quiet gasp, impacting him even more.

"I need a drink," she muttered, spinning around.

That made two of them.

"You want one?" she asked, as if reading his mind. "Whiskey?"

"Sure."

Disgusted by his reaction, he looked away, but the sudden memory of her silky skin prompted another swarm of heat in his blood. So she appealed to him. So she attracted him in a gut-deep, visceral way. He had to nip his reaction fast.

Needing some mental distance, he took stock of her kitchen, the pile of junk mail spilling out of her trash can evidence of a recent trip. Then he shifted his gaze to her front room. This room was messier, more lived-in with magazines scattered about and a red sweater tossed over a chair.

But what really snagged his interest were the photographs arranged in groups on the walls. He eyed the nearest group—half a dozen shots of abandoned buildings in various stages of ruin—and couldn't help but be impressed. She used shadow and light to bring out subtle details—peeling paint, ripples in the weathered wood—to stunning effect. The photos pulled at something inside him, managing to churn up his emotions somehow. The buildings seemed alive, forlorn, haunting in their decay.

Even more intrigued now, he slid another glance her way, watching as she fixed their drinks. Then he edged farther into the room, lured to a series of photos of street kids this time. The mix of innocence and betrayal in their faces slammed through him like a kick to the solar plexus, impossible to ignore. She'd captured the shocked dullness in their eyes, the weary cynicism made more poignant by their startling youth.

This woman didn't hold back. She didn't soften the brutal truth. She depicted these traumatized children with an intimacy born of experience, demanding a response.

Making him wonder who had betrayed *her*.

That rogue thought stopped him cold. He didn't care about her past. He didn't care why she'd run away from home. Somehow, this woman held the key to Tommy's death—and he couldn't forget that fact.

Turning back to the counter, he picked up the tumbler she slid toward him and took a sip, savoring the smoky taste as the whiskey glided down his throat. He arched a brow, impressed. "Great whiskey."

Her gaze tangled with his, another wild flurry of attraction tripping his pulse. This close, he realized her eyes weren't the green he'd originally thought, but a deep, slate-blue with golden starbursts—definitely unique. But nothing about this woman was typical, from her lethal street-fighting skills to the outrageous talent in her work.

Another flush suffused her cheeks. "I don't see the point of drinking rotgut."

She could definitely afford better, given the money her photos earned. "So what does the *B* in B. K. Elliot stand for?" he asked.

"Brynn."

That suited her. "Why the pseudonym?"

"I like my privacy."

"Most people would like the fame."

"I'm not most people. Is that a crime?"

No, but running away from a murder scene was. Not to mention pulling the trigger. "I'm here about Tommy McCall," he said, getting down to business. "What do you know about his death?"

"Nothing. I don't know him. I told you that before."

Right. He set the tumbler on the granite counter,

pulled his brother's old photo from his wallet and slapped it down. Then he pinned his gaze on hers.

For a minute she didn't move. Her gaze dueled with his, her chin rising to a stubborn angle as she held her ground. But several seconds later, she broke the connection and glanced down.

The color leached from her face. Freckles stood out on her suddenly pasty skin. Fearing she might faint, he lunged across the kitchen toward her, but she grabbed the edge of the counter and held on. Emotions rippled through her eyes—shock, sorrow, regret.

"Where..." Her voice cracked, and she cleared her throat. "Where did you get this?"

"He'd hidden it under the insole in his shoe." The shoe Parker hadn't inspected until years after his death, when he'd finally decided to dispose of his brother's clothes.

He'd shown the photo to the head of C.I.D.—by then, his boss—who'd agreed to reopen the case. But no one remembered the girl by then. The witnesses who'd seen her leaving the crime scene had long since disappeared. And after several futile months spent canvassing the area, the case was closed for good.

Until now.

He pocketed the photo again. "How well did you know him?"

Her hand shaking, she picked up her glass and drained it in a single gulp. "Not well. We talked a few times on the streets, that's all."

He doubted that. Tommy wouldn't have kept that photo unless she'd mattered to him. But she'd barely been a teenager back then, far too young to be his girlfriend. More of a kid sister, perhaps?

"So what can you tell me about his death?" he pressed.

"Nothing." She shook her head, the expression in her eyes still stark. "Why? What does it matter now? Why start asking questions after all this time?"

"His murder's never been solved."

"A lot of murders aren't."

True enough—which was exactly why the Colonel had made the homicide cold case squad his priority, allocating extra resources to the cause. But Parker had another reason to care. He took out his business card and tossed it down.

Brynn picked it up. Her face went pale again. "You're Tommy's brother?"

So Tommy had mentioned him.

"And you're a detective." She sounded numb.

"That's right. And I want answers. Justice." No matter how many years had passed.

"Justice?" She barked out a strangled laugh. "That would be a first, coming from a cop."

Parker gritted his teeth, her accusation striking home. His father had been corrupt. He'd paraded as a model citizen—a decorated cop, a dedicated family man—until a police corruption sting had stripped away the illusion, exposing the truth behind the facade.

And then he'd taken the coward's way out, leaving Parker to deal with the mess.

His suicide had ripped the family apart. Parker's mother had turned into a recluse overnight. Tommy had rebelled, lashing out against authority and getting hooked on drugs. As a rookie cop, Parker had battled to save his job, struggling to live down his father's reputation and prove that he wasn't the same—a doubt that still lingered in the force, even after all this time.

"All cops aren't bad," he said, his voice flat.

"No?" She jerked her chin toward the photos on her walls. "Ask those kids about that. They can tell you about *justice* and the police."

"They'd be wrong."

"The hell they would." Her voice turned hard. Her gold-flecked eyes darkened to steel. "They know a lot more about reality and *justice* than you do. They've been raped, robbed and abused—and the police don't give a damn. The only thing they care about is power."

He wanted to argue the point, to defend the life he led. But he didn't have to justify his choices to a suspect. He hadn't done anything wrong. And he wasn't about to let her distract him from his brother's murder—the reason he was here.

"You're entitled to your opinion," he said.

"That's generous of you," she snapped back. "But it's not an *opinion*. It's a *fact*."

"Regardless, I still want answers about my brother, and you were the last person to see him alive."

Her head came up. "What makes you think that?"

"Witnesses saw a girl matching your description running from the scene."

Her jaw went slack. "You think I *killed* him?"

"Didn't you?"

She stared at him, her eyes sparking with a kaleidoscope of emotions—shock, outrage and something else. Something that looked a lot like guilt. "Get out."

"The hell I will."

"I said to *get out* of my house."

"Not without answers."

"I don't have anything to say to you."

"I think you do."

"You're wrong."

Not this time. This woman knew what had happened to Tommy. And after fifteen years trying to find her, he wasn't going to back off now.

"Tommy was your friend," he fired back. "He carried that photo around in his shoe. Doesn't that mean anything to you? Don't you care what happened to him?"

"Care?" A flush climbed up her cheeks. Fury vibrated her voice. "You're the one stirring up trouble. You're going to get people hurt—innocent people who don't deserve this grief. So don't accuse me of not caring!"

"What people?"

Her lips pressed tight.

"What people?" he demanded again, stepping forward.

She bumped against the counter and stopped. "Leave me alone."

"I can't."

"Everyone has a choice."

And he'd made his. He'd vowed to bring his brother's killer to justice, and he refused to stop until he did.

A shrill ring split the air. Their eyes waged a silent battle, tension crackling between them as the telephone rang again.

"I need to get that," she said.

Parker braced his hands on his hips and scowled, refusing to let this drop. If Brynn hadn't killed his brother, she knew who did. He'd bet his badge on that. He *had* to convince her to talk.

The telephone trilled again. When he still didn't

move aside, she arched a brow. "Do you mind? I really need to answer the phone."

Cursing the interruption, he expelled his breath. "All right, but we aren't done yet." He inched aside, just far enough to let her pass.

Her eyes blazed into his for another heartbeat, her anger clear. Then she turned and stalked past the microwave to the phone. He lowered his gaze to her hands, tensing in case she tried to incapacitate him somehow. But in a move so quick he could hardly believe it, she lunged sideways, scooped up her coat and backpack then upended the table into his path.

He sprang into instant action, stumbling over the chair as he raced after her into the hall. But the split-second delay had given her a head start. She flung open the basement door and dove inside, slamming the dead bolt home just as he grasped the knob. Her steps thundered down the basement stairs.

Swearing, he rattled the knob. He rammed the door with his shoulder, but the thick wood didn't budge. Unable to believe his stupidity, he ran through the mudroom and out the back, searching the shadows for a cellar door. But there was no other exit in sight.

The toolshed. He sprinted to the corner of the patio. The side gate hung ajar. He raced through it to the sidewalk, then stopped and turned in circles, scanning the empty street. The cold air brushed his face. A siren wailed in the quiet night.

But B. K. Elliot was gone.

Chapter 3

Brynn pressed deeper into her neighbor's doorway, her entire body trembling as Parker McCall stalked into view. His sharp steps bludgeoned the brick sidewalk. Fury radiated off his powerful frame. He veered to a black pickup truck beneath a streetlight and leaped inside, then gunned the engine and roared away. Brynn held her breath, plastering herself flatter against the building as the truck's high beams swept past. The engine's growl faded into the night.

Thoroughly rattled, she sank to the cold cement door stoop and pulled her knees to her chest, her frenzied pulse refusing to slow. What a disaster. Her picture had appeared in the newspaper. Her identity had been revealed. Now Tommy's brother had found her.

And he was a *cop*.

Still quivering wildly, she dragged in a breath, knowing she'd had a lucky escape. Everything about Parker McCall reeked of danger—from the jut of his steel-hard jaw to those penetrating black eyes that scrutinized every move. He was too smart. Too determined. And there wasn't a chance he'd leave her alone.

Especially since he'd found that photo in Tommy's shoe.

She hugged her knees even tighter, unable to stop the rush of guilt. Seeing that photo had demolished her composure, bringing back a swarm of regrets. Of all the mistakes she'd made in her life, of all the hell that she'd been through, the day Tommy had died had been the worst.

And it was all her fault. That sweet boy was dead because of her.

Struggling against a tide of emotions, she forced the memory aside. She couldn't wallow in the past. God knew, she'd berated herself for it enough. She had to keep moving forward, keep the truth from coming to light and survive.

But how? Parker would never give up. And if he'd already found her, the others couldn't be far behind.

Her head jerked up at that thought, and she frantically scanned the street—but nothing moved, no one emerged from the row houses, not even a car drove past. Easing out a tremulous breath, she willed herself to calm down. Nadine was safe in Peru for now. But she had to warn Haley fast. And she'd better prepare her agent, Joan Kellogg, for the upcoming media storm.

Wishing she still had her cell phone, she grabbed her backpack and rose. Since her agent lived only a few streets over in the heart of Old Town, she would head to her house first. She could notify Haley from there.

Aiming another quick glance at the shadows, she scurried down the empty street. The cold wind blew, sending goose bumps down her neck, and she buttoned her coat to block the chill. Returning to the area had been a gamble, she'd known that. And it was one she'd been reluctant to take. After Tommy's horrific murder the three runaways had made a pact—they'd hidden the evidence, changed their identities and vowed never to reveal what had happened, no matter what the cost. Then they'd gone on the run, moving from city to city for years. Eventually Nadira—Nadine now—had moved to New York to get her medical degree. Haley had come to D.C. to start her shelter for pregnant teens.

And although she'd hated to admit it, Brynn had been lonely. Haley and Nadine were the only family she had. She'd finally decided to chance it, figuring enough time had passed. As long as she steered clear of her stepfather, as long as she avoided the Baltimore neighborhood where Tommy had died, no one would notice her here.

Her agent had helped. Although Joan didn't know the details of Brynn's past, she'd guarded her identity religiously from the start of her career—arranging her exhibits, appearing for her in public, hiring publicists to manage her website and promote her work. And no matter how intense the pressure—even after those awards—she hadn't cracked.

That safety had been an illusion, of course. Parker McCall had just proven that. Now she had to keep him from discovering the truth about Tommy's death before more innocent people got killed.

She darted across the road, the buzz of traffic on the distant beltway mirroring the hum of dread in her nerves. A few blocks later, she reached her agent's house. Still hurrying, she unlatched the iron gate, crossed the small brick patio and rang the bell. Then she shot another furtive glance behind her, relieved that no one had followed her here.

So far.

Seconds crawled by. Her agent didn't answer the door. Frowning, she stepped back and surveyed the windows, for the first time noticing that the house was completely dark. But Joan had to be in town. She always notified her clients before she took a trip. Brynn reached for the bell again, then froze.

The door was hanging ajar.

Inhaling swiftly, she spun around. The bare trees creaked overhead. The withered mums along the walkway bobbed in the frigid wind. Dried leaves tumbled across the bricks, skittering into the corners like frightened mice.

Longing for her missing handgun, Brynn nudged the door open wider and peered inside, but she couldn't make out much in the dark. Her heart stuttering wildly, she crept through the open door.

She waited a beat, letting her eyes adjust to the shadows, the destruction making her reel. Tables had been overturned. Glass covered the floor, remnants of the once-majestic chandelier. Ruined paintings lay amid the shards, their canvases slashed, their gilded frames snapped apart like twigs.

Appalled, she glanced from the ruined foyer into the equally demolished parlor and tried to breathe. Joan's row house had been trashed. But why? By whom? And where had her agent gone?

Her nerves coiling, she crept inside, inching past

the staircase into the kitchen while trying not to make any noise. But broken plates crunched under her feet. Smashed groceries littered the floor, adding to the senseless mess. Behind the kitchen, Joan's office looked as if a tornado had touched down with desk drawers ripped out, papers flung everywhere, her computer gone....

Along with any client information she'd stored on the machine.

Beating back a rush of panic, Brynn prowled back through the foyer and up the staircase, the creaking steps erupting like gunshots in the tomblike house. She checked out the vandalized guest rooms, then continued down the hall to the master bedroom and peeked inside.

Her heart skidded to a halt. Joan lay sprawled across the rug in a sliver of moonlight, her eyes closed, her skin sheet-white, her body completely still. Blood glistened on her forehead and matted her silver hair.

Horrified, Brynn raced to her side and knelt. "Joan." *Oh, God.* The sixty-year-old woman was far too pale.

She seized her agent's wrist, feeling frantically for a pulse. Each tortured second seemed an eternity before she detected a feeble throb. She was alive. But barely. Her skin felt much too chilled.

Desperate to save her, Brynn leaped to her feet, lunged for the telephone on the bedside table and punched in 9-1-1. "I need an ambulance. Fast," she added, reciting the address. "Joan Kellogg. She's been attacked in her bedroom upstairs. Hurry." Ignoring the dispatcher's questions, she hung up.

Then she dropped to Joan's side again. "Hold on," she pleaded. "Help's coming soon. I promise."

Her agent's eyes fluttered open. "Brynn?"

"Don't talk. Save your strength. An ambulance is on the way."

Joan fumbled to grasp her hand. "Man…black hair. Snake tattoo. Looking for you…"

"Shh. It doesn't matter now. Just rest." Her throat thick, Brynn gently squeezed Joan's hand, her clammy skin icing her heart. Where was the blasted ambulance? Why was it taking so long? She shot a desperate glance at the window, despising the feeling of helplessness—and guilt. Joan had nearly died because of her.

But who had sent the attacker? How had he connected Joan to her? Had he seen Brynn's photo in the newspaper—or found her some other way?

"Go. Hide," Joan croaked out.

"Forget it. I'm not leaving you alone." She'd already caused enough problems. The least she could do was stay and protect her from further harm.

A siren finally cut through the night, and Brynn expelled her breath. *Thank God.* The ambulance was nearly here. But then a new worry thrummed through her nerves. In seconds help would arrive—along with the police. They'd ask questions she couldn't answer, scrutinize her in ways she couldn't afford.

"Go," Joan whispered again, echoing her thoughts.

Red lights flashed outside the window. The siren abruptly cut off. Torn by conflicting emotions, Brynn dithered over what to do. She couldn't abandon Joan, not after her agent had worked tirelessly to safeguard *her.* But neither could she stay and let the authorities find her here.

"Hurry…"

"All right," she agreed. "I'm going. But I'll call you

later at the hospital. And I'm hiring you a bodyguard. I'm going to make sure you stay safe."

Voices filled the house. Footsteps hammered on the stairs. Her pulse accelerating, Brynn grabbed hold of her backpack and rose, then glanced around the room. The house had to have a servant's staircase. All these historic places did. Spotting a likely cupboard beneath the eaves, she rushed around the bed, flung the small door open and stepped inside. Then she felt her way down the unlit staircase, a steep, narrow passage with shallow treads. Seconds later, she emerged in the office behind the kitchen and exited the house through the alley door.

But as she blended back into the night, questions whirled through her mind. Who had attacked her agent? Not Parker McCall; he didn't fit Joan's description of that snake tattoo. And she couldn't see him harming a woman, no matter how angry he became. She'd repeatedly provoked him in the alley, and he'd refrained from hurting her.

So someone else was on her trail, someone connected to her past. Someone ruthless enough to harm an innocent woman to get to her.

The gang leader she'd witnessed executing his prisoner? Her stepfather? She shuddered hard at the thought. Both men were equally vicious. Both men wanted her dead.

And now that her photo had appeared in the newspaper, they would hunt her down, endangering anyone connected to her. And who would be next? Haley? The pregnant teenagers in her homeless shelter? Some unsuspecting passerby on the street?

But what could she do to stop them? If she spoke out,

if she broke her vow of silence and revealed the truth, she would jeopardize Haley and Nadine.

They were in danger either way.

She lurched to a stop at a lamppost, leaning against it as she caught her breath. What about Parker McCall? Was there any chance she could trust him?

Her nerves coiled tight at the thought. She'd be crazy to trust him. The police always banded together. He'd take her stepfather's word over hers.

Wouldn't he?

She started jogging again, slower this time, thinking back to Parker's face—his hot black eyes, the harsh angles of his square-cut jaw, that unbridled masculinity that seeped from every pore. The man was dangerous, all right, disrupting her equilibrium in ways she absolutely couldn't afford. And he clearly wouldn't give up. She hadn't missed the resolve in those lethal eyes.

But behind that determination she'd caught a glimpse of something deeper, darker. *Pain.* He'd cared about his brother. Really cared. And that gave her a glimmer of hope. If she could control the information he gleaned, if she could keep him from unearthing too much too fast, maybe, just maybe, she could use him to her own end.

And maybe she was insane. Trying to control Parker McCall would be like riding one of those sixty-foot waves she'd seen in Hawaii one year. If she made a mistake, if she had one second of inattention, he'd crush her alive.

But did she have a choice?

Spotting a convenience store with a pay phone, she stopped. For several long moments, she debated what to do, combing through her options again. But one thing was crystal clear. She could no longer run. Joan's attack had guaranteed that. She had to protect the people around her.

And Parker was her only hope.

Her belly tensing, she checked her watch. Less than two hours had passed since he'd left her house. She doubted he'd be asleep.

She was right. Two short rings later, his deep voice rasped into her ear. "Parker McCall."

She inhaled to steady her nerves. "It's me. Brynn Elliot. If you still want information about your brother, I'm willing to make a deal."

Silence crackled across the line. "What kind of deal?" he finally asked.

"I'll tell you in person."

"When?"

"Tomorrow at noon." She named a coffee shop on Wisconsin Avenue in Georgetown. "And Parker…"

"Yeah?"

"Come alone or the deal's off." Not waiting for an answer, she hung up. Then she leaned back against the glass and hugged her arms, feeling as if she'd just stepped onto a high wire over Niagara Falls. She'd taken the plunge—but she had to watch her step. She had to keep her head, stay in control and somehow manage Parker McCall.

Before the killers destroyed them all.

Parker drummed his fingers on the round metal table inside the coffee shop the following afternoon, convinced that he'd lost his mind. He'd spent years obeying the rules, trying to live down his father's legacy and prove he wasn't corrupt. And now he was risking everything to meet with a possible suspect in his brother's death—his reputation, his integrity, his job.

And for what? He already knew that he couldn't trust her. She'd lied about knowing his brother. She'd fled the scene of his murder, evading the authorities for years. Even now she was trying to conceal her identity, eschewing money and fame to escape scrutiny, a sure sign she had something to hide.

And those bizarrely cryptic comments she'd made... What "trouble" was he stirring up? Which "people" was he going to hurt? Nothing but vague innuendos designed to paint her as the victim and throw his investigation off course.

He gulped down the last swallow of his espresso and checked his watch, then let out a huff of disgust. *Insane is right.* He'd risked everything he believed in to meet her here, and she would probably stand him up. If he had any sense he'd walk out now, turn the case over to his supervisor like he was supposed to and let him investigate Tommy's death.

But then the door swung open and she strolled inside—her pale cheeks flushed, a black watch cap pulled low over her head, exposing the flame-colored ends of her hair. She still wore the same black peacoat and jeans and had that pack slung over her back. Her gaze collided with his, and she paused.

And damned if another shock of awareness didn't sizzle through him, like a lightning strike to the gut. His heart began to thud, a predatory kind of alertness pinning him in place. And judging by her startled expression, she felt it, too—this crazy, magnetic pull.

Disgusted at his reaction, he scowled back. Appealing or not, B. K. Elliot was a suspect—one he wouldn't underestimate again.

Her flush climbing higher, she gave him a cautious nod, then wove through the half-empty restaurant, heading his way. But as she neared, he picked up on subtle details—the slight crease puckering her brow, the grooves bracketing her lush mouth, the nervous way she kept scanning the restaurant like a criminal on the lookout for cops.

Even more on guard now, he watched as she took her seat. "You want something to drink?" he asked.

"No, thanks. I'm good." She pulled off her cap and shook out her tousled hair, the deep hues catching the light. Then she glanced around the room again.

"Something wrong?"

"What? No." Her gaze danced back to his.

She's lying. The woman looked spooked as hell. "Something's bothering you."

"I just thought… You came alone like I told you, right?"

"I said I would."

"And you didn't tell anyone you were coming here?"

He cocked his head. "You accusing me of something?"

"No, I…I just needed to be sure."

He worked his jaw, a spurt of annoyance hardening his voice. "I don't lie, and I don't go back on my word. I said I'd come alone, and I did. Now if you've got a problem with that, I need to know because I didn't come here to play games."

Hesitating again, she searched his eyes. "I thought someone followed me here. I guess I was wrong."

Not quite willing to believe her, he crossed his arms. "So what's this about a deal?"

She lifted her backpack onto her lap, pulled out a five-by-seven black-and-white photo and placed it on the table, facing him. "This girl. Do you know who she is?"

He dropped his gaze to the photograph. The girl was young, barely pubescent, with long blond braids and troubled eyes. He frowned, trying to place her, certain he'd seen her before. And then the memory broke loose. "You had a photo of her on your wall." She'd been part of the homeless group.

"But you don't know who she is?"

"Should I?"

Her eyes studied his again. She gave him a nod, as if he'd confirmed something she already suspected, and put the photo away. "Her name was Erin Walker. She was a runaway. I met her on the streets a while back."

"Pretty young for a runaway."

"Some kids grow up fast."

He couldn't argue that. "Go on."

"The police picked her up and took her home. Her parents have money, so they sent her to High Rock Camp. It's a place in western Maryland for at-risk youth, one of those wilderness therapy camps where they do survival things."

"I know it." In fact, his boss, Colonel Hugh Hoffman—the head of Baltimore's Criminal Investigation Division—had founded the camp. And it was a great success, generating so much positive publicity it had spawned imitations in other states. It had even impressed Senator Alfred Riggs, who'd taken the Colonel under his wing, fast-tracking his political career.

"Erin died there," Brynn continued. "Supposedly she committed suicide."

Parker nodded, not sure where she was going with this. "Sad, but it happens."

"Not usually with a girl that young."

He studied her blue-gold eyes. "You don't believe she committed suicide?"

"I don't know," she admitted. "I don't have enough information to decide. Her family refuses to talk. She was a minor, so the papers didn't release any details. And the camp doesn't want bad publicity, so they've kept everything hushed up."

Realization dawned. "You want me to look into her death."

"I'd like to see the autopsy report and photos so I know for sure."

"Why?"

Her gaze slid away. "She was a friend. I feel I owe her that much."

Another lie. Or at least not quite the truth. "Forget it."

Her gaze shot back to his. "What?"

"I said no deal."

"You're turning me down? But why?"

"Because you're lying."

"I'm not—"

"The hell you aren't. You've been lying to me from the start. You said you didn't know my brother. You claimed you didn't know about his death. You even lied about answering that phone. I doubt anything you've told me is true."

Her eyes went dark. A flush returned to her cheeks. "You can't expect me to tell you everything. I don't even know you."

"Baloney. If you didn't think you could trust me, you wouldn't have proposed this deal. Now you're sitting here telling half-truths while I've played straight with you from the start."

"I'm not lying about this girl."

"You expect me to believe that?"

"Believe what you want. But I'm telling you the truth, as much as I can right now."

Neither of them moved. Her angry gaze stayed locked on his. Tension crackled between them, like the atmosphere before a lightning storm.

And despite all evidence to the contrary, despite knowing that she'd lied, he realized she'd played him to perfection, piquing his interest about the case. Because if there was any chance she was right…

He shook his head, hoping the motion would dispel this lunacy and knock some sense back into his muddled brain. "It doesn't matter. There's still no deal."

"But—"

"It's not my case. It's not even in my jurisdiction." Questioning a potential suspect was one thing. But meddling in someone else's investigation… "I'd be putting my job on the line—and for what? To satisfy your curiosity? To pass some sort of litmus test you've devised?"

"You want *me* to take a risk and tell you about Tommy's death."

"It's not the same."

"You're right. It's not the same thing at all. You might lose your job. *Big deal.* I've got more to lose than that."

"Like what?"

"Nothing." She shrugged into her coat and stood. "Forget it. I should have known I was wasting my time talking to a *cop*." She swung her backpack onto her shoulder and stalked across the room, then shoved open the door to the street.

Parker scrambled to his feet, his temper mounting as he strode after her outside. What right did she have to test him? *She* was the suspect. He was the one who couldn't trust *her*.

He caught up with her on the sidewalk and grabbed her arm. She wheeled around and glared back. "Get your hands off me."

"Or what? You'll elbow me in the head again?"

"I should."

"Try it, and I'll haul you in right now."

"Fine. Go ahead and arrest me," she countered, shaking her slender arm loose. "But you'll never find out the truth that way."

"You don't think I can find out what happened to Tommy without your help?"

"I know you can't."

Parker opened his mouth to argue, but damned if she wasn't right. She knew what had happened to Tommy. She'd been the last one to see him alive. For all he knew, she'd pulled the trigger and run away.

But what if she hadn't? What if she'd witnessed his death instead—and knew who the killer was? What if innocent lives really were at risk? Could he give up the chance to find out?

And what if—God forbid—that kid at the camp had been murdered as Brynn thought? He'd sworn to obtain justice for victims, no matter how inconvenient the case. He was duty-bound to pursue the truth.

But he *couldn't* do what she'd asked. Hoffman would fire him in a heartbeat—unless his supervisor canned him first. Delgado would leap at the chance.

"Look." He tried to sound reasonable. "It's not that I don't want to help you—"

"Then do it." Her eyes challenged his. "You've heard my conditions. I've told you what I want."

He glowered back, his anger rising again. She didn't understand what she was asking. Bad enough that he'd gone behind Delgado's back, contacted the possible suspect in his brother's death and then failed to bring her in. That alone could get him suspended. He could try to spin his involvement and claim he was verifying Brynn's identity before handing the case to his boss. No one with half a brain would buy the excuse, and for all his faults, Delgado wasn't a fool. But it might be enough to let Parker escape with a reprimand instead of losing his badge.

But he had no business snooping in Erin Walker's file. It wasn't his case. It wasn't in his jurisdiction. This wasn't even remotely connected to him.

Even worse, the kid had committed suicide at Colonel Hoffman's camp. If the C.I.D. chief learned Parker was meddling in his affairs—and sharing sensitive information with an unauthorized civilian—there wasn't an excuse on earth that could save his ass.

But he'd already failed his brother once. He couldn't renege on his promise to find his killer, too.

And he'd searched for this woman for fifteen years. He'd be damned if he'd turn her over to Delgado, then be forced to beg his supervisor for details about his brother's case.

Or worse, have him refuse to reopen the investigation and forfeit forever his chance to learn the truth.

Quelling his protesting conscience, he sighed. "All

right. Give me your phone number. I'll look into it and get back to you."

She shook her head. "We're doing this together."

"Forget it. You'll just have to trust me."

"I'm not that big a fool."

"And yet, you expect *me* to trust *you*."

Her mouth turned flat. She folded her arms, her eyes still trained on his. And his grudging respect for her rose. She certainly wasn't a pushover.

"You can't come with me," he said. "Her records won't be stored here. They'll be in Washington County—the district where she died. I'll have to make some calls, see if they'll fax a copy to me." Assuming he could fabricate a plausible excuse—without his boss finding out. "But I'll meet with you as soon as I'm done. That's *my* final offer."

Still looking reluctant, she managed a nod. "Fine. Then we have a deal?"

She offered him her hand. Against his better judgment, he enfolded it in his, the soft, feminine feel of her skin sending a spasm of heat through his blood. Grimacing at his reaction, he dropped her hand and stepped back.

He'd definitely lost his mind. This woman was a danger on too many levels to count. And he'd better keep his wits about him if he hoped to survive.

Chapter 4

Parker wasn't naive. He understood the need to bend the rules at times if it contributed to the greater good. The problem was, once a man crossed into that gray zone, once he'd blurred the distinction between right and wrong, it became harder to redraw the line.

His father had proven that.

But now here he was, following in his doomed father's footsteps. Because he couldn't sugarcoat his actions. He was breaking the rules, pure and simple— the one thing he'd sworn he would never do.

For Tommy's sake, he reminded himself fiercely. He was fulfilling his promise to his brother and trying to find his killer the only way he could.

But that still didn't make his actions right.

Cursing the predicament Brynn had put him in, he neared the homicide office—with its fax machine—and glanced around. So far so good. No one had paid any attention to him. Now he just had to slip inside, grab the faxed file off the machine and leave before anyone noticed him here.

Then he'd be done with this subterfuge for good.

He shot another glance back, then stepped inside the room, the din of ringing phones and voices quieting a notch. Getting the file faxed over hadn't been easy. The overworked people out in western Maryland hadn't wanted to fill his request. He'd had to use the Colonel's name, claiming that Hoffman wanted to check the file because of the potential scandal involving the camp. Three uncooperative people later, Parker finally found someone willing to take the time to send him the file without verifying it with Hoffman first.

Picking up his pace now, he walked past the massive copier, dodged the boxes of paper stacked beside a work table and headed to the fax machine. But a rail-thin, silver-haired woman blocked his path, and his hopes instantly tanked. Terry "The Terror" Lewis. The woman who'd investigated his father. She stood beside the machine, holding a sheath of papers—the file he'd requested, no doubt.

His luck had just run out.

She turned at his approach. "Detective McCall," she rasped in her smoker's voice. She held up the papers, disapproval on her narrow face. "What are you doing with this?"

So she'd noticed his name on the cover sheet. He couldn't feign ignorance now. "Just checking the records for a case."

She frowned, her ice-blue eyes nearly level with his. "Which case is that?"

Parker hesitated. Technically, he didn't have to answer. Even though she outranked him, Lieutenant Lewis worked in the Criminal Intelligence Section and wasn't in his chain of command. But she was smart. She'd sniff out any deception fast. Better to sprinkle in enough truth to allay suspicions—and lend his answer legitimacy in case she checked.

"Susie Smith."

"The kid they found in the Inner Harbor?"

"Right. She was from Emmitsburg. I'm checking the deaths in that general area during the past few years to see if they're related."

She arched a brow. She wasn't buying it—and he didn't blame her. The connection was ludicrous at best. And this woman was nobody's fool. Even Hoffman knew better than to take her on.

But he had no choice but to brazen it out. He held out his hand for the file. "Do you mind?" he asked.

She hesitated, obviously reluctant to give it up, then she slapped it into his hand. Parker tucked it under his arm, giving her what he hoped was a civil nod.

He didn't dislike Terry Lewis, exactly. He probably would have admired her if she hadn't tried to bring him down. She'd simply been doing her job, conducting an investigation into a towing scam in the traffic unit when she'd stumbled on an even more serious plot. Defying warnings from her fellow officers, she'd persevered, bucking the hallowed Blue Code of Silence to uncover the truth, that his father had extorted payments from prostitutes and drug dealers—a revelation that had rocked the force.

But then she'd turned her suspicions toward *him*.

And, suddenly, the irony struck him hard. After all

those years obeying the rules, after all those years trying to show that he wasn't the criminal she believed,
he was finally proving her right.

Without a word, he exited the room. Then he strode
down the corridor to the stairwell, feeling her eyes bor-
ing into his back. *Perfect.* He'd managed to get a copy
of the dead girl's file. But he'd tipped off Terry "The
Terror" Lewis.

He hoped it was worth the cost.

"This had better be worth it," he muttered an hour
later as he slid into the seat across from Brynn. He'd arranged to meet her at a fast-food restaurant far enough
from police headquarters to avoid running into anyone he knew.

"Problem?" She tilted her head to meet his eyes.

"No." *Not yet.*

"Then you got the file?"

"I got it." But at what price? Trying not to dwell on
the potential fallout, he set the folder on the table and
opened it to the top page.

She leaned across the booth to see. Her hair swung
loose, strands a deep, rich shade of chestnut mingling
with the brighter red. And despite his vow to keep his
distance, her beauty swamped his senses; the subtle,
feminine scent of her seeping into his blood. His gaze
dropped to her sensual lips, the elegant line of her slender throat, then back to her glorious hair. He curled his
hands, the urge to plunge them through that thick mass
hard to resist.

She turned her head, and her gaze collided with his.
Her eyes turned wide and dark. Her breath made an
audible hitch, propelling his pulse into a sprint. So she

wasn't immune. So she felt the chemistry zinging between them—no matter how inappropriate it was.

He jerked his gaze back to the file and frowned. It didn't matter what she felt. Having an affair with her would be nuts. He'd already jeopardized his career by accessing the deceased girl's file. He wasn't about to compound his mistakes by getting involved with a potential suspect, too.

No matter how intriguing she was.

"Here's the initial incident report," he said, his voice brusque. "She was reported missing at 7:00 a.m. They searched the grounds, and a staff member discovered her body by the old Forest Service lookout tower at ten. The paramedics arrived at 10:35."

"That seems slow." She kept her eyes averted, but pink patches flagged her cheeks.

"The camp's in the mountains, in an isolated area." He checked the report. "The ambulance came from Emmitsburg. That's the nearest place. But it wouldn't have made a difference either way. She was already dead."

He waited while Brynn finished reading, still struggling to keep his gaze from her. Then he continued paging through the report—the interviews with the other children, statements from the counselors, the psychologist's assessment of her mental state.

A picture gradually emerged. Erin Walker had gone to bed at 9:00 p.m., the official lights-out time. She'd been in her cabin an hour later, presumably asleep, when the counselor had conducted her nightly rounds. No one had guessed her plans. No one had seen her leave her bed. No one had even missed her until reveille the following day. She'd been quiet in the days preceding her disappearance, but her behavior hadn't raised any flags. In fact, she'd been making progress—staying off drugs, participating in the camp activities, cooperating with the other kids.

Parker turned to the photos next. The first shot showed the historic lookout tower in a clearing amid the trees. Next came a close-up of the dead child's body— her skull bashed, her neck at an unnatural angle, the ground around her saturated with blood.

His stomach pitching badly, he spared a glance at Brynn. Every trace of color had fled her face. "Are you all right?"

She swallowed visibly, her eyes huge in her bloodless face. "It's not easy to look at."

"Death never is." The wooden tower was ninety feet high, and the girl's small body bore the results of her fall. "It's worse when you know the person. The photos I saw of my brother..." He shook his head, not wanting to revisit the horror of Tommy's death. But those crime scene photos still plagued his nightmares, even after all this time. Not to mention the gruesome memories of his father's death.

Brynn's gaze connected with his. And the compassion in her eyes caused a sliver of warmth to unfurl in his chest. She'd cared about his brother—which begged the question: *What role did she have in his death?*

But they would discuss Tommy soon enough. He had to fulfill his part of the bargain first.

Steering his mind back to Erin Walker, he flipped to the next photo. Even though he'd braced himself, the close-up view made his stomach clench. How much worse would this be for Brynn?

"You said you met this girl on the streets?" he asked, hoping to distract her from the gore.

"That's right."

"Any idea why she ran away?"

Her face still chalky, she managed a shrug. "The same reason they all do, I guess. They're desperate. Some are neglected or abused. Or their parents have started a second family and don't want them around. Or sometimes they've made a mistake—committed a crime or gotten pregnant—and they're afraid their parents will go berserk. In Erin's case, she used drugs."

"Like Tommy."

"Yes, like Tommy." Sympathy softened her eyes. "They're confused, angry, ashamed. They can't control their feelings and don't know how to repair the damage they've done. And they don't think anyone will help."

Guilt fisted in Parker's throat. He shifted his gaze to the plate-glass window and stared unseeing at the afternoon rush-hour traffic whizzing past. He and Tommy hadn't been close. The five-year gap in their ages had kept them apart. When he'd gone off to college, his brother had still been in junior high. But to think that Tommy preferred the violence of street life to asking him for help...

"I tried to help him," Parker said, his voice low. "I took him to counselors, enrolled him in programs. But nothing worked." Their battles had only grown more heated until his brother had split for good.

"It's hard to reach an addict. The chemicals change how they think. I tried to help Erin, too. But in the end I only made things worse."

"How do you figure that?"

Her eyes turned pained. "I convinced her to go to a shelter, a place I know for teenage girls. She was there for a couple of days, and then her parents picked her up. I thought I'd done the right thing. She told me she wanted to get clean. And her parents had the resources to help her. They got her into that expensive camp."

"You don't think you caused her death?"

A bleak look filled her eyes. She opened her mouth to speak, then shook her head. "Maybe not directly. But she'd probably be alive right now if I hadn't persuaded her to go home."

He could relate to that. How many times had he second-guessed himself, wishing he'd done something—anything—different with Tommy, something that might have saved his brother's life?

His gaze stayed on hers. And something shifted inside him, like a long-locked door creaking open to admit the light. And he knew that she understood. She carried the same burden of guilt, the same unending remorse.

Suddenly, his mind flashed back to the image of that scrawny girl standing beside his brother, and he wondered again what had driven her from home.

He tamped down on the question hard. He didn't need to know Brynn's life story. He didn't need to forge a connection with her. And he definitely couldn't afford to desire her, not when she could be a suspect in his brother's death.

Although he was beginning to have doubts about that.

Alarmed, he jerked his gaze back to the file. What was he thinking? He was breaking the fundamental rule of police work, letting her get to him. He had to keep his distance, hold on to his objectivity to find out the truth about Tommy's death.

"Here's the autopsy," he said. Still appalled at the direction of his thoughts, he checked the diagnosis at the top. "She died of blunt force trauma, consistent with falling from that tower. The toxicology studies show she'd taken meth."

Keeping his gaze fastened on the file, he skimmed the various sections of the report—the internal and external exams, the degree of rigor mortis, the evidence taken from the scene.

"Who did the autopsy?" Brynn asked.

"The State Medical Examiner in Baltimore. That's standard procedure in a case like this."

"I didn't see anything about sexual activity."

"She was twelve."

"And she'd spent time on the streets."

True enough. And runaways rarely stayed innocent for long. He flipped back to the internal exam, then checked the diagnosis again. "Here it is. She had scarring consistent with sexual activity. But there was nothing to suggest it was recent—no semen present, no abrasions or inflammation that would indicate a rape."

He spread his hands. "The cause seems obvious. She was a drug user with meth in her system, and she either jumped or fell from that tower."

But Brynn didn't look convinced. "You mind if I look at the file again?"

"Go ahead." He slid the folder her way. "But there's no evidence to suggest foul play—no bruising on her neck, no signs of any force. No other footprints around the tower. The surveillance camera was down that night, but even so, the case looks cut-and-dried."

"She swore she was getting off drugs."

"So she had a relapse. It wouldn't be the first time an addict did that."

"I know. But I still have a feeling…" Pulling the

folder closer, she began leafing through the pages again, her delicate brows drawn down.

He understood her reluctance to accept the truth. It was always easier to blame someone else than live with relentless guilt. But unless she had evidence she wasn't revealing, her suspicions had no basis in actual fact.

Suddenly, she sat upright. He snapped his gaze to hers. "What is it?"

It took her a moment to answer. She thumbed back through the photos again, nibbling her bottom lip. Then she slid a photo toward him. "Did you see this?"

Parker focused on the dead girl's face. Around her neck she wore a necklace, a silver disk on a matching chain. On it was a design—hearts within a heart. "What about it?"

"It's not in all the photos for one thing." She flipped back through several shots. Sure enough, in every other photo, her neck was bare—a detail he couldn't believe he'd missed.

"Maybe it fell off when they moved her."

"It isn't mentioned in the report. It isn't listed with her personal effects."

He frowned at that. "You think someone stole it?"

"I don't know. Why would they? It doesn't look valuable enough."

True. It looked like costume jewelry, something a young girl would wear. "Maybe one of her friends kept it as a memento."

"What friends? She didn't have any, according to those reports. And that design." She went back to the necklace again. "See how irregular it is? The lines aren't even straight. It looks as if she engraved it herself."

"Maybe she did. Maybe she made it at the camp."

"Maybe." Heavy doubt laced her voice. "But I've seen something like it before…."

She pulled her laptop from her backpack, placed it on the table and turned it on. Then she opened a folder in her portfolio and started browsing through various shots.

Parker returned to the Walker girl's file and carefully reread the reports, but Brynn was right. There was no mention of the missing necklace. So where had it gone—and why?

Still not sure it mattered, he switched his attention to Brynn's computer as she searched her files. Faces paraded past, hundreds of poignant faces of emaciated, runaway kids. Everyone looked tormented. Everyone looked lost. Everyone had that unnerving cynicism in his waiflike eyes.

And once again, Brynn's amazing talent leaped from the screen, the juxtaposition of innocence and despair wrenching the viewer like a primal scream.

No, it was more than talent, he decided. She had the rare ability to erase the distance between the subject and herself. She knew these kids. She *was* these kids. Their lives had been her own.

Which revealed more about *her* than she probably knew.

Brynn paused. "Here. Take a look at this."

Leaning even closer, he studied the photograph she'd brought up. It showed a young girl standing in a row house doorway, her tight top and skimpy shorts emphasizing the stark angles of her sticklike frame. Heavy black makeup rimmed her drugged-out eyes, giving the impression of a child playing dress-up in her mother's clothes.

But this wasn't a game. This girl lived a hellish existence, enduring unspeakable acts of depravity to survive.

And she wore the same type of silver necklace with that same multiple-heart design.

"Her name's Jamie," Brynn said, enlarging the shot. "I met her a couple of months ago near Ridgewood Avenue."

Parker scrutinized the necklace. The engraving on this one looked as amateurish as the first. "What do you think it means?"

"Maybe nothing," she admitted. "It just strikes me as odd that two runaway girls, both drug addicts, are wearing the same hand-engraved necklace. Now one of them is dead—and her necklace has disappeared."

"You think they both went to that camp?"

"Maybe." But her skeptical tone belied her words.

"You think someone killed Erin Walker there?"

"I don't know."

But she suspected foul play. *At the C.I.D. chief's camp.* An allegation that could create a firestorm and torpedo the Colonel's career.

Not to mention *his.*

And unless he missed his guess, her doubts didn't only spring from the missing necklace. She had another reason she wanted to pursue this case, something she didn't want to divulge. But exactly what that could be, he didn't know.

"I just want to find out for sure," she added.

"How?"

"Ask this girl, Jamie, where she got her necklace to start with."

Parker sat back and rubbed his jaw, mulling over

what to do. He didn't have to help her. He'd fulfilled his part of the bargain and shown her the Walker girl's file. There was no reason to drag this out, no reason for him to stay involved.

Except that necklace had disappeared. That kid had died at his boss's camp. And she had meth in her system, despite having sworn off drugs. None of which proved any wrongdoing. None of which was necessarily suspicious or pointed to any crime.

But Brynn was right. Something about this case felt off. His instincts were clamoring hard. And it was his duty to investigate a murder—even if it cost him his job.

"All right. I'll go with you," he decided, hoping he wouldn't regret it. Brynn was dragging him into this case deeper, leading him down a path he might lament.

But he couldn't back out yet.

A short time later, they parked in the alley behind a flophouse near the intersection of Ridgewood Avenue and Garrison Boulevard where the young prostitute plied her trade. His weapon drawn, Parker took the lead through the basement entrance, picking his way over tarps and sheets of plywood to the stairs.

"Police!" he shouted, heading up the musty, unlit staircase to the lower floor. No answer. His heart thudding hard, he called out again. "Police! I'm coming through the door!"

His gut tense, every sense alert for danger, he stepped into the trash-strewn hallway and aimed his gun around. Damn, but he hated dealing with junkies. They'd jump him or stab him with a needle before he could even blink.

A muffled sound came from a nearby room. *Bingo.*

"I know you're in there. I want to see your hands. Have them up where I can see them. Now I'm coming in."

He waited a beat, giving the occupants a chance to get their hands up, then kicked open the door and stepped inside. A young girl huddled on the floor atop a threadbare blanket. Her scrawny arms were scabbed, her legs swollen from shooting heroin through her toes. She appeared to be alone.

To be sure, he scanned the room, taking in the spray-painted walls, the bottles and needles littering the floor—evidence that the action picked up as the sun went down. Smells he didn't care to identify assaulted his nose. "Is anyone else here?"

She gave him a sullen look. "No."

"You're sure?"

"Yeah."

Still watching for sudden moves, Parker kicked aside her purse. Her mild-mannered appearance didn't fool him. He'd seen far meeker junkies than this kid suddenly snap. "Keep your hands in your lap," he warned.

Brynn pushed past him into the room. Ignoring the potential danger, she went to the girl's side, clutching a grease-soaked fast-food bag. His nerves still edgy, Parker reluctantly lowered his gun.

But as hesitant as he was to pursue this case, he couldn't help but admire Brynn. She'd charged down the street, ignoring the thugs hanging out in the shadows as she scoured the boarded-up row houses for the teenage girl. And she had the uncanny ability to blend in. In the newspaper she'd looked like a wealthy shopper strolling through the upscale shops. Now she looked younger, scruffier, almost like a street kid herself in her sneakers and faded jeans.

"Hey, Jamie. Remember me?" Brynn asked.

The teenager blinked at Brynn. "Yeah. You're that photographer."

"That's right." Brynn handed her the bag of food.

Her eyes bloodshot, the teenager propped herself against the wall. She tore open the bag, then pulled out a fistful of French fries and crammed them into her mouth.

Parker turned his head to hide his distaste. Not that her hunger shocked him. During the months he'd searched for Tommy, he'd spent time questioning the prostitutes who worked the streets. He understood the desperation and addictions that drove them, the terror that chained them to their vicious pimps—even when it cost them their lives.

But that didn't make their suffering any easier to take, especially in a girl this young.

And he wondered how Brynn could stand it, documenting this horror every day. But that was the point, he realized, his respect for her rising even more. She knew that most people went about their lives ignoring anything that disturbed their peace. They didn't want to see the misery lurking in the shadows, the ugly reality these runaways faced. But her photos ripped them out of that complacency, refusing to let them turn their backs on these abandoned kids.

"I need to ask you something," Brynn said to Jamie. "It's about that necklace you had. The one with the hearts."

Not bothering to look up, the girl continued to scarf down the fries.

"Do you still have it?" Brynn asked.

Jamie touched her neck, then shrugged. "Nope." She tore the wrapper from the hamburger and took a bite.

"Do you remember where you got it?"

Her gaze flew to Brynn's. "I didn't steal it."

"I know that," Brynn said, her tone soothing. "It's just…I wanted to get one like it, but it looked handmade. I thought maybe you'd remember where you got it."

The teenager continued eating, but the wariness didn't leave her eyes. "A friend gave it to me."

"What friend?"

Jamie took another bite. "A girl I know."

"Any chance she went to a place called High Rock Camp?"

"I don't know."

"Can you find out?"

"Maybe," she said around another mouthful of food.

Parker hesitated. He hated giving money to junkies, knowing they'd only spend it on drugs. But he needed to ensure her help. And maybe it would keep her from turning a trick. He pulled a fifty-dollar bill from his wallet and held it out. "We'd really like to find out where you got it."

Jamie shot him a startled glance, as if she'd forgotten he was there. Then she quickly sized him up, her gaze far too worldly for her tender years. Parker curled his lip, revolted at the thought of the depravity this girl endured.

She reached up and snatched the bill. It disappeared into her blouse. "All right."

"We'll come back tomorrow afternoon," Brynn said. "Does that give you enough time to find her and ask?"

Polishing off her burger, Jamie let out a muffled

grunt. Then she turned her attention to her milkshake, sucking furiously on the straw.

Catching his eye, Brynn motioned for him to wait. She opened a side pocket on her backpack and pulled out a business card. "Listen, Jamie. A friend of mine runs this shelter for girls in D.C. Always Home. We'd like to take you there."

"I don't need help."

"It's a safe place. She has beds, food…" When the girl didn't answer, she sighed. "Keep the card anyway, in case you change your mind. She'll even send someone to pick you up. And if you don't need it, you might know someone who does."

Jamie took the card with a shrug. She slipped it into her pocket, then continued drinking her shake.

Turning, Brynn signaled for them to leave. Realizing the girl would only come back if he tried to evict her, Parker decided to forget it and led the way down the stairs. "Any chance she was telling the truth?" he asked when they'd reached the alley again.

Brynn swung her knapsack onto her shoulder and made a face. "I don't know. Maybe. You never know with an addict."

He slanted her a glance as they started walking toward the corner, their feet crunching over broken glass. The sun dipping behind the buildings added shimmers to her fiery hair, enveloping her in a glow. "You seem to know a lot about drug addicts."

"I wasn't a user, if that's what you're asking. I've just dealt with them on the streets."

Which once again brought up the question—why had she fled her home? Before their partnership ended, he was going to learn what made this woman tick.

"Is that how you met my brother?" he asked instead. "On the streets?"

She nodded. "A guy was hassling us. Tommy intervened."

"Us?"

She squinted into the waning sunshine. A car rumbled past on the nearby street, the deep drum of its subwoofers vibrating his chest.

"Two girls I knew," she finally said. "We hung out together near the Inner Harbor. Tommy became our protector. He watched out for us when he could."

"You're saying he helped you?"

She came to a stop. Tilting back her head, she met his eyes. "Why are you so surprised? He was a good guy, Parker. He had problems, and he made plenty of mistakes, but he was still a good man at heart. You should be proud."

Proud? Parker shook his head, trying to reconcile this version of his brother with the defiant teenager who'd run away from home. "I don't know. He'd changed so much toward the end. I hardly knew him anymore."

"That was the drugs. Addicts become obsessed. If you threaten their addiction, they lash out. But he admired you, Parker. He mentioned you sometimes."

His heart wobbled hard. He struggled to draw a breath, his chest suddenly too tight. The year after his father died had been pure hell—coping with his father's treachery, dealing with Tommy's addiction. All they'd done was fight. He'd figured that Tommy despised him, that he'd lumped him in with his father, considering the accusations he'd hurled his way.

"Helping a runaway isn't easy." Her voice was gentler now. "You can only do so much. After that, it's up to them."

Still grappling with his emotions, he met her eyes. And despite his vow to keep his distance, her understanding reeled him in. Tempting. Soothing. Making him ache to pull her closer and bask in her healing warmth.

Making him realize exactly how many years he'd felt alone.

His cell phone chimed. Returning to reality, he struggled to clear his head. What was wrong with him? Why couldn't he stay objective around Brynn? He was falling under her spell, breaking the most basic rule of law enforcement and letting her get to him.

And he *never* got involved with a suspect. He never even dated a woman connected to the force. He kept his private life completely separate, what little there'd been of it these past few years.

His phone rang again. Grateful for the distraction, he pulled it from his jacket pocket and checked the screen. Delgado had sent him a text message. His pulse quickened as he pulled it up.

Donut break's over. Get back here ASAP. The Colonel's pissed.

He muttered a curse. Lieutenant Lewis must have contacted Colonel Hoffman and revealed that he'd requested a copy of the Walker girl's file.

"Is something wrong?" Brynn asked.

Wrong? He'd just been caught in a lie. His job could be on the line. "I need to get back to the office."

"I've got things I need to do, too," she said quickly. "Why don't we meet again tomorrow afternoon?"

Instantly suspicious, he snapped his gaze to hers. "Why not sooner?"

"I've got errands to run. I need a new cell phone, for one thing. And Jamie won't be awake in the morning. I thought I'd visit that camp in the meantime and try to get an impression of the place."

Not without him. He was already in this case too deep. And if there was any chance that kid had been murdered, he needed to know. "I'll go with you. I'll drive."

Hesitating, she searched his eyes. "All right, we'll go together. Ten o'clock?"

He nodded. "At your house?"

"No. I'm not going back there tonight." She named a place downtown.

"Good." Knowing that he owed her, he plunged his hand through his hair. "Listen, Brynn. About my brother—"

"Let's talk about it tomorrow, okay? When we've got more time?"

"Tomorrow, then."

She spun on her heels and walked away. He watched her merge into the shadows, her slender hips swaying, her russet-colored hair a beacon in the encroaching night. And suddenly, he realized he was reluctant to let her go.

And it had nothing to do with his brother's death.

Chapter 5

"I don't know what you did," Delgado warned as Parker tossed his jacket over the back of his desk chair half an hour later. "But you've really pissed the Colonel off."

No kidding. The hush that had followed in his wake as he'd walked the gauntlet through his office had already clued him in.

"Your timing sucks, too." Delgado leaned back against the cubicle's upholstered wall, a smirk on his dusky face. "What with that gang leader's release from prison and all."

Parker shot him a scowl, annoyed at his gleeful tone. Bad enough that Delgado had charmed his way up the career ladder, getting promoted over far more deserving men. But listening to the smug man crow… "Old news, Delgado."

"And it just got worse. The media's on a witch hunt, claiming we're incompetent since we haven't brought him in."

Parker bit down hard on a curse. Bad timing didn't begin to describe it. Last week a prisoner named Markus Jenkins, the leader of the notorious Ridgewood gang, had mistakenly been released from the Roxbury Correctional Institution in western Maryland—then disappeared. The pressure to recapture him had been extreme. If the media had started bad-mouthing the police, the Colonel would go berserk. He'd crucify anyone who caused another problem and put his reputation at risk.

Realizing it was futile to postpone the inevitable, Parker left Delgado gloating beside his cubicle, crossed the hallway into the new building, then rode the elevator to the Colonel's floor. The receptionist waved him through, her eyes wild as she tried to deal with the ringing phones.

"Come in," Hugh Hoffman's deep voice boomed out when Parker knocked on his office door.

Parker squared his shoulders and went inside. The C.I.D. chief stood at his corner window, peering through the open slats on the miniblinds. A shade under six feet tall, Hoffman was built like the lineman he used to be with a thick, stocky neck, massive shoulders and thighs, and a barrel chest padded with fat. He'd worked his way up the ranks of the police force, his unflagging work ethic and passion for fighting crime earning him widespread respect. Even Senator Riggs had recognized his potential and had begun grooming him for a future congressional run.

He turned at Parker's approach. "Detective." His eyes were devoid of warmth.

Stopping beside a chair, Parker braced himself for the coming storm. He didn't have long to wait.

"Just what the hell do you think you're doing?" Hoffman demanded.

Parker stiffened his spine. This didn't bode well. He'd seen Hoffman in a lot of moods but never this livid before. "Sir?"

"Don't act dumb. Lieutenant Lewis called me. She says you've been looking at the Walker girl's file."

"I was exploring a lead that didn't pan out."

Hoffman's face turned a mottled red. A vein bulged in his florid cheek. He gripped the back of his desk chair, as if it cost him to stay in check. "Do you have any idea who that kid was? Erin Walker. Daughter of Dean Walker, head of Walker Avionics."

Which sold weapon systems to the military, both home and abroad. Parker's heart took a nosedive. "Big money," he guessed.

"Big?" Incredulity rang in the Colonel's voice. "We're talking billions of dollars a year. And he's a bundler for Senator Riggs, the single biggest donor to his campaign. And in case you haven't been paying attention, the senator's up for reelection next year."

Parker closed his eyes. *Hell.* No wonder the Colonel was ticked.

"Now you listen to me," Hoffman continued, his voice a dangerous growl. "Because I'll only say this once. That case is closed. That girl took drugs and died—whether by accident or suicide, we'll never know. Now leave it alone. That family doesn't need you stirring things up after the grief that they've been through.

And neither do I! If Walker gets a whiff of this, all hell is going to break loose. And I've got enough trouble right now with the media breathing down my neck."

"I understand."

"You'd better. I'm giving you an order, Detective. *Leave that case alone.* And I don't think I need to remind you what will happen if you don't."

Parker's face burned. "No, sir." The message couldn't be clearer. Hoffman would fire him if he disobeyed.

Hoffman held his gaze, letting his warning sink in. Then he pulled out his desk chair and sat. Parker fixed his gaze on the window, his pride still smarting as he waited to be dismissed.

But Hoffman seemed determined to make him squirm. He unwrapped a roll of antacids and popped several into his mouth. An eternity later, he sighed. "Sit down, Detective."

Expecting another lashing, Parker lowered himself into a chair. The Colonel continued to watch him, as if debating what to say. Then he reached down and pulled a folded newspaper from his desk drawer.

"Since you seem to have time on your hands, I've got a project for you. A favor, if you will." Shifting his big body forward, he held the paper out.

Curious, and relieved that the Colonel's temper had run its course, Parker took the paper and opened it to the front page.

On it was the photo of Brynn. Parker forced himself to breathe.

"The woman in that picture," the Colonel continued. "She goes by a pseudonym, B. K. Elliot. But her real name is Hoffman."

Parker jerked his gaze to his. "You're related?"

"She's my stepdaughter."

Parker's jaw dropped. He stared at the C.I.D. chief, too stunned to speak.

Hoffman folded his hands, his eyes turning pensive now. "You've probably heard the stories. She ran away from home when she was twelve. She was a troubled kid, to say the least. We tried everything—tough love, counseling…but nothing we did seemed to help. God knows we tried. She snuck out at night and lied, accused us of all sorts of terrible things. The situation got ugly, I'm afraid."

He let out a heartfelt sigh, as if the memories still caused him pain. "She directed most of her anger at me. That was normal enough, I suppose. I was her stepfather—I'd taken her father's place when he died.

"She's the reason I started that camp. I was determined to help these kids, even though I'd failed with her."

Feeling completely staggered, Parker tried to process this news. Everyone knew the C.I.D. chief's story. Hoffman's walls were covered with the awards he'd won for his work with troubled teens. But to think Brynn was that runaway stepdaughter…

"She's a photographer now," the Colonel said, nodding toward the newspaper in Parker's hand. "Quite a good one from what I've read. But she's still unstable. A mental illness like that doesn't go away on its own. And that's where you come in."

"Me?"

"I'm worried about her, Parker. She's a very troubled young woman. And she needs help—counseling, medication… Now that she's finally surfaced, I want you to bring her in. Quietly, of course. I don't want to scare her off. And none of us needs the publicity right now. But it would mean the world to her mother and me."

Parker grappled with what to say. The Colonel wanted him to find Brynn. He obviously didn't realize that Parker had already contacted her. But if Brynn was his missing stepdaughter…

Still unable to believe it, he gave his head a shake. "She's the girl in my brother's photo. The one we found in his shoe a few years after his death. You saw it. You reopened the case and searched for her. You never mentioned the relationship then."

Hoffman winced. "I figured you'd make the connection." He heaved himself from his desk chair and went to the window again. Twisting the wand on the miniblinds, he adjusted the slats to maximize the dwindling light.

"You're right, of course. I knew who she was at once. But you have to understand how desperate I was. She was sick and needed help. And I didn't believe for a minute that she'd killed your brother. At least I hoped not. She manipulated people and lied, but stooping as low as murder…"

He turned around with a sigh. "I didn't want to think she'd sunk that far. It would have killed her mother if she had. I figured I'd bring her in, then turn the case over to someone else on the off chance that her testimony could help. I doubted it would do any good, though. She never told the truth, even when she wasn't high on drugs.

"But when we couldn't find her…well, it didn't seem important to mention it then."

He retook his seat, his expression pained. "In hindsight, it was a mistake, one of my many regrets. I should have revealed who she was. It wasn't fair to you to keep a secret like that. If I could do things over…" He spread his beefy hands.

Parker dropped his gaze to the photo, not knowing what to think. He could hardly criticize Hoffman for making a mistake. He'd made plenty of errors of his own. But deliberately concealing that Brynn was his stepdaughter… It wasn't a minor detail. Parker couldn't help but feel betrayed.

And why hadn't Brynn told him who Hoffman was? She knew he ran that camp. What kind of game was she trying to play?

Hoffman opened his desk drawer again. He pulled out a bulging accordion folder and slid it across the desk. "I'd like you to help me find her. Quietly, off the record. We'll ask her about your brother when we bring her in, but, frankly, you shouldn't get your hopes up about that. Even if she remembers, she'll probably lie."

"Right." Aware that the Colonel was waiting for an answer, Parker managed a nod. "I'll do my best."

"I know you will. I respect that about you, Parker. I took a chance on you back when you were a rookie, and you haven't let me down so far."

"I appreciate that." Hoffman had been one of the few officers willing to go out on a limb and vouch for Parker when his father's criminal activities had threatened to sink his budding career. And he hadn't stopped there. He'd helped Parker make detective, followed his progress through the force. And when Parker had applied to join the homicide cold case squad, he'd made sure that he got in.

The Colonel cleared his throat. "I've done some preliminary research and found out that she has an agent,

Joan Kellogg. The agent lives in Old Town Alexandria. You might start your inquiries there."

"I will."

"Report your progress directly to me. I don't want any risk of this leaking to the press. Those damned hyenas are already out for blood. And with her high profile, we'd have reporters hounding us from around the globe. We'll release a public statement after we bring her in. Now you're dismissed."

"Yes, sir." Parker stuck the newspaper into the file and rose. Still dumbfounded by the bombshell, he crossed the office, the industrial carpet absorbing his steps.

"Oh, and Detective?"

Parker turned around.

"I mean what I said. Leave that other case alone. If word gets out…"

Parker would lose his job. "I understand."

"Good. Now get to work."

Parker exited the C.I.D. chief's office. Ignoring the curious gazes of his fellow officers, he made his way back to the older section of the building and his cubicle on the sixth floor.

Brynn Elliot was Hoffman's stepdaughter.

What the hell was going on?

Feeling completely off-kilter, he tossed the file onto his desk and slumped into his chair. He stared at the stains on the ceiling, the Colonel's words still spinning through his mind. Then, determined to get some answers, he opened the accordion folder, pulled out the contents and began to read.

The file chronicled Brynn's childhood from kindergarten on, which was when her father had died. It contained elementary school report cards, notes from parent–teacher conferences and psychologists' reports. By middle school it included records of truancy and repeated attempts to run away.

And every report stated the same thing. Around age seven, when her widowed mother had remarried, Brynn had become angry, unstable. A liar, but stated in more socially acceptable terms. She disrupted class, picked fights with her classmates and refused to do her work. And her problems worsened as she aged— stealing, skipping school, running away from home. The documents didn't leave room for doubt. The Colonel's stepdaughter, Brynn Katherine Hoffman, had been a severely troubled child.

Was she any more trustworthy as an adult?

Parker's doubts increasing, he worked his way through the file. He read articles about the C.I.D. chief. The groundbreaking ceremony at High Rock Camp. Interviews with Hoffman about his stepdaughter. His public pleas for her to come home. Photos of him receiving awards the camp had won. A photo op with Senator Riggs.

An hour later, his head pounding with a vengeance, Parker shoved the file aside. He leaned back in his chair and massaged his eyes, unable to deny the facts. The evidence supported Hoffman's allegations about Brynn. She had a volatile history. She'd run away, resisted everyone's efforts to help her and refused to tell the truth. All the experts agreed.

And everything Parker knew about Hoffman backed that evidence up. He waged a tireless war on crime. His reputation was superb. He'd even fought for additional funding to beef up this homicide cold case squad, determined that no murder, no matter how old, would remain unsolved. And no one had done more than he had for at-risk youth.

Whereas Brynn...

Parker opened his eyes on a sigh. She'd obviously concealed the truth from him. To be fair, she probably didn't know he worked for her stepfather. Parker's business card only listed his rank—detective—not the office where he worked. And even if she nosed around, asking questions, no one would give that information out. But she knew her stepfather ran that camp. He'd founded the place for her sake! So why hadn't she told him that?

Unless she had a hidden agenda...

He stilled. Was that what this was about? Was she using him to carry out a personal vendetta against the Colonel? Was she investigating that Walker girl's death, hoping to uncover some sort of wrongdoing that would bring her stepfather down?

And what if she was? Could he honestly help her damage the Colonel's career? Hoffman had supported him, giving him a chance to prove himself when he was a rookie, despite his father's crimes. How could Parker betray that trust?

Feeling manipulated from both sides, he slipped the file folder into his desk, snapped off his desk lamp and rose. Then he stalked through the nearly empty office, his heavy footsteps echoing in the gloom.

He knew what he *should* do. He should tell Hoffman the truth—that he'd already located Brynn—and let him handle her. That way there'd be no ambiguities, no subterfuge or guilt. He'd just follow the Colonel's orders and turn her in.

But he couldn't erase that niggle of doubt. Because

the truth was, the Colonel had misled him before. He'd withheld information about Brynn when they'd found that photo in Tommy's shoe. And even if his intentions had been altruistic, even if he regretted his actions now, Hoffman had clearly lied.

And what if Brynn was right? What if those irregularities in the Walker girl's file signified something bad? What if the C.I.D. chief was hiding something important, suppressing details about her death—just as he'd hidden his relationship with Brynn? Could Parker take that chance?

He pushed open the door to the parking lot and stepped outside. Still thinking hard, he stuffed his hands in his jacket pockets and headed across the deserted lot toward his truck. On the surface, the case seemed straightforward. Erin Walker had suffered a relapse, taken drugs and died, just as the autopsy said.

But Hoffman couldn't afford any scandals. That camp was the cornerstone of his budding political career. At the slightest whiff of any wrongdoing, Senator Riggs would withdraw his support, and Hoffman would go from rising political star to pariah overnight.

Which provided Hoffman a motive to keep anything unflattering from coming to light.

But did Parker dare defy the Colonel's order and continue to investigate this death? He'd have to lie to his boss about his activities. He'd have to hide his relationship with Brynn. He'd risk arousing the anger of the dead girl's parents, the wrath of a powerful senator. If he got caught, his career would end.

He'd also have to deceive Brynn. Because if she learned that he worked for her stepfather—and that he'd asked him to bring her in—she'd never trust him again.

And he'd give up his chance to discover the truth about Tommy's death.

He unlocked his truck, feeling trapped. Because if he was going to be brutally honest, there was another factor at work—beyond his sworn duty to an innocent victim, beyond his loyalty to Hoffman, beyond his promise to find out how his brother had died.

The truth was that he liked Brynn Elliot—or whatever her real name was. And not only because of the unruly attraction tying his gut in knots. He admired her amazing talent, her attempts to help those runaway kids.

And damn it, he wanted to believe her, no matter what proof Hoffman tossed his way. He wanted to believe that she'd cared about Tommy, that she understood his loss and pain, that the compassion in her eyes was genuine.

Grimacing at his gullibility, he climbed into his truck and slammed the door. She'd gotten to him, all right. But both Brynn and the Colonel were keeping secrets.

And he'd be damned if he'd play the fool.

Chapter 6

Something had changed between them overnight.

Brynn slid an uneasy glance at Parker's profile as he drove them through the mountains of western Maryland toward High Rock Camp. He'd sat in brooding silence since he'd picked her up an hour earlier, his lean hands cradling the wheel, his jaw bunched tighter than a boxer's fist. And when he'd looked her way, he'd eyed her with an alert kind of stillness, a wary intensity that set off warning bells in her head.

Had he spoken to her stepfather? Had he learned something damaging about her past? Nerves tightened in her belly at the thought. Exactly what had happened to cause this tension, she didn't know. But it had erased the bond they'd begun forging between them. That tentative trust was gone.

But what could she do? She couldn't back out of their

agreement. She had too many enemies to fight this war alone. And to have any chance of exposing the truth about her stepfather, she needed Parker's help.

He slanted her a sideways glance, his mesmerizing eyes so like Tommy's that her heart made a little flip. And that was another problem right there. Bad enough that he had the power to arrest her. Worse that he appealed to her in a decidedly carnal way. His rumbling, low-pitched voice, the potent magnetism of his handsome face evoked thoughts she had no business entertaining right now. And his resemblance to Tommy disconcerted her completely, bringing back a flood of regrets.

Still badly unsettled, she turned her face toward the windshield; the colorful trees lining the two-lane road barely registered as they sped by. She couldn't think about the past right now. She couldn't keep agonizing over Tommy's death. She had to focus on discovering what had happened to Erin Walker. Because if what she dreaded proved true, she had more blood than Tommy's on her hands.

"We're almost there," Parker said, his deep voice drawing her attention back to him. "So how do you want to play this?"

Inhaling deeply to quiet her nerves, she turned her thoughts to the task ahead. "We'd better keep it simple so we don't goof up. Let's say we're the parents of a troubled teenager, and we want to check their program out."

He quirked a brow, his hot, dark gaze scrambling her pulse. "Aren't you young to have a teenage daughter?"

"Not technically. I'm twenty-eight." But there was no point raising scrutiny they didn't need. "We can make her our niece instead. Her parents died in a car accident, and we have custody."

"Name?"

"Amber. She's fifteen. She's been sneaking out of the house at night and running around with a fast crowd. And we just found pot in her room. If they ask us anything else, let me handle it. We won't contradict each other that way."

"You're good at making things up."

Good at lying, he meant. She pulled her gaze back to the windshield, determined to ignore a nasty little stab of hurt. It didn't matter what Parker thought. No one had ever believed her—not her teachers, not the social workers who'd paraded through her childhood and definitely not the police. So why should she expect anything different from him? Just because he was Tommy's brother, just because they had this mind-boggling chemistry ricocheting between them didn't mean he was on her side.

Besides, he was right. Living on the streets, she'd had to reinvent herself continually to survive.

"I've been around a lot of runaways," she said by way of explanation. "I know the profile well."

Parker didn't answer. He just continued to watch her, scrutinizing her with those wary eyes. Cop eyes. Eyes that took in every detail but gave nothing of his thoughts away. She turned her face toward the passenger-side window again. He was dangerous, all right. And no matter how tempted she was to trust him, she couldn't forget that fact.

Seconds later, they crested a hill and the sign for High Rock Camp came into view. Brynn leaned forward, her heart beating double-time as Parker turned in at the gravel drive. The gate hung ajar. The guard shack stood unmanned, allowing them to pass unimpeded into the camp. But the security camera mounted on the high, steel fence took her aback. She hadn't expected to be caught on film.

They drove past the gate, then followed a meandering track through the woods, gravel crunching under their tires. A squirrel bounded into their path. Leaves fluttered from the trees, doing cartwheels across the truck. A quarter mile later they reached a one-story log building bearing an office sign. Parker pulled into the parking lot beside it and stopped.

And suddenly, a clammy sweat broke out on her brow. Dread slithered through her veins, the terror she'd suppressed for years surfacing again. She'd entered her stepfather's world. But she was older now. Smarter. Far less vulnerable.

And she would never suffer that abuse again.

Beating down the instinctive panic, she climbed out of the truck and shut the door. Then she forced herself to inhale, taking long, steadying gulps of the mountain air. A cardinal whistled overhead. A stream gurgled nearby. She turned her attention to the office, the freshly painted logs and flower boxes brimming with chrysanthemums giving it a tidy, welcoming look.

The setting was tranquil. Picturesque. Perfect. But then, her stepfather always had excelled at creating the right facade.

Still trying to calm her heart rate, she waited for Parker to join her, then started up the flagstone path. But he caught hold of her arm and tugged her to a halt before she'd taken a dozen steps. Startled, she tipped her head back to meet his eyes. "What's wrong?"

"We're concerned parents, right?"

"So?" This close, she could trace the razor stubble emerging on his jaw, the intriguing hollow at the base of his muscled throat, his disturbingly sexual mouth. The woodsy scent of his aftershave teased her senses, disquieting her even more.

"So we need to look the part." He linked their hands, and the feel of his warm, calloused skin set off a rush of heat in her blood. Then he pulled her into motion, adjusting his pace to hers. She was still trying to regain her equilibrium as they neared the office door.

Appearances, she reminded herself firmly. They were only playing a part. But the banked strength in his massive hand, the coiled power in his easy strides, had the oddest effect—making her feel sheltered, protected. *Safe.*

Which didn't make the least bit of sense. Parker was a cop, and he clearly distrusted her. So why did she have this insane urge to burrow against him and let his broad shoulders shield her from harm?

At the door, he released her hand. More off balance than she cared to acknowledge, she swept past him and went inside. Then she stopped and glanced around, determined to quit worrying about Parker, quash the intense dread threatening to consume her and concentrate on the reason they were here—finding out the truth behind Erin's death.

The office looked like an upscale lodge. A huge stone fireplace dominated one wall. Thick wooden beams yawned overhead. Generously sized leather armchairs surrounded a coffee table made of antlers, while a Western rug covered the wide-planked floor, adding splashes of color to the muted room. Nature sounds fluted over the sound system, the soft chirping of birds and a splashing stream designed to calm.

A blonde woman about Brynn's age rose from the corner desk, a gracious smile on her face. She wore a white silk blouse, a classic pencil skirt. She had her hair pulled up in a sleek chignon. "May I help you?" she asked in a pleasant voice.

"We hope so," Parker said. He shot the receptionist a lazy smile that completely transformed his face, making him look younger, friendlier and far, far sexier. Brynn blinked at him in surprise. When he put on the charm, he was a lethally attractive man.

"We'd like information about your camp," he added.

A blush crept up the receptionist's cheeks. "Please make yourselves comfortable. I'll see if Mrs. Gibson is available." She flashed Parker another smile, then padded across the rug to an adjacent office and tapped on the door. When a woman called out, she slipped inside.

Still stunned by the change in Parker, Brynn wandered across the room, needing to put some distance between them to clear her mind. So what if he'd poured on the charm? So what if that wicked smile made her heart pound and sparked an avalanche of lust in her blood? She was here to investigate a young girl's death, not ogle Parker McCall—no matter how gorgeous he was.

Determined to conquer her wayward reactions, she circuited the room, studying photographs of teenagers engaged in typical camp pursuits—hiking through the woods, riding a zip line over a canyon, climbing rocks and paddling canoes. There were other shots of them at work—cooking, erecting tents, building a campfire and clearing trails. The last few photos showed overjoyed parents reuniting with their kids, relief in their teary eyes.

Brynn's heart twisted, a sudden yearning curling inside her, a longing she'd buried for years. As a child, she would have bartered her soul for parents like that—parents who actually cared.

Appalled at the direction of her thoughts, she crossed her arms. What was wrong with her today? Coming even this close to her stepfather had stripped away her defenses, making her vulnerable in ways she couldn't afford. She had to stay alert and concentrate on investigating Erin Walker's death. This could be her only chance to get the proof she needed to stop her stepfather's abuse.

To her relief, the receptionist returned just then with a short, dark-haired woman in tow. "Good afternoon. I'm Ruth Gibson." The director reached out to shake their hands, her level gaze and no-nonsense manner indicating a woman used to taking charge. She ushered them into her office and motioned toward the armchairs beside the desk. "Please have a seat."

Brynn pulled out the chair beside Parker and sat, then surreptitiously glanced around, taking in the map covering the back wall, the whiteboard displaying cabin assignments—information she was dying to see. She swept her gaze over the awards dotting the walls to the corner file cabinet behind the desk. A framed photo stood on top.

It was a photo of *her*.

She gaped at it in horror, so shocked she could hardly breathe. But it was her, all right. She was eight years old, fishing with her stepfather at Deep Creek Lake.

Now what was she going to do?

"You look familiar," the director said, taking her seat behind the desk. "Have we met before?"

Oh, God. This was all she needed, for the director to recognize her. And what if Parker noticed the photo? How would she explain it to him?

Praying that neither would look toward the file cabinet, she tried to sound offhand. "I don't think so. I'm sure I would have remembered."

Mrs. Gibson nodded, but speculation lingered in her eyes. She folded her manicured hands on her desk. "So how can I help you?"

While Parker answered, Brynn struggled to gather her composure and play her part. She should have anticipated this. Her stepfather had founded this camp because of her—or so he claimed. Of course he would display her photo. It helped him maintain the charade.

She couldn't let Parker see it. He would recognize her stepfather at once. Hugh Hoffman was a colonel in the Baltimore Police Department, head of the Criminal Investigation Division, for heaven's sake. He was famous in the community, thanks to this camp and his connection to Senator Riggs. And while her appearance had obviously changed, Parker might still notice the resemblance. He was far too astute.

But maybe he would miss it. From where he sat, there was a spider plant blocking his view. If she could just keep the director from making the connection until they were gone...

"How old is she?" the director asked when Parker had finished telling her about their "niece."

"Fifteen." Parker paused convincingly. "We aren't sure what to do. We've tried counseling, but it hasn't worked. We heard great things about your program and thought we'd check it out."

"Of course." Getting down to business, the director handed them each a set of glossy brochures. "This is a residential program for at-risk youth. The courses we run vary in length, from several months for the older teenagers to shorter sessions for younger kids. Our goal is simple, to help them understand the cause of their negative behaviors, such as their drug use or poor choice in friends.

"Our advantage here is the setting. Removing a child from her home environment forces her to adjust. We help her change in a good way, to learn positive coping skills she can apply to other areas of her life."

Pretending to focus on the director's spiel, Brynn flipped through the slick brochures. She had to appear attentive. She couldn't give Mrs. Gibson any reason to scrutinize her and wonder where she'd seen her before.

The director continued talking, covering the importance of family involvement, the technology that enabled parents to follow their child's progress at the camp online. Brynn wanted to dislike the camp, but in truth it sounded great. The director was intelligent and concerned. She looked and sounded sincere. And the program appeared top-notch.

"You say the children spend several months here?" Parker asked when she paused.

"The older ones do. It takes time for them to incorporate the lessons they learn. The setting speeds up the process, but change still doesn't happen overnight. Our younger kids, the ten- to fourteen-year-olds, come for shorter lengths of time. We run those sessions throughout the year. The next one starts up in a couple of weeks."

Mrs. Gibson handed them each another brochure. "Here you'll find some sample schedules."

Parker shifted forward, drawing Brynn's gaze as the director launched into another speech. He sat with his forearms braced on his knees, his eyes locked on the director's face as if hanging on every word. And a sudden wistfulness curled inside her, the desire to believe that he really cared.

She mentally rolled her eyes. Of course he didn't care. This was an act, a ploy to get information about the camp.

But he'd worried about his brother. He'd tried to save Tommy's life.

"Could we get references?" Parker asked. "I'd like to talk to some parents who've sent their kids here recently and find out what they think."

"Certainly. We can provide you with a list of families who've given us permission to release their names. I'll have the receptionist print that out. You'll also find testimonials on our website and in the brochure."

"I'd like to hear more about your activities," Brynn cut in, determined to get to the point so they could leave. "Our niece is very artistic. Do you offer painting or jewelry design?"

"We do." The director swiveled around, pulled a three-ring binder off a low shelf beneath the window and paged through. Then she handed the open binder to Brynn.

Parker leaned closer to see. Brynn struggled to ignore his nearness, the way his solid shoulder bumped against hers. Trying not to look affected, she thumbed through pictures of teens using a potter's wheel, developing photographs in a darkroom and painting beside a stream.

When Mrs. Gibson launched into a discussion of outcome studies, Brynn passed Parker the notebook and sat back. So the camp offered art classes. That didn't prove the necklace came from here. But neither did it rule it out.

Regardless, she needed more concrete information if she hoped to learn how Erin had died. She had to find out how often her stepfather came here, get a look at those cabin assignments—uncover *something* that could lead to a clue.

Her opportunity came a moment later when the receptionist knocked on the office door. "I'm so sorry to interrupt," she said, directing her words to her boss. "May I speak to you for a moment?"

"Of course." Her smile apologetic, Mrs. Gibson rose. "Excuse me. I'll be right back. Feel free to look through the photos while I'm gone. I'll get that list of names for you, too." She left and closed the door.

"You have your cell phone?" Brynn asked Parker.

"Yeah."

"Can you get a picture of that map and whiteboard?" She gestured toward the back wall. "I'm going to check the desk."

Not waiting for an answer, she beelined to the corner file cabinet. She snuck a quick glance back, relieved to see Parker heading across the room. Then she flipped the photo over and shoved it behind the plant. Breathing easier now, she tested the drawers of the file cabinet, but they were locked.

She had no better luck at the desk. The computer was

password-protected. The desktop was absurdly neat with no appointment book in sight. Growing desperate, she opened the top desk drawer and rifled through the papers, then started on the next.

In the bottom drawer she hit pay dirt—a digital camera, the same brand she used, lying atop a stack of brochures. Working quickly, she removed the memory card and slipped it into her pocket, then stuffed the camera back into the drawer.

Knowing the director could return any moment, she hurried back to her chair. "Did you get the pictures?" she asked, slightly breathless, as Parker retook his seat.

"Yeah."

"Good." They could examine those after they left.

"How about you?" he asked.

"I found a camera and took out the memory card."

"What good will that do?"

She gestured to the three-ring binder on the desk. "These photos are for show. I want to see what goes on behind the scenes, the shots they didn't print."

He took that in. "So what do you think of the camp?"

"Typical sales pitch. She reels you in, trying to hook you on the camp before she springs the price."

"I doubt most parents care about that."

"Unless they're rich, they do."

He shook his head. "They're too desperate." He picked up the three-ring binder and flipped through the pages, stopping on a photo taken at the course's end. A girl was crying and hugging her parents, and the love and joy on their faces wrenched even Brynn's jaded heart.

"These parents have been through hell," Parker continued. "They've tried everything to save their child.

By the time they get here, they'll pay anything. They'll mortgage the house, take out a loan, do whatever it takes."

The sudden pain in his eyes drew her attention, and she realized he was talking about himself. He'd been that desperate. He'd tried everything he could think of to save his brother's life. And he thought he'd failed.

But Tommy had died because of her.

Unable to bear Parker's scrutiny, she looked away. But she couldn't deny the truth. She'd killed Tommy McCall as surely as if she'd fired that gun.

"Wouldn't you pay anything?" he prodded.

"Of course." A dull ache lodged in her throat. A terrible weight pressed on her chest, making it hard to breathe. But as much as she wanted to ignore it, she couldn't deny the evidence staring her straight in the face. Parker had loved his brother. He blamed himself for Tommy's death. And she had no right to make him continue to suffer for something he didn't do. She had to confess her role in that awful affair.

Because Parker was a decent man. He was loyal, protective. The kind of man a person could depend on. The kind of man who'd spent fifteen years trying to track down his brother's killer, refusing to give up. The kind of man she'd once fantasized about.

The fact was, there *were* good men in the world, honorable, trustworthy men who sheltered their children and loved their wives. Tommy had been like that. Parker appeared to be the same. Just because she'd had a lousy childhood, just because she'd witnessed the worst depravity on the streets didn't mean those good men didn't exist.

They just didn't exist for *her*.

The door swung open, interrupting her thoughts. Brynn struggled to compose herself, to ignore the pain roiling deep in her soul. Her past didn't matter now. She'd made peace with her life long ago. And she no longer yearned for things she could never have—like love.

"Sorry about that," Mrs. Gibson said, retaking her seat behind the desk. "Did you have any other questions?"

Still feeling raw, Brynn met the director's gaze. But the woman's carefully modulated voice, that annoyingly pleasant smile pushed her over the edge. She was so damned tired of the unfairness, so damned tired of the hypocrisy of people like this director who pretended to lead such respectable lives—while ignoring the evil in their midst.

"Just one," Brynn said, an edge to her voice. "What's your safety record here?"

"Excellent. We have a nurse practitioner on-site full-time. The injury rate is what you'd expect at an active camp, the occasional sprains and cuts. But serious injuries are rare."

"That's not what I meant. I heard you recently had a suicide."

The director went still, her professional smile freezing in place. "I can't discuss an individual case," she said, her eyes like ice. "But we do a complete evaluation of the children before we accept them in our program. We consult with everyone involved—social workers, counselors, school psychologists. And unless they're cleared clinically and medically, we don't allow them to come."

She folded her hands on the desk, her knuckles turning white. "I'm not going to lie. These children are troubled, and we can't always predict how they'll react. If they have medical issues that could complicate their progress, say, bipolar disorder or depression, they need to address that with their pediatrician before they attend the camp."

And what if the child wasn't the sick one? What if the problem was at the camp?

Brynn opened her mouth to argue, but Parker caught hold of her arm and pulled her to her feet. "Thank you, Mrs. Gibson. You've been an enormous help. You've given us a lot to think about."

The director rose as well, her smile back in place—but it didn't reach her eyes. "It's not an easy decision. Not every child belongs in a residential program like this. Read the brochures, visit our website. It explains the program in depth. If you're still interested, we'll be happy to make an appointment and introduce you to the staff."

His hand hovering at the small of her back, Parker guided Brynn out the door. Then he frog-marched her to the parking lot. "What was that about?" he demanded when they reached his truck.

Still struggling to control her temper, Brynn clutched her stack of brochures. "I got tired of listening to her sales pitch. She sounded like some kind of infomercial, making everything sound so ideal."

"She's the director. It's her job to promote the place. And why shouldn't she brag? The camp's reputation is great."

"That's just it. It's *too* good." She gestured toward the office. "Look at this place. There's no peeling paint, no weeds growing around the bushes. Nothing's out of place." It even smelled like the perfect camp—a faint trace of wood smoke mingling with the scent of the pines. "It's like some fairy-tale version of rehab. I wanted to shake her up."

"Yeah, you did that. I doubt she'll forget us anytime soon."

Oh, God. He was right. She'd made them memorable, and not in a positive way.

And for what? Exactly what had she accomplished here? Sure, she'd found a map and a camera's memory card, but they might not yield any clues. And at what cost? The director would remember her now. The minute she went to her file cabinet, she'd make the connection—and tip her stepfather off.

Suddenly feeling deflated, Brynn sagged back against the truck. Maybe she'd been wrong to come here. Maybe she was mistaken about Erin's death. Maybe she was simply too biased against her stepfather to accept the truth—that Erin Walker had taken drugs, then suffered an accident or killed herself, just as the autopsy report said.

She rubbed the dull ache forming between her eyes. Because even though she hated to admit it, the program did sound great. The staff seemed committed to helping those troubled kids.

"I'm sorry. I know it was dumb to provoke her. It's just…I keep thinking that something's off. That Erin's death wasn't what it seemed."

Parker leaned back against the truck beside her and crossed his arms. For a long moment he didn't answer. The cool breeze ruffled his hair. Dried leaves rustled over the ground. A chipmunk watched them from a nearby tree stump, then picked up a nut and scurried away.

Parker turned his head to meet her gaze. "You really think that girl was murdered?"

"I don't know."

"But that's what you think."

She nodded. "Yes, that's what I think."

He lapsed into silence again. A long moment later, he dragged his hand down his face. "There's no evidence."

"I know. But something else is going on here. I'm sure of it, Parker. I just can't prove it yet."

His gaze swung back to hers. Several seconds ticked by. His scrutiny made her uneasy, the intensity in his eyes making it impossible to breathe.

And, suddenly, she suspected he knew more than he'd let on—about her relationship to her stepfather, about her troubled childhood, about the horrific abuse that drove her from home. That he was simply biding his time—like the trained interrogator he was—waiting for her to confess the truth.

She couldn't believe how tempted she was to do just that—to forget that he was a cop, to ignore the danger hounding her footsteps and tell him the unvarnished truth.

But then, his expression changed. His eyes were just as intense, but hotter, more hypnotic, like whirlpools dragging her under—in a decidedly sensual way.

Her pulse battered her throat. He pushed away from the truck and moved even closer, trapping her against the cab. And that insane attraction rippled between them, that unruly maelstrom of need.

Her breath backed up in her lungs. Her belly tightened, acute tremors of excitement tripping along her nerves. She tore her gaze from his jet-black eyes to the black stubble shadowing his granite jaw, and stalled on his gripping mouth. Then he reached out and stroked his finger down her cheek, sending a torrent of pleasure streaming through her veins.

Was he going to *kiss* her?

His gaze dropped to her mouth. Her heart nearly leaped from her chest. And for a wild moment she wondered if she should push him away—or pull him close.

But then a gunshot erupted in the distance, jarring her back to earth. *Hunters.* A reminder that predators prowled in the forest—like the enemies pursuing her.

Parker stepped away. "We'd better go."

"Right." Somehow, she managed to breathe. But as she climbed into the truck, her pulse still wildly out of rhythm, she had the feeling that something had changed inside her. A decade of survival instincts were now at war with her heart.

And for the first time, she didn't know which would win.

Chapter 7

He'd nearly kissed a potential suspect.

Parker leaned against his kitchen counter in his condo on the outskirts of Baltimore a short time later, unable to believe what he'd just done. He knew he had to stay detached. He knew he had to keep a level head. And yet he'd ignored his protesting conscience, let his hormones override his judgment and nearly blown his impartiality to shreds. If that gunshot hadn't stopped him, he would have violated every principle he believed in—his oath of honor, the police officer's code of ethics, the high moral standards that had kept him from becoming his father's clone.

Thoroughly disgusted at his behavior, he speared his hand through his hair. He'd nearly screwed up, all right. But now he had an even bigger problem on his hands. He'd seen that photo of Brynn on the file cabinet, the one she'd taken pains to hide. And Ruth Gibson was nobody's fool. The next time she looked at her file cabinet, she'd link that photo to Brynn. Then she'd notify Hoffman that his long-lost stepdaughter had been nosing around the camp with a man fitting Parker's description, asking questions about the dead girl's case—the case Hoffman had warned him to leave alone.

And Parker could kiss his job goodbye.

Searching for a way to contain the damage, he put the tuna fish sandwiches he'd made on the table, then added napkins and plates. Maybe he could spin his involvement with Brynn, pretend he was following Hoffman's orders and trying to earn her trust. That might mollify the Colonel, buying him enough time to investigate this case.

Assuming Brynn didn't catch on first.

He glanced at the door to the downstairs bathroom, the sound of running water signaling that she was still busy freshening up. Deciding he had to chance it, he took out his cell phone and punched in Hoffman's number. The administrative assistant answered on the second ring.

"Hi, Debbie. This is Detective McCall," he said, keeping his voice low. "Is the Colonel in? He's expecting my call."

The assistant put him on hold just as the bathroom tap cut off. Not wanting Brynn to hear him, he strode down the hall to the guest bedroom and shut the door.

"Hoffman here," the C.I.D. chief said a second later.

"I found your daughter."

A pause pulsed over the line. "Already? Good work." Pleasure suffused his voice. "I knew I could count on you."

"But I can't bring her in yet," Parker added quickly.

"Why not?"

"She doesn't trust me yet. I need more time."

"How much time?" Hoffman sounded annoyed now, and Parker winced. His boss wasn't a patient man.

"Not much. A few days at most. She's still nervous. If I make a move now, she'll bolt."

Hoffman didn't answer at first. "Two days," he finally said. "I want her in custody by then. If she won't come in freely, we'll haul her in for questioning for your brother's death. But I'm hoping it won't come to that."

"I'll call you as soon as I can."

"You'd better. And Parker..." Hoffman paused. "Watch out. She's clever. She'll play on your sympathies and twist the truth until you don't know what to think. Make sure you don't fall for her act." He disconnected the line.

Parker slipped his phone back into his pocket, suddenly besieged by doubts. Was Brynn manipulating him? Was she doing exactly what Hoffman had warned him about and playing him for her own ends? Or was the Colonel lying to him?

Even more unsettled, he strode back into the kitchen. Brynn stood at the counter, holding her camera, and she raised her gaze to his. And that quick lurch of attraction tripped through him, that inevitable surge of adrenaline that knocked his pulse off course. His belly went taut, his breath quickening.

And damned if he didn't feel guilty, as if he'd betrayed her somehow.

But that was ridiculous. He didn't owe her a blasted thing. So what if her talent intrigued him? So what if her uncommon beauty provoked instincts hard to resist?

He was a cop, a professional. He knew better than to let his hormones rule his head. And his duty was clear— rule out foul play in that young girl's death, get Brynn to fulfill her part of their agreement and then hand her over to her stepfather and be done with her for good.

No matter how much she tempted him.

He motioned toward the kitchen table. "I made some sandwiches. Help yourself if you're hungry."

"Thanks." Her gaze skidded away. A blush tinged her cheeks, more proof that she felt this reckless pull. But she seemed determined to resist it, which was good. Because when she found out he worked for her stepfather…

She sank into her seat and set down her camera, then took her laptop from her bag. "I'll transfer those photos to my computer while we eat. We lucked out with their camera. It uses the same kind of memory card mine does." She inserted the memory card into her camera and got to work, still not quite meeting his gaze.

Needing a distraction, he took the seat across the table and devoured half of his sandwich in a few quick bites. Then he uploaded the photos he'd taken to his own tablet computer and turned his focus to finding clues.

He examined the camp's map first. The grounds were bigger than he'd expected, sprawling for several hundred acres over South Mountain where it merged with the Catoctin range. The main cabins were near the office. They consisted of half a dozen buildings clustered around a central dining hall. Trails fanned out from the compound, meandering through the hills like crooked spokes. One path led to a river, where kayaks and canoes were stored. Another went to a rock climbing area and zip line course. The bulk of the trails ended at a lake, where there was a fishing dock, beach, several rustic campsites and a shower house.

The old Forest Service lookout tower where Erin Walker had died was in the opposite direction, near the southern perimeter of the camp. Next to it was an abandoned farmhouse. A faint line connected the farmhouse to the nearest road.

Parker frowned. "Look at this." He angled the tablet so Brynn could see. "There used to be a road to this farmhouse. If it's still there, you can enter the camp near the lookout tower."

"Is that important?"

"Possibly. A couple things have been bugging me about this case. One is why Erin went to the tower. It's not near her cabin. And it was dark. Why would she hike that distance through the woods at night alone?"

"We don't know that she *was* alone."

"True." Although the absence of other footprints would suggest as much. "Either way, it's quite a trek. The other question is where she got the drugs. The autopsy said she had meth in her system. So she either brought it in herself—"

"No." Brynn sounded sure. "The staff would have searched their bags. They'd want to make sure the kids weren't smuggling in alcohol or drugs."

"Then someone else brought it in." But who? "We know she ended up at the tower. So maybe she met her drug supplier near there. That gives her a reason to make that hike."

Brynn studied the map, her eyes reflecting her doubt. "You're right about the distance, though. That's a long hike in the dark. And she had to cross that creek. I wonder if there's a bridge somewhere."

"It isn't on the map." Curious now, he rose and retrieved Erin's file, then took his seat again. He skimmed the autopsy report, pausing on the description of her clothes. "Her shoes and socks were wet. So she probably waded through the creek."

Brynn looked even more skeptical now. "She was twelve years old. Those woods would be scary at night. And then to wade across a creek with the water all black and cold?" She shook her head. "I don't see it."

"She was on meth. She probably felt invincible. That could explain why she climbed that tower."

"Maybe." Brynn didn't sound convinced. "But I still can't see her going all that way alone."

"You think another kid went with her?"

She hesitated, her gold-flecked eyes reflecting her doubt. "Or someone chased her there."

That made even less sense. "If she was in danger, why would she run away from help? Why not go to the counselors' cabin and find an adult?"

"Maybe one of the adults was chasing her."

Parker arched a brow. "That's quite a leap." And they didn't have a shred of proof. Still, something compelling had convinced Erin Walker to make that trek. "Let's gather the evidence first, then start drawing conclusions."

Determined to follow his own advice, he returned his attention to his computer, bringing up the cabin assignments this time. He listed the campers' names in a separate document, highlighting the kids in Erin's cabin. Not that it did much good. He couldn't interrogate those kids without their parents' consent—and alerting his boss.

He blew out a frustrated breath. "Any luck with the photos?"

"Not yet. There are thousands of pictures on this card. I've skipped ahead to the ones taken around the day she died."

Taking sips of water, she continued studying the screen. He watched her drink, the erotic lilt of her lush lips like a cattle prod on his nerves. He took in the high, sweet curves of her breasts, the graceful line of her throat. And the urge to plunge his hands through her fiery hair, to plunder the heaven of her moist lips, nearly did him in.

Dangerous thoughts, he warned himself. He had to resist Brynn Elliot, not fantasize about how good she'd make him feel. Now if he could just convince his body of that…

"Here, take a look." She turned her computer toward him, and he forced his attention to the screen. The photos were what he'd expected—kids clowning around and doing the usual camp activities, such as swimming and pitching tents. His interest lagged until she brought up several shots that included adults—the director, counselors. *His boss.* There were several shots of Hoffman playing football with the kids, which made sense. He'd been a high school football star.

Brynn paused on a picture of the campers roasting marshmallows over a campfire. Hoffman was there, sitting beside a skinny, preteen girl with a long black ponytail. The scene looked ordinary enough…except his knee rested against her thigh. He sat so close that their shoulders touched. And she was clearly trying to lean away, her legs curled up in a fetal position, her face averted from his.

A funny feeling took hold in Parker's gut, and he glanced at Brynn. She stared at the screen, her face suddenly pale, her fingertips pressed to her mouth, as if she was trying not to get sick.

She dragged her gaze to his, the horror in her eyes catching him off guard. Her reaction seemed way out of proportion to seeing a photo of her estranged step-father sitting beside a child. Unless...

"You're not saying..." He could hardly voice the thought, it disgusted him so much. "You don't think Hoffman and that child..."

Brynn didn't answer. She didn't have to. The revulsion in her eyes said it all.

She believed Hoffman was a pedophile, that he'd sexually molested this kid.

Stunned, Parker jerked his gaze away. *A pedophile? Was she nuts?* The Colonel was everyone's role model, the most upstanding man he knew. And he'd warned Parker not to believe her. Brynn had a history of making false accusations against him. But the horror in her eyes looked real.

And sometimes even the wildest allegations proved true.

His emotions in total upheaval, he stared at the screen as Brynn scrolled through several more shots— Erin paddling a canoe, erecting a tent with the black-haired girl. She was smiling at the camera and looked content.

Then another shot filled the screen, this one of Erin Walker standing beside the lake, the Colonel at her side. He had his arm slung over her shoulders, an easy smile on his face. Erin was dressed in a one-piece swimsuit, clutching a towel to her scrawny frame. She looked ready to cry.

Parker's heart sank. Oh, hell. This did not look good.

"The date is July 14, two days before she died," Brynn said. She zoomed in on the doomed child's face. Sunglasses hid her eyes, but her mouth wobbled down at the corners. She had the necklace on.

Parker stared at the screen. Disgust warred with dread in his gut. "You think Hoffman is abusing these kids. You think he caused Erin Walker's death."

"I think there's a good chance, yeah."

Parker pushed away from the table, then paced around his kitchen, too agitated to stay in his seat. A murder at the camp would be scandalous enough. But sexual abuse… This was huge, explosive—and not just because Hoffman was a cop. Not even because he was the head of C.I.D., a man with formidable power. Hoffman was the protégé of an influential senator. Various politicians had stakes in his success. The repercussions would ripple up through the highest circles, destroying families and careers.

He met Brynn's eyes, knowing she was wondering how he'd react. But what should he think? He'd read her file. She had a history of inventing tales.

But what if her stories are true? What if no one had believed her back then? Could the system have screwed up that much?

He wanted to believe her. She came across as sincere. But he had a weak spot when it came to Brynn. And the Colonel was a model citizen with a stellar reputation, a paragon in the community.

Just like Parker's father.

And look how corrupt he'd been.

"If she was abused, then how come she didn't report it?" he asked. "It's not as if there's no one there to talk to. There are counselors all over that camp."

"Fear. Shame. Maybe he told her no one would believe her, or worse, that they'd say it was all her fault."

Still not convinced, he shook his head. "Why didn't the counselors notice something was wrong? They're sensitive to that these days, especially if they work with kids. They're trained to spot the signs."

"They see what they want to see, especially if the guy has power."

Was that true? Parker leaned back against the sink, trying to keep an open mind. Would the staff overlook a pedophile if he was important enough? He had to admit Hoffman fit the profile. Pedophiles often coached and ran camps to have access to their target kids.

But to prey on children that young... His belly churned. He couldn't stand to think it. A predator like that was a total slime bag, the lowest of the low. And if Hoffman had taken advantage of that poor child's addictions to molest her...how much worse could he get?

Brynn rose and joined him at the sink. "You don't believe he abused her?"

"I don't know."

"You mean you don't want to know."

"That's not what I said."

"You didn't have to. He's a cop. He's so high up he's out of reach. He can do whatever he wants, and no one gives a damn, no matter who his victims are."

Parker's jaw went hard, the accusation hitting too close to home. His father had been above the law—or so he'd thought. "That's not true."

"Right." She scoffed in disbelief.

His own temper flared, her poor opinion of the police force rankling him. "Listen, Brynn. I don't care who he is, whether he's the head of C.I.D. or some derelict on the street. If he's guilty, I'm going to find out. But I have to follow the law. I can't accuse him without proof."

"Proof?" Incredulity rang in her voice. "You saw that photo."

"It isn't enough. It's *not*," he continued when she opened her mouth to argue. "I agree that it looks bad. And I'm willing to investigate. But an accusation like this could destroy his life. I can't do that to him until I'm sure."

Her eyes flashed. She propped her fists on her hips. "And what about the children he's destroyed? Don't you care that he ruined their lives?"

"Of course I do." The thought of a helpless child suffering such depravity made him ill. "But I still have to have some proof."

Knowing he hadn't convinced her, he shoved his hand through his hair. "Listen. My dad was the perfect father. He coached Little League and soccer. He led my Cub Scout troop. He was a cop, a hero. Everyone thought he was great, especially us—until the news came out that he had this whole police bribery thing going on."

She went still. "You're saying he wasn't guilty?"

"No. He was guilty as hell. There wasn't any doubt. And when he realized he couldn't hide it…" He inhaled, anger and sorrow churning through him, even now. "He ate his gun. He took the coward's way out, leaving me to deal with the mess."

She pressed her hand to her throat. "You're not saying… You didn't find him?"

"Yeah." He closed his eyes, struggling to block out the memory of the gore. "I heard the shot and went inside the house."

"Oh, God. I'm so sorry, Parker. I didn't know."

"Tommy never told you?"

Her eyes still huge, she shook her head.

"The point is that it ruined our lives. My mom just shriveled up. Her mind went AWOL overnight. She died soon after that. And you saw what happened to Tommy. He'd been using drugs before, but the suicide pushed him over the edge. He got hooked and ran away."

"And you?" she asked, her voice wavering slightly.

"I dealt with it."

"It couldn't have been easy."

"No." They had been the worst years of his life—his mother in full retreat, his brother determined to self-destruct, Parker's integrity under fire at work. "But I know what it feels like to have your world fall apart. I know what an accusation like this can do—not just to the person who's accused, but to everyone around him. And I can't inflict that on anyone until I'm sure."

Her gaze held his, the sympathy in her eyes reeling him in. And a sudden longing whispered through him, the temptation to tug her close, to bask in her comfort and warmth and feel that he wasn't alone.

She reached up and stroked his jaw, the slight touch jump-starting his pulse. And another emotion washed through him, a need so sharp it stole his breath. He grabbed her wrist, stilling her hand, keeping her soft, delicate fingers trapped against his jaw.

His heart tapped a ragged beat. Sudden heat thickened his blood. And, without warning, far more than sympathy crackled between them. That hunger simmering beneath the surface exploded to life, too potent to ignore.

His gaze fell to her mouth. She moistened her lips with her tongue, sending a swift shaft of heat arrowing straight to his groin. His body went taut, the insistent urge to touch her flaying his blood. He wanted to inhale her arresting scent, make her breath turn jagged and fast, feel her bare skin slick against his.

Unable to resist, he pulled her against him.

"This is a bad idea," she whispered, her gaze fastened on his mouth.

"Really bad." But then why did it feel like the only thing he'd done right in a long, long time?

He released her hand, then slid his thumb along her jaw, tilting her chin toward his. He plunged his other hand through her hair, wrapping the silky strands around his fist the way he'd ached to, the shimmering satin igniting his nerves.

Her eyes fluttered closed. He bent his head, the erotic scent of her filling his senses, her nearness weakening his restraint. Then he slanted his mouth over hers, her thrilling taste turning his blood hot. Wreaking havoc on his good intentions. Incinerating his resolve.

Her lips parted, allowing him entry. Making a low, rough sound of approval, he hauled her more fully into his arms, taking her lips in a hungry kiss. His body went rock-hard, the alluring feel of her blurring his mind. He dropped one hand to the small of her back, aligning her lower body more firmly against him, and the feel of her hips cradling his shaft nearly sent him over the edge.

She was sultry, delicate, soft, as exciting as he'd imagined, her intoxicating taste driving him wild.

But this was nuts. She was a suspect, a person of interest in his brother's case, no matter how crazed she made him feel.

With effort, he broke the kiss. His breath sawing, his heart thundering, he pulled her head to his chest. Then he closed his eyes, struggling to regain control, but it took every ounce of willpower he possessed not to forget his honor—or his sanity—and give in to the explosive hunger riding them both.

After a moment, he eased back farther, putting some badly needed space between them. He couldn't screw this up. He had too much at stake. But the sight of her kiss-swollen lips and her eyes dark with desire nearly brought him to his knees.

She cleared her throat and stepped back, a soft flush staining her cheeks. "Listen, Parker. I can't… This isn't…"

"I know. Bad timing."

"Yeah," she agreed, but the raw need in her eyes contradicted her words, tempting him to forget his good intentions and yank her back into his arms.

She nodded. "But about Hoffman—"

"I still need proof."

"I know. But I'm worried about those kids." Fear crept back through her eyes. "I'm scared he'll hurt someone else."

Parker understood. And without warning, snippets from Brynn's file flitted through his mind, hints at the evil she must have endured—assuming her accusations were true. But he didn't dare go there just yet. It would make him way too crazy to think of what she'd suffered and how badly she'd been betrayed. He had to try to stay impartial for now.

But he had the sinking feeling it was far too late

for that. That kiss had just blown away any objectivity he'd had.

"We'd better go," she said. "It's time to meet with Jamie."

"Yeah." They had to find that prostitute, the one with the borrowed necklace—their only clue right now. "But Brynn…"

Pausing, she glanced back.

"I give you my word. We'll get to the truth." Because if someone had killed Erin Walker, Parker intended to bring him down.

No matter who the hell he was.

Brynn snuck a glance at Parker's profile as they walked along a side street in search of Jamie, her head still spinning from that kiss. She'd spent the thirty-minute drive from Parker's condo to downtown Baltimore in a haze of lust, unable to focus on a single thought. Even traipsing through the chilly evening air hadn't helped. Just the sight of his hard-planed face, the memory of that wicked mouth on hers, sent thrills shuddering and skipping through her veins.

But it was learning about his background—the crushing disillusionment he'd suffered about his father, how he'd struggled to hold his family together after that weak-willed man checked out—that really demolished her equilibrium, making it impossible to stay detached. Parker was more complex than she'd expected, more human, a man she was rapidly coming to respect.

But she couldn't afford to think like that. That killer might be searching for her. A dangerous predator was on the loose, preying on innocent kids. And getting involved with a cop could be suicidal, no matter how much she wanted to trust him—or how delirious he made her feel.

But oh, that man could kiss…

Still struggling to pull herself together, she glanced down the darkened street, noting how oddly empty it seemed. No hookers sauntered past. No men loitered or milled around. An occasional car drove by, heading to Garrison Boulevard a block away, but the street was strangely subdued. Across from a broken streetlight, two teens loitered on the steps of a row house, talking on their cell phones. But Jamie was nowhere in sight.

Brynn braved a peek at Parker, another sizzle of awareness scattering her pulse when he met her eyes. "I'll ask those guys if they've seen her," she said, hoping that putting some distance between them would get her mind on track.

"I'll do it." He loped up the sidewalk. She followed more slowly, her gaze roaming from the impossible width of his shoulders in his leather jacket to the sexy fit of his faded jeans. She stifled a sigh. She had it bad, all right. Just looking at Parker put her hormones in overdrive. But it was time to get a grip.

The two boys rose as Parker approached. But then they took off running, slipping into the shadows beside the house. "Hey!" he called, but they vanished into the night.

Parker swung back around, a scowl on his handsome face. "What the hell?"

"They probably realized you were a cop." Not a popular profession in this part of town. But where was Jamie? And why were the streets so deserted? This time of night, more people should be hanging around.

Brynn frowned at the murky shadows, apprehension

plucking her nerves. Smashed glass littered the street. A gang-tagged car sat rusting by the curb. A black cat slunk past, then squeezed under a chain-link fence, disappearing into a weed-choked lot.

Something is about to go down here. The street was too quiet. Tension screamed in the air. "I don't like this."

"I agree. Something's off. Let's get out of here."

Glad he hadn't resisted, Brynn turned back toward Parker's car. But then a woman emerged from an alley half a block away. Heading in the opposite direction, she strutted down the sidewalk, her high-heeled boots and spandex skirt advertising her trade.

Brynn placed her hand on Parker's arm. "Hold on a minute. Maybe I can get her to talk."

She jogged after the woman to catch up. A lone car rumbled past. The hooker ran into the street to flag it down, then let loose with a stream of obscenities as it sped off.

"Excuse me," Brynn called out. She hurried past the junked car.

The hooker spun around to face her, her heavily made-up eyes narrowing to slits. She looked about sixty, but was probably closer to Brynn's own age, with tri-colored hair resembling a rat's nest atop her head. Her huge breasts swayed in her halter top.

"I'm looking for Jamie," Brynn said. "She hangs out near here. Do you know her?"

The woman backed up and shook her head. "I got nothing to do with her." She spun around to leave.

"Wait!" Brynn lunged forward and stopped her, unwilling to give up yet. "Please. She's my friend. I really need to talk to her."

The hooker blinked. "How you going to do that?"

This time Brynn went still. "What do you mean?"

"She's dead."

"Dead?" Brynn gaped at her in disbelief. "But… that's impossible. I talked to her yesterday, and she was fine."

"Gangbangers," the hooker told her as a deep rumble drummed the air. "They…"

A low-riding car turned onto the street, its headlights cutting through the gloom. Suddenly all business, the hooker pulled down her top to reveal more cleavage, stepped off the curb and thrust out a heavy hip. But then her dark eyes bulged. Her jaw went slack, her face turning stark with fear. Swearing, she whirled around and fled, moving faster than Brynn thought possible on her spiked heels.

"Wait!" Brynn called, but the hooker darted between two sagging porches and disappeared.

Still reeling from the news about Jamie, Brynn headed back down the sidewalk toward Parker, one eye on the approaching car. She couldn't believe that Jamie was dead. Why would gang members kill a young prostitute like her? Unless Jamie's murder had something to do with *her*…

The lowrider car puttered closer. The deep blast of its subwoofers vibrated the ground. The feeling of imminent danger mounting, she hurried to catch up to Parker, anxious to get off the street.

But then the lowrider drew even with them and stopped. The passenger window rolled down.

The barrel of a gun appeared.

Parker lunged forward and knocked her down, shoving her to the sidewalk behind the gang-tagged car just as they opened fire.

Chapter 8

Brynn lay plastered under Parker, bullets thudding and pinging into the car beside them, his heavy body pinning her down.

Gangbangers were trying to kill them. They had to get out of there fast. She shoved against Parker, her survival instincts shrieking at her to run, but his dead weight kept her trapped.

"Don't move!" he shouted into her ear. "Stay behind the engine block." Pulling his pistol from his back holster, he leaped to his feet and returned fire, the deafening barks making her flinch. She crawled to a crouch, the cement rough on her palms, and searched for a way to escape. But they'd never make it. The nearest house was half a dozen yards away—and they'd be dead before they ran three feet.

Parker ducked behind the car again, a battle raging in his dark eyes. "I said to stay down," he growled, whipping out his cell phone. He lifted it to his mouth.

Brynn's heart stopped. He was going to call the police. She grabbed hold of his wrist. "No, don't!"

"What?"

"Don't call," she begged as incredulity flooded his eyes. "I can't… I'll explain later. Please," she added, praying he'd listen.

He stared at her for a heartbeat. Then another barrage of gunfire broke out, and he swore. He pocketed the phone and waited a beat, then jumped to his feet and pumped out several more rounds. Brynn clapped her hands to her ringing ears.

She knew Parker thought she was insane. It was lunacy to resist calling for backup when they were pinned behind this car. But the police meant involving her stepfather—a danger she couldn't afford.

Wishing desperately that she still had her handgun, she scoured the street, frantic to find a way out. But the narrow trees wouldn't offer protection. The nearby porches were too exposed, assuming they could make it up the steps. Farther down the street was that empty lot—but it was still too far away.

She beat back a swell of panic, the feeling of helplessness she most despised. She was *not* going to die here. She refused to let these street punks do her in after everything she'd endured. She spotted a bottle in the gutter and grabbed it, marginally reassured. It wasn't much of a weapon, but at least she could try to fight back.

Parker crouched beside her. He ejected his spent magazine, took another from his holster and slammed it into his gun. Something moved at the edge of Brynn's vision. Her panic exploding, she whipped up and hurled the bottle at their assailant—just as a shot barked out. The bullet went wild, and she flung herself back down. Parker jumped up and got off several more rounds.

The car's engine roared. Tires screeched, a thick, choking cloud of exhaust billowing past as the driver gunned the accelerator and peeled off. Her heart still stampeding wildly, Brynn rose and peered around. Smoke swirled through the haze from a nearby porch light. The stench of sulfur permeated the air. She drew in a breath, the abrupt silence reverberating in her eardrums, her legs trembling so badly she could barely stand.

"Why didn't you stay down?" Parker raged. "You could have been killed."

"He was going to shoot you." She heaved in another breath. "Did you get him?"

"Yeah." His expression still fierce, he took her arm. "Come on. We need to get out of here before they come back."

The gang would retaliate, all right. Parker had just provided them with another reason to want them dead.

But why had the gang attacked them to begin with? And why had they done Jamie in? Her thoughts winging back to the teenager, she raced after Parker down the empty street, her feet crunching over broken glass. This couldn't be a coincidence. That gang had gone after Jamie right after Brynn had talked to her.

Jamie was dead because of her.

Hardly able to grasp it, she hurried toward Parker's truck. He beeped it open, and she dove inside, but she couldn't avoid the truth. All these years she'd guarded her secrets. It had been the only way to keep her friends safe. Even now, years of ingrained caution were clamoring at her to run, stay quiet, *hide*. But that strategy no longer worked. Innocent people were dying because of her. First Tommy. Now Jamie. Even her agent had nearly lost her life.

She might even be responsible for Erin's death. Her continued silence had enabled a dangerous predator to operate undetected, harming untold numbers of kids.

She stole a look at Parker's profile, her stomach a flurry of dread. But no matter how much it scared her, she knew what she had to do. She had to reveal what she'd witnessed that awful night, why she didn't want him to call the police.

And how she'd caused his brother's death.

Parker cranked the truck's powerful engine and sped away from the curb. Fastening her seat belt, she scoured her mind for another option, but that gang had forced her hand. She had to make a leap of faith and confess the truth.

She just prayed that Parker would believe her—or neither of them would survive.

Brynn was still gathering her courage half an hour later as she huddled on the leather sofa in Parker's condo, clutching a throw blanket over her shoulders in a futile attempt to warm up. Her hands were like blocks of ice. The adrenaline dump from that shooting had left her so shaken she could hardly hold on to a thought. But she had to pull herself together fast.

Parker came through his kitchen doorway, cradling a crystal tumbler in each big hand. "Vodka," he announced, handing her a glass. He took his seat on the sofa beside her, making the cushions sink. He'd removed his leather jacket and pushed up the sleeves of his faded blue Henley, exposing the sinews of his muscled arms. Warmth beckoned from his solid frame, making her yearn to lean close.

Instead she sipped her vodka, shuddering as it burned her throat. "Did you find out anything?" She'd heard Parker phoning his coworkers for information as he'd poured their drinks.

He nodded, his dark eyes grim. "They received a discharge call, a report that shots were fired. They sent a patrol unit to investigate."

"Do they know that you were involved?"

"They'll figure it out eventually. They can trace the shells to my gun. But unless they find something that connects it to Jamie, they won't investigate it for a while. They've got too many homicides to deal with first. That buys us a couple of days, at least."

Brynn took another swallow of vodka. Baltimore was a violent city. Unless there was a victim, a simple report of shots fired would be a low priority. "What about Jamie?"

"They found her in Lincoln Park. That's a standard spot for a dump job. Rigor mortis puts her death at around six last night. She still had money—several hundred bucks—so it wasn't a robbery. All signs point to the Ridgewood gang."

"That's what the hooker said, that the gang killed her." Like the execution she'd witnessed years ago. Brynn closed her eyes, bile swarming through her belly at the thought. She could only pray that Jamie hadn't suffered, that the end had been mercifully swift.

"It's my fault," she admitted, feeling sick.

"Why do you say that?"

Brynn shifted her gaze to him. She took in his dark, knitted brows, the stark, steely planes of his thoroughly masculine face. He looked dependable, invincible, strong.

Leap of faith, she reminded herself. She had to trust him. She could no longer do this alone. She took a gulp of vodka for courage and shivered hard. "I didn't tell you, but the night you found me, the night you came to my house, my agent, Joan Kellogg, had been attacked."

"The one in Alexandria?"

"You know her?"

He shook his head. "Just her name."

Of course he would know all that. He was a detective—a darned good one since he'd managed to track her down.

"That's where I went after you left my house," she continued. "I wanted to warn her that you'd shown up and that the media could be next. But when I got there, she'd been attacked. She said the guy was after me. He was Caucasian, with black hair and a snake tattoo."

"The Ridgewood gang. That's their symbol."

Brynn nodded, then choked more vodka down. "That's not all. I thought someone was following me when we met at the coffee shop the next day. But I figured I'd imagined it. Or that maybe I'd lost him. I must have been wrong. He must have followed me to Jamie. Although I don't know how...."

"Why would the gang be after you?"

Good question. Knowing the time had come to answer, she swallowed hard. "I'm not exactly sure. It's a different gang. But I think it's connected to a gang execution I witnessed fifteen years ago." She forced herself to meet his eyes. "That was the day your brother died."

Parker went stone-still. His gaze didn't veer from hers. A clock ticked in the kitchen, in time to her thumping heart. "I told you I met Tommy on the streets," she continued. "We were friends. Just friends," she added in case he was wondering. "I was really young. And I…I was a real mess back then."

She'd been so incredibly damaged, so utterly alone. So terrified and furious at the world. Betrayed by everyone who should have helped her. She'd gone berserk whenever a man came near.

But Tommy had been different. He'd never looked at her in that sick, sadistic way she'd come to associate with men. He'd wormed through her defenses, renewing her hope that good people still existed, even if a monster had preyed on her.

"I had two other friends, two girls I hung around with," she continued. "They'd run away, too. Haley got pregnant, and her family disowned her. Nadine was a little older, seventeen, I think. Her family was Middle Eastern. They were trying to force her into an arranged marriage. They threatened to kill her if she didn't obey." A threat they intended to carry out, even now, if they ever caught up to her.

"We stayed together for protection at first. It's not easy to survive on the streets without a pimp." And Brynn would have killed herself before she'd let a man touch her again.

"None of us knew how hard it would be. The hunger, the violence… We weren't prepared for that. So we stuck together to survive."

She slid Parker a glance. He sat immobile, tension rippling from his steel-hard frame. "Tommy watched out for us, too. He kept the men away, made sure they knew we weren't alone. He was kind to us." She paused. "You have no idea how rare that is on the streets."

Parker looked away, his Adam's apple working in his whiskered throat. Her heart rolled, knowing how painful this had to be for him to hear.

"We tried to help him, too," she said, her own chest tight. "We made sure he had blankets and food. We took him to the needle exchange. He…he wasn't alone, Parker. We'd formed a family of sorts."

Parker set his glass on the coffee table, then pressed his fingertips to his eyes. The slump of his broad shoulders, the anguish seeping from his powerful body made her yearn to console him, to wrap her arms around him and hold him close. But she had to tell him the rest before she lost her nerve.

Even if he despised her when she did.

"I had a camera, an old thirty-five-millimeter Yashica. It belonged to my father—my real father. He was an amateur photographer. He mostly took nature shots. We used to go on long hikes through the woods… He taught me how to see things differently, to look at the colors and light. He made everything seem beautiful, magical." She'd only been five or six, but she still remembered those days vividly—the enchantment, the wonder, the joy. They'd been the best days of her life.

"That camera…it meant the world to me." It was her prized possession, her only link to her beloved father, and the only thing that had kept her sane. "Anyhow, I got it in my head to photograph an abandoned warehouse near Orleans Street. It had the most amazing historic details. And it…affected me somehow, how sad and ruined it was. I wanted to capture it on film.

"It was dumb. The C.D. gang owned the streets

around there. The City of the Dead. They ran the heroin trade back then. Tommy tried to convince me not to do it. So did Haley and Nadine. But I wouldn't listen. I thought I'd be safe if I went early enough in the day.

"I went the next afternoon. Nadine and Haley insisted on coming with me, even though they didn't approve. But we'd gotten a late start. Haley had found a stray cat." Even then Haley had been a nurturer, trying to rescue everyone in sight.

"And Tommy?" Parker asked, his voice unsteady.

"He wasn't around when we woke up. I didn't know where he'd gone. When we got to the warehouse, Haley and Nadine refused to go inside. They were smart." Brynn stared, unseeing, at her glass, a cold pit forming around her heart. How many times had she wished she could relive that moment and listen to them this time? "I thought I'd be okay."

She'd never been more wrong.

She drained her glass of vodka, set it on the coffee table and pushed it aside. Then she pulled the blanket closer around her in a useless attempt to warm up. "I started taking pictures. It was a big place, the walls all covered with gang tags." Another warning she'd ignored. "I kept going in deeper, where there wasn't much light. The shadows brought out the textures in the walls, little fissures and defects that the sunlight hid…."

Just like with people. Their real nature emerged in the dark.

Shivering, she pulled her mind back on track. "Then I heard voices. I thought it was just a drug deal. I should have turned around." Another fatal mistake.

"The next room had a big window along one wall, the glass all busted out. It looked out at an inner courtyard. The voices were coming from there, so I went to see. A man was kneeling on the ground. He had his back to me, and I could see that his hands were tied. He was crying."

She closed her eyes, trying to block out the memory of that horrific, high-pitched sound. A man reduced to his most primitive instinct, whimpering and pleading for his life.

"I couldn't see his face, but he looked older, middle-aged. He had a bald spot, and he was wearing a blue plaid shirt and slacks. Not the kind of clothes someone younger would wear."

"He was forty-five." Parker sounded numb. "His name was Allen Chambers. He was a heroin addict from Dumfries, Virginia. His hands weren't bound when they found him, but there were bruises on his wrists."

Brynn nodded. Of course Parker would know the details. The dead man had been found near his brother's body. "There were a couple of gang members with him. Two, for sure, but I only saw one man's face. He was facing in my direction. He was Caucasian, with tattoos on his cheeks and neck. Crosses. He was in his early twenties, I'd guess. I couldn't see the other person from where I stood, just his weapon. There was a pillar blocking my view. But they both had guns."

She clasped her hands and curled forward, the terror of it flooding back. "I was so scared. I couldn't move. I was just…frozen. I don't know how long I stood there, probably only seconds, but it felt like hours. The kneeling man kept sobbing and begging for them to let him live.

"And then…they shot him. I'm not sure who fired the gun. I thought it was the other man, the one I couldn't see, but it happened so fast I couldn't tell. There was this enormous bang and the man flew back."

She hugged her arms and rocked, trying to block out the images. The blood. The dead man's vacant eyes. The dreadful silence of a life abruptly gone.

"They realized I was there. I don't know how. Maybe I cried out, or I moved and it caught their eyes. But the guy with the tattoos looked up. He raised his gun. That's when I turned and ran."

Her palms turned slick with sweat, her heart thudding against her rib cage as she relived that frantic flight, the wild hysteria fueling her steps. "They chased me. I knew they wouldn't give up, that they'd never let me live. I'd just seen them murder that man. And they were fast. I could hear their footsteps pounding behind me. All I could think was that I had to warn Haley and Nadine.

"And then, out of nowhere, Tommy leaped out. He must have been coming to find me."

She dragged her gaze to Parker, meeting his tormented eyes. "He saved my life. He got in their way on purpose, stopping them so I could escape. I heard the shots…."

Parker closed his eyes. The stark pain on his face twisted inside her, like a knife cleaving her heart, bringing a sting of tears to her eyes. "I'm so sorry, Parker. It was all my fault. If I'd only listened to him and not gone there…"

For a long moment, he didn't answer. He hung his head, anguish radiating from him in waves. And then he scrubbed his face with his hands, the tension in his shoulders giving way to a weary slump. Acceptance. Resignation. Despair.

"It wasn't your fault," he said, his voice raw. "You didn't pull that trigger."

"I might as well have. He never would have been there if it weren't for me. And I was a coward. I kept running. I didn't even go back to help." To her everlasting shame.

Parker shook his head. "You were how old? Eleven? Twelve?"

"Thirteen by then." She'd just been small for her age.

"You were a child."

Not in the ways that counted. She'd lost her innocence long before that. "Still…"

"What good would it have done? He probably died instantly. And if you'd gone back they would have shot you, too."

But at least she would have deserved it. And leaving Tommy alone like that after all he'd done for her… "I should have been there for him. He was my friend." A friend she'd left lying dead in an abandoned warehouse after he'd sacrificed his life to save hers.

"So what did you do?" Parker asked, emotions roughening his voice.

"I caught up with Haley and Nadine, and we ran for blocks." Racing through the streets in abject panic, frantic to save their lives. "We finally found a drainage pipe and hid. We huddled there for hours. Later, when it was dark enough and we were sure they'd left, we came back out."

"Why didn't you call the police?"

"The police?" She shot him a look of disbelief. "We were minors. Runaways. The cops were our enemies. They would have hauled us in for questioning and sent us home."

"And that would have been so bad?"

"Weren't you listening? Nadine's father had vowed to kill her. We couldn't let her identity come out."

His gaze narrowed. "And you?"

Her stomach tensed. She chose her words, knowing she had to tread carefully now. "My stepfather was a cop. He had…things he needed to hide. He would have made sure I didn't talk."

Not that the police would have believed her. They never had before. Still, he couldn't take the chance that she'd finally get through to someone and expose him for the monster he was, blowing his facade of respectability to shreds.

Parker cocked his head, his eyes narrowed on hers. "You're saying he would have hurt you?"

"I know he would have."

"And that's why you didn't want me to call for backup today? Because he's still around?"

"Yes." She picked up her empty glass, then set it down, scrambling over what to say. "It's…complicated. I can't tell you the details right now." And she prayed he wouldn't press her yet. "But even if I'd talked to the police back then, it wouldn't have done any good. I only saw the one man, the one in the photo. Haley and Nadine didn't see anything, either, so they couldn't help. But I'm sure that the shooter saw us. And he knew I'd caught the execution on film. That's why we had to hide."

Parker's head came up. "Whoa. Back up. You're saying you took pictures?"

She frowned. "Didn't you see them?"

"How could I do that?"

It was her turn to be confused. "I mailed them to the police."

He shot to his feet. "What?"

"I didn't mean to take them. It was a reflex. That's why they ended up blurred and underexposed. But I wanted to help the police catch the killer, so I made prints."

"You took photos," Parker repeated, sounding incredulous. "And you mailed them to the police?"

"Right. I'd been doing odd jobs at a photography store on Charles Street for a while part-time. I'd figured out the code for their alarm system, so I snuck inside that night and developed the film. I wrote Tommy's name on the back of the pictures and sent them to the police. I figured someone would know what to do with them and get them to the right place."

Parker still looked thunderstruck. "They weren't in Tommy's file."

"Maybe they were in the other guy's file—Allen Chambers, the one they executed."

He shook his head. "I followed that case. His body was found near Tommy's, so they assumed the deaths were linked. I would have known if they had evidence like that."

"But...that doesn't make sense. I thought for sure they'd get there." It was the only thing that had assuaged her guilt, believing she'd provided the police with evidence—imperfect though it was.

"So if you never saw them, where did they go?" she asked.

"Good question."

"They were out of focus and dark. You could sort of

see that one guy, but that was it. Maybe the police figured they were worthless and threw them out."

"Not a chance. They would have run them for prints, probably sent them to forensics to see if they could clean them up. They'd never toss evidence like that out."

"So what are you saying? That someone kept them out of the file on purpose?"

Parker's mouth turned grim. "It's a possibility."

"But that means…" If a cop had destroyed those photos… Her heart beat faster. A chill snaked through her blood, sending prickles slithering over her spine. All this time, she'd believed she had two dangerous enemies, two men who wanted her dead—her stepfather and Tommy's killer. But what if she didn't? What if the two men were the same?

Parker's gaze connected with hers, the stunned realization in his eyes mirroring hers. There was only one reason the police would have destroyed that evidence. A cop must have been involved in his brother's killing.

And her stepfather had worked in Homicide at the time….

Chapter 9

Parker stared out his condo window at the gathering night.

A cop might have killed his brother. Someone he'd worked with. Someone he respected and trusted. *Someone he might even work with now.* A coldhearted murderer could be masquerading on the police force, a man who'd violated his vow to protect and defend the innocent, sullying the integrity and responsibility of the badge. A man who defied everything Parker believed in—honor, justice, truth.

And he might have worked in the homicide unit at the time of Tommy's death, destroying evidence, compromising his brother's investigation, committing any number of other crimes.

Still not willing to believe it, Parker braced his forearm on the glass and struggled to marshal his thoughts.

He knew better than to rush to conclusions; he had to stay objective and let the evidence build his case. There might be a logical explanation why those photos had disappeared, one that didn't implicate a cop.

But what the hell it was, he didn't know.

He turned his head toward Brynn. "You're sure you sent those photos to the police?"

Her eyes troubled, she gave him a nod. "I looked up the address in a phone book—the Baltimore Police Department on East Fayette Street. Then I went to the post office and bought a bunch of stamps from the machine. I'm sure it was enough."

So those photos must have reached the department. And someone had either mislaid or destroyed them. The queasy feeling inside him grew. "Did you keep a copy?"

"No, but I hid the negatives. I wanted Haley and Nadine to be able to find them if something happened to me."

His pulse began to race. "So they still exist?"

"Hopefully."

"Where did you hide them?"

She hesitated a beat. Her distrust stung, but he understood her reluctance to speak. Someone could be trying to kill her to keep that evidence from coming to light. And it appeared to be a cop.

"In the Central Library," she finally said. "The Enoch Pratt Library on Cathedral Street. I used to go there a lot to study their photography books."

He glanced at his watch. "They'll be closed by now. We'll have to look for them tomorrow."

"They might not be there," she cautioned. "It has been fifteen years."

But if those negatives still existed, he intended to

find them. Because if they could provide a clue to Tommy's death...

Suddenly needing another drink, he walked over and retrieved his glass. "More vodka?"

When she shook her head, he returned to the kitchen and poured himself a refill, still mulling over the case. He'd been a patrol cop when Tommy had died. He hadn't known many people in the homicide unit back then, aside from Hoffman and Vernon Collins, the lead investigator on his brother's case. It wouldn't hurt to check his background for a possible connection to that gang.

Parker knocked back a slug of vodka and swore. Complicated didn't begin to describe this case. Implicating Hoffman in Erin Walker's death was risky enough. If Parker tried to tie him to his brother's crime scene, he'd ignite a firestorm, thrusting the entire Baltimore police department into an uproar, causing repercussions that could last for years.

And what if he was wrong? What if a cop wasn't involved in Tommy's death? All Parker had were random incidents he couldn't connect—two dead girls, missing photos from his brother's crime scene, a mysterious, hand-engraved necklace and a gang who wanted them dead. And he couldn't accuse anyone without proof.

Brynn strolled through the kitchen doorway and set her glass in the sink. She leaned against the counter beside him and crossed her arms. "So what do you want to do next?"

"I'll make some calls, find out who worked in Homicide when Tommy died. We can see if anyone had connections to the C.D. gang."

A frown creased her brow. "What I don't get is why

the Ridgewood gang is after me. They weren't even around back then. Why would they care what I'd seen?"

"Good point." And a disturbing one. "I doubt many City of the Dead members are still alive. Fifteen years is a lifetime on the streets." So how were the two gangs linked? And if they *weren't* connected, why was the Ridgewood gang after Brynn? Unless they wanted Jamie's necklace… But that made even less sense.

"My supervisor transferred over from the gang unit," he told her. "I'll ask him what he knows."

Brynn tilted her head, her eyes curious. "Where *do* you work? You never said what unit you're in."

Realizing what he'd let slip, he took a swallow of vodka to buy some time. "Homicide," he said, deciding to stick close to the truth. "But I didn't join the unit until years after Tommy died, and there'd been a lot of turnover by then. The burnout rate is pretty high."

It wasn't a total lie. He *had* worked in Homicide until Hoffman had decided to prioritize the cold case squad and invited Parker on board. Still, deceiving Brynn felt wrong.

But he couldn't tell her the truth. She'd never trust him if he did. And she was keeping secrets, too. She hadn't revealed that Hoffman was her stepfather. She hadn't told him why she'd run away from home—even if he'd guessed the reason behind her flight.

But could he blame her for not coming clean? If no one had believed her before…

He skimmed her glossy, auburn hair, the beckoning lilt to her bowed lips, the sweater molding to her slender curves. Then his mind flashed back to the photo of her standing in the alley beside Tommy—a scrawny, underfed kid with torn jeans and untamed hair. She'd been so damned young, her eyes so wounded and hollow, with the same raw, traumatized look of the victimized kids she photographed now.

His thoughts swerved back to her file, and the doubts he'd been harboring returned with a vengeance, impossible to ignore. What if she'd told the truth about the sexual abuse? What if no one had believed her back then? What if no one had looked for the cause behind her angry behavior and listened to her cry for help?

And what if no one had stopped a dangerous predator who'd continued racking up victims for years while he pretended to champion their cause?

That thought shuddering through him, he gazed into her blue-gold eyes. And despite not having proof, despite Hoffman's warning that Brynn would manipulate him, the temptation to believe her grew. It explained why she'd acted out, why she'd run away from home. She'd been desperate. Abandoned. Alone.

He ran his gaze over her face, the delicate lines of cheeks and jaw. She was so beautiful. So determined. So strong.

Because if he'd guessed right, the terrified child who'd fled an abusive home had not only survived; she'd grown into a formidable woman—a woman who'd dedicated her life to helping the hopeless. A woman who championed forgotten kids. A woman who confronted hypocrisy head-on, refusing to let society brush these victims aside, no matter how dirty or inconvenient the truth.

But he wasn't blameless, either. He'd always prided himself on his integrity. He'd vowed not to repeat his father's mistakes. But he'd never questioned Hoffman.

He'd let the man's position and reputation blind him to his sleazy crimes—enabling him to destroy more lives.

But could Hoffman really be that evil? Could he really be trying to quiet Brynn permanently, as she claimed? Could a man he'd put on a pedestal—who even Senator Riggs lauded as a hero—have molested children for all these years?

"Listen, Parker...I'm so sorry about Tommy," Brynn said, pain lacing her soft voice.

Realizing she'd misunderstood his silence, he sighed. "I know."

She took another step closer, her eyes searching his. "I wish... I'd do anything to go back and relive that day, to make it right."

Her sincerity humbled him. Even now, after everything she'd suffered, she was worried about hurting *him*.

His throat thickening, he reached out and tucked her fiery hair behind her ear. "It wasn't your fault. And what you told me... It means a lot to know how he died." To know his brother's death hadn't been wasted, that he'd died a hero, saving her.

"I wish I'd listened to him," she whispered, her full mouth wobbling, her eyes shining with tears. "I wish I hadn't been so stubborn. You don't know how many nights I've lain awake wishing so badly he hadn't died. If I could just go back and do it over..."

He understood. The same guilt had tormented him for fifteen years. "I tried to hold my family together after my father died," he admitted. "But I couldn't do it. Tommy ran away no matter what I did. I keep wondering what I did wrong, if there was something I should have changed. Maybe if I'd found a different counselor, maybe if I'd quit my job… And I'd give anything to do it over, to do things differently this time."

She rested her hand on his arm. Her luminous eyes stayed on his. "Tommy didn't talk about his family much, but he admired you, Parker. He knew he'd let you down. I think he wanted to go back home, but he couldn't conquer the drugs."

Oh, hell. Parker tipped back his head and closed his eyes, emotions piling up on him, the horrible grief he'd harbored threatening to break free. If only he could go back. If only he could see his little brother one more time. If only he could convince him that he wasn't a failure, that everything would be all right.

A huge lump blocked his throat. He pinched the bridge of his nose, struggling against the crushing remorse. Then he heaved out a breath and looked at Brynn, the compassion in her eyes swamping his heart.

And once again that connection shimmered between them, the awareness that she understood. *That she cared.* And something around his heart unwound, his self-blame easing up a notch.

The sympathy in her eyes held him captive. A tumult of emotions gripped his heart. Gratitude that she was here. Sorrow for what she'd endured. Regrets that he couldn't redo the past.

And he realized something else. His feelings for her had gone beyond admiration for her considerable talent, beyond attraction to a beautiful woman, beyond respect for what she'd endured. They'd morphed into something at once primitive and complex.

He stroked the curve of her throat, her slight pulse pattering against his palm. He drew in a breath, filling his senses with her calming scent. He'd never expected her to be like this. He'd never dreamed that the girl whose photo he'd carried in his pocket could touch his heart. He never expected to feel this bond, this rapport, this heat.

He knew he should resist her. He knew she was keeping secrets. He shouldn't get involved with a potential suspect until he was sure of what was going on. And he had a duty to follow the rules, an obligation to bring her in and let her stepfather handle this. But memories of that kiss muddled his brain, beating down his resistance. And he'd be damned if he could walk away.

Their eyes remained locked. His heart stuttered through several beats. And the need to possess her drummed through him with primal urgency, demolishing his restraint.

She dropped her gaze to his mouth, making his belly clench. He slowly stalked around her, backing her against the sink.

"This is still a bad idea," she whispered, the raw hunger in her voice thickening his blood.

"I know." His voice came out low and rough. "But damned if I can make myself care." He skimmed his hands down her arms and hips to the base of her slender spine. Then he moved in close, his blood rocketing through his veins.

Her breasts grazed his chest. The heady scent of her filled his lungs. Her lips parted in invitation, and everything male inside him took charge.

"Parker," she said, but whether it was a protest or a plea, he couldn't tell.

He lifted his hand and bracketed her jaw. The memory of her taste flooded through him, deleting his thoughts. He traced the contour of her lips with his thumb, the seductive curve of her pale throat. Damn, but he wanted her. He wanted to feel her naked skin, to plunder her tempting mouth, to delve so deeply inside her that they both lost the capacity to think.

Unable to resist, he dipped his head. He waited one last heartbeat, giving her time to come to her senses and move away. But her eyes fluttered closed. Her hands clutched his arms. And instead of acting sanely, she pulled him closer still.

His lips met hers, the sweet, downy feel of her inciting a riot of need in his blood. Her mouth was warm, tender, soft. Endlessly intriguing. A mouth he could spend forever exploring. He shivered hard, his body and soul blazing to life.

And it wasn't nearly enough. He took the kiss even deeper, giving rein to his burgeoning need. He rocked his hips against her, desperate to feel her softness cradle his rigid length. She gasped against his mouth.

Knowing he was moving too quickly, that he was teetering on the edge of losing control, he broke the kiss with effort, then pulled her head to his neck. His breath came in uneven rasps. His body tightened and throbbed.

But beyond the hunger was something more—tenderness, protectiveness, the need to keep her safe. This thing between them had gone beyond wanting to find Tommy's killer, beyond wanting to find the truth. It had changed into something far more complicated, feelings he didn't understand.

Making a final grasp at sanity, he reminded himself that this wasn't wise. He had no proof that she was a victim, no proof that Tommy had died the way she'd said. For all he knew, she'd fed him a pack of lies.

And he hadn't been forthright with her. When she

found out he worked for her stepfather, she would detest him. If he had any sense of decency, he'd tell her the truth right now.

Lowering his hands to her hips, he eased away, giving them some badly needed room. "Listen, Brynn…"

She lifted her gaze to his. And the sudden wariness filling her eyes—as if she expected him to reject her—stopped him cold.

He couldn't tell her. He couldn't put that hurt and disillusionment back into her eyes. Instead, he wanted to prove that he wouldn't betray her, that he was a man she could depend on, that he deserved her loyalty.

"I want you so damned much," he said instead—because it was true.

Stepping forward, she wrapped her arms around his neck. Then she dragged his head down to hers. He had one final thought, that maybe this was how his father had begun his downward slide, one mistake compounding another until he'd reached his doom.

But for once in his life, he didn't care.

Brynn sank into the kiss, the glorious feel of Parker's mouth on hers making it impossible to think. His kiss was hot, insistent, arousing, his stark urgency igniting hers, eroding any vestiges of her self-control.

She knew she should resist him. *He's a cop.* The warning flitted through her mind, then disappeared like dust in a swirling wind. The hard feel of him thrilled her. His rough, whiskered jaw, his iron muscles flexing under her hands, the magic of his mouth on hers made everything inside her go wild.

She ran her hands through his thick, short hair, over the tendons bunching his neck. He growled deep in his throat, the feral sound torching something primitive in-side her, making her want to climb right into his skin.

She'd never expected this frantic hunger. This over-whelming desire to breathe him in. The longing to take refuge in his strong arms, to let him battle the world on her behalf. *To trust.*

He slid his hand under her shirt and up her back, the warm, calloused feel of his skin sending frissons of ex-citement dancing along her nerves. Then he cupped her breast, and she gasped, her heart kicking like mad, her nipples pebbling into tight little peaks of need.

The hunger was relentless, insistent, insane. She had a gang hunting her down. Her stepfather wanted her dead. And Parker was a cop, dedicated to his badge.

But logic no longer mattered. Pleasure and instinct took charge. Everything inside her narrowed to her overwhelming hunger for this man.

She wanted to forget the past, forget the danger and fear. Forget the repercussions she'd suffer when reality came roaring back. She wanted to lose herself in the oblivion he offered, just glory in the moment and live.

He ended the kiss, and a moan escaped her throat. Then he rained kisses along her neck, the erotic rasp of his whiskers sending shivers cascading like fireworks over her skin. She ran her hands over his shoulders and back, thrilling at the shudders racking his taut body, his intensity inflaming hers.

Then suddenly, he hauled her into his arms. She gasped, then locked her legs around his waist, admir-ing his impressive power as he strode with her down the hall. He kicked open the door to his bedroom, and after a few short strides, deposited her on the king-size bed. He followed her down to the mattress, settling his weight over her.

But then he stopped. Propping himself up on his forearms, he gazed deeply into her eyes. "Are you okay with this?" he asked, his voice husky.

Does he know about the abuse? The sudden worry skittered through her, but she brushed her concerns aside. How could he possibly know about that?

"More than okay," she answered truthfully, running her hands down his arms and back. It had taken years of therapy and hard work, but she'd finally freed herself from the sordid past.

And she'd never been more glad.

His lips grazed her neck. She let out a breathy sigh. She needed to feel his hands stroking her body, his naked skin on hers. He slid his hands beneath her shirt, and she arched with pleasure. His wicked mouth was driving her beyond control. Unable to stand the torture, she squirmed and thrashed against him, suddenly desperate for more.

As if reading her mind, he rose to his knees, ripped off his T-shirt one-handed and tossed it aside. "I need to see you," he said, the roughness of his voice causing an answering spasm of heat in her blood. She peeled off her jeans and shirt, then flung her underwear onto the pile while Parker grabbed protection from the bedside table and made short work of his remaining clothes.

She paused, admiring his magnificent body, his beautifully roped tendons and sculpted muscles drying her throat. But it was his absolute focus on her, the stark hunger blazing in his eyes that threatened to do her in.

"You're beautiful," he growled. He moved over her again, his masterful mouth devouring hers. Then he kissed his way down her body, worshipping her, arousing every inch of her, drowning her in sensations so intense she wanted to sob.

She fisted her hands in his hair, lost to sensations. She tried to hurry him up, her frustration unbearable, and he chuckled against her skin.

Then his humor abruptly ended. He spread her legs with his knees and bracketed her face with his hands, his eyes fixed on hers. And suddenly she had the oddest sensation, as if he could see straight through to her soul.

As if he saw *her*.

The world fell away. She stayed trapped in his heated gaze, a riot of emotions thickening her throat. Because beyond the rampaging hunger, beyond the need erupting like a wildfire between them, was something else. Something deeper. A sense of connection. A feeling that she'd finally found a man she could depend on. A man who would guard and protect her. A man she could trust with her heart—a thought that both thrilled and terrified her.

Then his body drove into hers, the pleasure so exquisite that she cried out. And then she stopped thinking altogether, giving herself over completely, and surrendered to the shocking bliss.

Chapter 10

Brynn regained consciousness with a start, feeling disoriented and strange. She jerked open her eyes and searched the shadows, her gaze stalling on Parker lying facedown beside her in the bed. His thick black hair was mussed. Heat simmered from his powerful frame. His head was turned her way, his harsh face slack in sleep, the morning stubble on his jaw pronounced. The sheet rode low on his hips, exposing the breadth of his muscled back, the mesmerizing play of shadows on his shoulders and arms, and her heart made a crazy lurch.

God, but he was gorgeous with that steel-hard body and scruffy face. She curled her hands, fighting the urge to stroke her palms down his heated skin and relive the ecstasy she'd experienced in his arms. Instead, she closed her eyes and listened to him breathe, the sound slow and steady and strong. She felt relaxed and thoroughly sated, hardly a surprise given the incredible night they'd had.

But beyond the lingering pleasure, there was something different about the morning, a niggling feeling she couldn't quite shake, as if something were missing or wrong. She frowned, trying to figure out what it was.

And then it struck her. *The fear was gone.* She didn't feel that usual hum of panic, that wariness that buzzed through her nerves. For the first time that she could remember, she felt safe.

Safe? Horrified by the thought, she sat up. Safety was an illusion. She hadn't been safe in decades, not since her father had died.

And the only way she'd survived since then was by constantly staying alert—watching her back, keeping her identity secret, monitoring who she met and what she said.

But Parker had snuck through those defenses almost from the start, burrowing straight to her most vulnerable part—tempting her to forget the past, forget the enemies who wanted her dead and let him shelter her from harm.

Spooked now, she clutched the sheet to her bare breasts and stared at Parker, aghast. He opened his eyes, his gaze arrowing straight to hers, and the blast of carnal hunger knocked her heart off course. Her breasts began to throb. Her groin moistened and ached. She skimmed the sexy grooves bracketing his mouth, the hollows of his whiskered cheeks. And he looked so incredibly appealing, so much like everything she'd ever dreamed of that she wanted nothing more than to crawl back into his arms, succumb to the fierce need coiling inside her and lose herself in the excruciating wonder of this man's embrace.

But that was insane. She couldn't afford to let down her guard again. Not now. Not with her enemies circling close. Not ever—because Parker was still a cop. A cop with the power to turn her over to her stepfather. And no matter how sexy he was, no matter how protected he made her feel, she couldn't forget that fact.

The silence yawned between them. Parker's eyes narrowed a fraction, a sudden stillness banking the heat.

"Regrets?" he asked in a carefully neutral voice.

She shifted her gaze to the window, where a glimmer of daylight seeped through a crack in the blinds. "No." It was impossible to regret the most glorious night of her life. "Last night…was wonderful. Amazing." A blush heated her cheeks.

"But?" His voice took on an edge.

"But I don't… I can't…." She inhaled deeply, then released the words in a rush. "We can't do this anymore."

Parker didn't move. His eyes never veered from hers. But a muscle in his square jaw bunched, and her heart made a sudden swerve. She'd offended him—the last thing she'd wanted to do.

"And why is that?" he finally asked.

Her belly doing gymnastics, she tugged the sheet higher against her breasts. "We just can't. Last night was…fun. But we have to focus on the case."

"Fun." His voice went flat. His eyes turned flintier yet. And the tension between them mounted, shattering any remnants of the intimacy they'd shared.

He tossed off the sheet and rose from the bed, his arousal obvious as he stalked naked across the room.

"There are extra towels in the bathroom closet," he said, yanking open his dresser drawer.

Oh, God. She'd totally mucked this up. Feeling miserable and confused, she tried again. "Parker, I—"

"Help yourself to a shower. I'll put the coffee on. After breakfast we can head to the library and find that film." Not bothering to glance her way, he pulled on his faded jeans, grabbed a T-shirt from the drawer and left the room. Several seconds later, a cupboard in the kitchen slammed.

Her belly churning, feeling as if she'd just made a huge mistake, Brynn stared at the empty hall. She wanted to call him back. She wanted to forget the world, forget the killers dogging her steps and hold on to this precious thing growing between them before she lost it for good.

But she couldn't chance it. The fear was too ingrained, the price of betrayal too high.

Buffeted by regrets, she climbed from the bed and gathered her scattered clothes. She'd healed physically from her stepfather's attacks long ago. And while it had taken years in counseling, years working to put the victimization behind her, she'd also recovered enough to finally find pleasure in sex. Casual sex. As long as she stayed detached, as long as she stayed in control and distanced herself emotionally from the encounters, she could enjoy her body's demands.

But trusting someone was different. It made her far too vulnerable. And having a relationship with a cop…

She dragged herself into the bathroom, then sagged back against the door. It was impossible. She'd had to end the affair. She couldn't let her desires blind her to danger with so many lives at stake.

Feeling thoroughly weary, she set the showerhead to its strongest setting and turned it on. Then she stepped beneath the spray, counting on the pummeling water to banish her doubts. She'd done the right thing. She hadn't made a mistake. She'd had to cool things with Parker before he got too close and she did something she'd regret.

So why did she want to cry?

The problem with reality, Parker decided as he set two coffee mugs on the kitchen counter, was that every time he tried to ignore it, it came back to bite him in his sorry ass.

He never should have let last night happen. Making love to Brynn had been foolhardy at best, morally wrong at worst, given that he'd concealed the truth from her. She still didn't know that her stepfather had ordered Parker to bring her in, a revelation that would destroy her trust.

Thank God she'd wanted to end it, even if her rejection had stung his pride. Bad enough that he'd let down his guard last night. He didn't need to compound the problem by prolonging the affair.

Even if it had been the best sex of his life.

She strolled into the kitchen a second later, grabbed her camera from her backpack and started fiddling with the lens. Parker dumped silverware beside the mugs, vowing to keep his distance and let reason dictate his actions for once. But her fresh, soapy scent flooded the room, bombarding him with erotic memories—the tempting texture of her skin, the ripe fullness of her naked breasts, the soft moans she'd made as he'd filled her, her nipples pebbling and pouting for his touch.

His blood rushed south. A sweat broke out on his brow. And despite his vow to resist her, it took every ounce of effort he possessed not to haul her into his arms and plunge so deeply and thoroughly inside her that he'd brand her as forever his.

He tried to clear the gravel from his voice. "Coffee?"

"Thanks." Still clutching the camera, she inched closer to his side. "Listen, Parker, about last night..."

"Forget it." He didn't want to do a detailed post-mortem, not in his current state. Struggling to appear unaffected, he made himself meet her gaze. But the uncertainty in her eyes did him in. Right or wrong, stupid or wise, Brynn affected him in ways he'd never expected. This wasn't just sex anymore; it wasn't just a release of physical needs. She meant something to him now, something important.

Something he sure as hell didn't want to name.

Needing to reassure her, he moved in close. Then he reached out and cupped her face, gazing into those gorgeous eyes. "You were right to cool things off. We need to concentrate on solving this case."

"It's just...I don't want you to be angry."

"I'm not." He tucked her silky hair behind her ear, felt her quiver beneath his touch. "Let's focus on finding those negatives, all right? We can sort out the other stuff later on."

She searched his eyes. "All right." Her mouth wobbled into a smile.

He curved his hand, giving her neck a gentle squeeze, then made himself step away. But he realized he was doomed. Brynn had gotten to him. He couldn't bear to hurt her, couldn't bring himself to tell her about her step-father and put that disillusionment back into her eyes.

But deception always came at a cost. And someday soon he'd have to pay the price.

The central branch of the Enoch Pratt Free Library was in a massive, three-story building in downtown Baltimore, just blocks from the Inner Harbor. Still trying to corral his feelings, Parker left his pickup truck in an hourly garage a block away and followed Brynn down the stairwell to the street. Then he walked with her toward the library, trying not to notice how the cold breeze tousled her shiny hair, the way her snug jeans molded her thighs.

Or how right she felt by his side.

Stuffing his hands in his jacket pockets, he stopped at the crosswalk at Cathedral Street and waited for the light to change. "Why did you hide the negatives here?" he asked, determined to exert some mental discipline and keep his mind on task.

She didn't answer at first. A trash truck barreled past. The flags atop the library snapped in the gusting wind. Several homeless men loitered near the book drop, smoking cigarettes while they waited for the library to unlock its doors.

"I used to hang out near here," she said when the light changed and they started across the street. "One day I was walking past the library and noticed a display they had." She nodded toward the tall, rectangular windows gracing the building's facade. "They were showcasing the work of A. Aubrey Bodine, the famous photojournalist. Those pictures blew me away. The way he used texture and light…" A note of awe filled her voice. "I *had* to go inside. I came here all the time after that to study his work. I read all the photography books I could, trying to improve my craft. I didn't have much money, so I couldn't afford to waste film. I figured the more I learned, the fewer mistakes I'd make."

Parker watched her speak, mesmerized by the passion in her voice, the way her eyes lit up as she discussed her work.

He'd never met anyone so intriguing in his life.

As if realizing she'd gone off on a tangent, she shot him a rueful smile. "Anyhow, I spent a lot of time here, back in the stacks."

"Did you always want to be a photographer?"

She nodded. "It was a way to stay connected to my father at first. Taking photos helped keep him alive in my mind. And then…it consumed me. It became part of who I was, something I had to do. And when I started winning contests and showing my work…"

"How did that happen? It couldn't have been easy on the run."

"My friends showed my work to a gallery owner in San Francisco. That's where we were living at the time. He suggested I get an agent, so I did." She shrugged. "My agent helped me a lot after that."

Mulling that over, Parker walked with her to the entrance just as people started filing inside. He hung back, letting her precede him through the turnstiles, then stopped in the central hall.

The place was impressive, he had to admit. A huge glass ceiling soared several stories above him. Spotless terrazzo floors gleamed in the brilliant light. Rectangular marble columns formed a loggia around the periphery, while in the center sat a large information desk flanked by potted trees.

"It's changed," Brynn said with a frown. She motioned toward a glassed-off section to one side. "That used to be the newspaper room. I just hope they haven't remodeled upstairs.

"I didn't dare hide the negatives outside," she continued, leading the way around the elevators to the stairs. "The weather would have ruined them. This was the only place I could think of where they might be safe."

Parker slid her a glance as they started up the staircase, curious about how she'd gotten by. "Where did you get your film? You couldn't have had much money."

"I didn't steal it, if that's what you mean." Her voice turned defensive now. "There was a photography store on Charles Street, not far from here. I used to search their trash at night to see if they'd thrown away any supplies. One night the owner caught me. Mr. Fowler. He was a crotchety old guy and scared me half to death, but he was a marshmallow inside." A smile ghosted across her face and warmed her eyes.

"He took pity on me when he realized how badly I wanted to learn. He let me sweep floors and do odd jobs in return for film and darkroom supplies. And he taught me what he knew."

Parker gazed at her face, attuned to the quirk of her brow, the way she scrunched her nose when she thought, the mesmerizing fullness of her soft lips.

He was doomed, all right. Last night had demolished any impartiality he'd had. Even more alarming, he didn't seem to care.

"That's where I developed the pictures I took at the warehouse," she added, heading up another flight of stairs. "I'd watched him open the store and knew the code for his alarm, so I snuck inside that night and developed the film. The next morning, as soon as the library opened, I hid the negatives here. Then I mailed the prints to the police and left town."

They reached the top of the stairs. She paused, a shadow flickering through her eyes. "I've always felt bad about that, that I left without saying goodbye after all he'd done for me. But I couldn't drag him into my mess."

Parker's heart rolled, impressed like hell that she'd tried to protect her friends while her life was on the line. "You ever talk to him again?"

She shook her head. "He's retired now. His nephew took over the shop. But I stopped by a few years ago and left him a package with some of my original prints." Another smile crinkled her eyes. "I'm sure he already knew who I was, though. He would have recognized my technique."

And considering the price her photographs now commanded, she'd more than repaid him for any supplies.

But as Parker accompanied her down the hall to the Fine Arts room, he couldn't shake his growing unease. Because the truth was, the more he learned about Brynn, the less he believed the Colonel's claim that she was mentally unhinged. On the contrary, he admired her. She'd managed to survive despite formidable odds.

But if she didn't have psychological problems, if she wasn't the lying manipulator his boss claimed, why had he asked Parker to bring her in?

Not sure he liked the conclusions he was beginning to draw, Parker set that problem aside. He'd think about Brynn and her stepfather later, after they'd found that film.

"This way," she said, her voice low.

Parker nodded to the librarian manning the Fine Arts

desk, then followed Brynn down the carpeted aisle past multiple stacks of books. On the back wall was a built-in cabinet, consisting of dozens of narrow drawers.

"This is it," she said, coming to a stop.

"You put them here? In this cabinet?"

"It's where they store their sheet music. I was afraid to put the negatives inside a book in case it got checked out. I was looking for someplace permanent where they wouldn't be disturbed. So I decided to hide them behind a drawer."

Admiring her logic, Parker surveyed the wooden drawers. "I don't suppose you remember which one?"

"Not exactly. I know it was close to the floor. I didn't think anyone would notice it if I put them down low."

She knelt on the rug and opened a drawer while Parker did the same. Both drawers were empty. Brynn frowned. "It looks like they moved the music. I hope they didn't inspect the cabinet and look behind the drawers."

She removed the drawer and set it aside, then peered into the empty space. She reached in and felt around, then put the drawer back in. "They're in an envelope. I was going to tape it to the bottom of a drawer, but I noticed that part of the panel on the wall was loose, right where two sections joined. So I slipped the envelope inside the loose part, with just the edge sticking out."

"Good thinking. Tape probably wouldn't have lasted this long."

He started on the row above her, removing the drawers, checking for signs of an envelope, feeling the back panel for give. The minutes ticked quietly by. A few curious patrons strolled past, but no one questioned them.

Parker's thoughts wandered back to the case—the

missing necklace and photos, Erin Walker's death, the murdered prostitute. But despite his attempts to connect them, the clues still didn't make sense. He needed to call his supervisor, Sergeant Delgado. As much as the man annoyed him, he had worked in the gang unit. Parker needed to find out what he knew—before their time ran out and that gang caught up.

"Parker." Her urgent whisper drew his gaze. Excitement brimmed in her eyes. "I found it!"

He closed his drawer and knelt beside her. His anticipation mounting, he watched as she reached into the cabinet and pulled out a yellowed, business-size envelope. She flipped it over and broke the seal, then took out a handful of plastic sleeves, the negatives still inside.

His heart skidded hard. He suddenly found it hard to breathe. *At last.* He could see what had happened in that warehouse the day that Tommy had died.

"I'm not sure how much they're going to tell us," she cautioned.

But he finally had a chance to find out.

It took a while, but they finally located a photography shop near Carroll Park that had a professional-grade drum scanner, which Brynn insisted they needed to get the highest resolution to view the film. Parker flashed his badge to ensure priority treatment from the manager and forestall questions about any violent images the film contained.

A short time later, Parker sat inside a coffee shop in a partially boarded-up strip mall, drumming his fingers on the table while Brynn set up her laptop and inserted the CD. *This is it.* He was finally going to find out why Tommy had lost his life.

Brynn transferred the digitalized files into Photoshop and pulled the first shot up. Parker hunched forward, not sure what to expect. But two teenage girls filled the screen. The one on the left looked Middle Eastern. She had straight black hair, exotic eyes, a breathtakingly beautiful face. The other girl was softer, still pretty, but less intimidating with her thick hair piled in a messy knot atop her head. He couldn't tell her hair color from the black-and-white photo, but guessed she was a brunette. "Are those your friends?"

Brynn gave him a nod. "The one on the left is Nadira—Nadine. She's a plastic surgeon in New York now. The other one is Haley. She runs a teen shelter in D.C."

She scrolled through several shots—Haley smiling and cuddling a kitten, Nadira taking shelter in a doorway to escape the rain. But despite their smiles for the camera, their eyes looked wounded and stark. Brynn had captured the essence of her subjects even then.

Then Tommy's face appeared on the screen, and Parker's heart stumbled to a halt. He took in his brother's gaunt cheeks, the shaggy hair flopping over his brows, the dark circles underscoring his spiritless eyes. He'd been so young. So addicted. So lost.

Trying hard to swallow, Parker stared at the screen as Brynn paged slowly through the shots—Tommy clowning around with Brynn. Tommy sprawled on the ground amid a pile of trash. Tommy slumped against a wall, his eyes wasted, looking weary beyond his years.

Unable to bear it, Parker squeezed the bridge of his nose, a burn forming behind his eyes. If only he could have saved him...

"I'm sorry," Brynn whispered. "I shouldn't—"

"No." He let out an uneven breath. "I want to see them." These were the final images of his brother's life.

A terrible pressure crushing his chest, he forced himself to watch as more images of his brother marched across the screen. Tommy laughing at the camera. Tommy feeding a stray dog. Tommy shooting up in a flophouse, his eyes tormented, enslaved by addictions he couldn't defeat.

And Brynn hadn't held back. She'd showed the harsh reality of Tommy's life—no matter how much it tortured him to see.

Parker scrubbed his face, grief welling up inside him, the pain too sharp too endure. But Brynn reached out and touched his hand. And the warmth of her skin was like a lifeline, enabling him to hang on.

"Are you all right?" she asked in a soft voice.

It took him a moment to answer. "Not really."

"That's the last shot I have of him."

Which seemed to make it worse.

Releasing Parker's hand, she hurried through the rest of the photos—shots of unknown kids this time. Grateful for the reprieve, Parker struggled to compose himself and ease the brutal tightness that had a stranglehold on his throat.

Then a warehouse appeared on the screen. "This is it," she said, her voice low.

Parker tensed, his gaze glued to the screen. Brynn continued clicking through the shots, and despite the inconsistent exposure, he could see the effect she'd been trying to create. She used the shadows to highlight subtle details, making even cracked paint seem alive. And while the photos were rough, her technique not yet refined, her talent was evident in every shot.

Then a dark, blurry image came on the screen. Parker frowned, trying to make sense of the picture, but he could barely make out any forms. "What's that?"

"You'll see." Her brows knitted, Brynn began manipulating the picture, increasing the contrast, sharpening the focus, using the toning tool to lighten the shot, until the image of a kneeling man took shape on the screen.

"Allen Chambers," Parker murmured. The heroin addict the City of the Dead gang had executed that day.

Then he blinked, his brain catching up with his eyes. *Hell.* Chambers wasn't only kneeling; he was falling backward. She'd snapped the shutter at the exact moment he'd been shot.

His heart racing, he scrutinized the violent scene. Chambers knelt in the center of the patio. Across the patio and facing the camera stood a young man holding a gun.

"Zoom in on that guy," Parker said, shifting forward.

A second later the gang member took up the screen. He was tall, thin, Caucasian, in his late teens or early twenties with crosses tattooed on his cheek and neck. Parker studied his long, thin face, thinking something about him looked familiar, but he'd be damned if he knew what.

"Can you copy this part of the picture and email it to me?" he asked. "I want to send it to my supervisor and see if he can identify this guy."

"Sure. I'll crop it and copy it to a separate file."

Parker turned his attention to the other gang member, but he was standing behind a pillar, hidden from view. Only the barrel of his gun appeared on film.

"Did you see who fired the shot?" he asked Brynn.

She shook her head. "I think it was the other guy, the one we can't see. But it happened so fast...."

"I'll check the case file, find out the angle of the shot." Then they could pinpoint the shooter for sure. "Can you get a close-up of the victim? I want to see what's binding his hands."

Brynn expanded the shot to full screen, then closed in on the kneeling man. Parker couldn't tell exactly, given the angle of his body, but something metallic seemed to bind his wrists.

"Those could be metal handcuffs," he said, sitting back.

"The kind the police use?"

"Maybe. But that doesn't mean a cop was involved. Even back then you could buy handcuffs in pawn shops and surplus stores."

But it didn't rule police involvement out.

"That's the end of the film," she said, her eyes on the screen again. "I developed the film after I took that shot."

After Tommy died.

The words hung unspoken between them. And for the first time, Parker could imagine the scene—a terrified young girl hiding in the shadows as cold-blooded killers executed that helpless man.

And then they'd turned their guns on her.

His emotions in sudden turmoil, he looked away. All these years he'd blamed Brynn for Tommy's death. Witnesses had seen her running from the warehouse, convincing him she'd been involved. But now, after seeing that photo, he could imagine her absolute panic as she'd fled the scene, trying desperately to protect her friends and survive.

Instead, she'd seen Tommy die.

He inhaled again, trying to block the gruesome images that sprang to mind. But he'd seen his brother's crime scene photos. He knew what had happened next.

And, frankly, there was no way he could blame her for Tommy's death. In her case he would have done the same.

"Go ahead and email me that shot," he said, trying to steady his voice. "If we're lucky, someone will recognize him. Send me the uncropped version, too. I'll forward it to Forensics, see if they can work their magic on it and get more clues."

Brynn got to work with a nod. As soon as the cropped shot showed up on his cell phone, Parker deleted the header and forwarded it to Delgado, not wanting him to know that Brynn was involved. Then, still struggling to come to grips with what he'd learned, he punched in his supervisor's number and rose.

"Where are you?" Delgado demanded when he answered the phone. "Colonel Hoffman's been asking for you."

Parker shot Brynn a glance, hoping she hadn't heard. To be safe, he walked across the nearly deserted coffee shop to the plate-glass window and peered out at the parking lot. "Over by Carroll Park, following a lead. I'll call him right away. But I need some information first. I just emailed you a photo of a gang member with cross tattoos on his cheek and neck. It was taken near Orleans Street fifteen years ago. Can you take a look, see if you can identify him?"

"Hold on." Parker gazed at the street as he waited, watching the traffic zip past. A couple minutes later Delgado came back on the line. "That's Dustin Alexander. He belonged to a gang called the City of the Dead. They were a small group, mostly Caucasian. They operated mainly around the Inner Harbor."

That fit. "Doing what?"

"Mostly drugs. They controlled the heroin coming in from South America. Baltimore was their East Coast distribution point."

"They still exist?"

"No. They disbanded about ten years ago when the New York gangs started moving in. Most of their members were dead by then."

"What happened to the guy in the photo, Dustin Alexander?"

"I'll look it up." Delgado went off the line again. As the minutes stretched, Parker glanced at Brynn, then scanned the other patrons in the café—an elderly man reading a newspaper, a teenage girl chatting on her cell phone, the college-age barista behind the counter arranging muffins in a case.

"Sorry," Delgado said. "It took me a minute to find the record. He was killed in 2002 by a rival gang."

"This gang, City of the Dead. Who was their leader?"

"Nobody knows. They were a tight-lipped group. We never found out, and believe me, we tried."

Parker mulled that over. "You said some of them survived?"

"A few. We think they got absorbed into the Ridgewood gang."

Parker caught his breath. That was the gang with the snake tattoo—the gang that had killed Jamie, the gang that had attacked Brynn's agent, the gang that was after Brynn. "Tell me about them."

"The Ridgewood gang? They started off as a subset of the Bloods. They took over the C.D.'s heroin route."

"So they deal drugs?"

"Drugs, weapons. They're allied with a South American cartel. The leader of their Baltimore operations is Markus Jenkins, the guy they released from prison by mistake last week."

Parker went still. This complicated mess was starting to make sense. If Tommy's killer—the guy behind the pillar—had survived and now belonged to this Ridgewood gang…it would explain why they were after Brynn.

"Why do you want to know?" Delgado asked.

It was Parker's turn to stall. He couldn't tell Delgado the truth. His supervisor would yank him off the case. "It's a long story. I'll fill you in when I get back. But I have another question first. It's about a symbol I saw on a runaway's necklace. Multiple hearts, one inside the other. Any idea what it means?"

"Not offhand. Hold on while I check with vice."

Parker stared out the window, surprised that Delgado would take the time. Normally his supervisor would make some cutting remark accusing Parker of being lazy and hang up.

Switching Delgado to hold, he used the time to check his missed calls. He was stunned to discover that Guerrero, who had the next cube over in the cold case squad, had tried to reach him seven times in the past two hours. Frowning, he phoned him back.

"For God's sake," Guerrero exploded. "Why haven't you answered your phone?"

Parker frowned. "I was busy." He'd turned off his

phone in the library and hadn't switched it back. "I thought you were still on leave."

"Delgado called me in early." He lowered his voice. "Christ, McCall. Do you have any idea of the mess you're in? Colonel Hoffman got a tip that you're dealing drugs."

"What?"

"They're tracking you on your GPS. Delgado just pinpointed your location. He's sending the SWAT team out to bring you in."

"The SWAT team? Are you nuts?" Parker gave his head a hard shake, sure that he'd misunderstood. "That's crazy."

"They're nearly there. I don't know what the hell you're up to…"

A squad car careened into the lot. Parker gaped out the window, adrenaline pumping through him as two more unmarked police cars followed suit. The cars screeched to a halt, and officers boiled out, donning their bulletproof gear.

Swearing, he spun around, lobbed his cell phone—with its GPS—into a trash can, then bolted back toward Brynn. He had to get her to safety fast, before all hell broke loose.

Chapter 11

Still unable to believe that someone—maybe even Delgado—had set him up, Parker charged across the room toward Brynn. What the hell was going on here? Hoffman had asked him to find his stepdaughter—and now he was trying to bring *him* in?

He pulled his Glock from his back holster. "Police! Get down!" he shouted at the customers. They screamed and dove to the floor. Taking in the situation in an instant, Brynn leaped up and grabbed her supplies, then darted behind the counter. Parker hurried to catch up.

They were outnumbered, out-armed. The police would surround the building. They'd block the exits and roads. To have any chance at escaping, they had to get out now, before the cops realized they'd been tipped off.

He lunged behind the counter, then raced down the hall after Brynn. The barista cowered in the corner of the rear office, his face a pasty white. "Don't shoot!" he cried, raising his hands.

Parker skidded to a stop and glanced around the small room, searching for a way to escape. The door to the alley was out. The police would block that first. "Is there another exit?" he demanded, flashing his badge.

The barista's eyes were wild, his Adam's apple bobbing in his gangly throat. "N-no."

Parker swore and whirled around. There had to be another way out. He refused to surrender until he knew what this was about.

"What's in here?" Brynn asked, pointing to a door half-buried behind a stack of supplies.

The barista shook his head. "I don't know."

Parker frowned at the door. It was in the common wall connecting the buildings. If there was a chance it led next door...

He pushed through a stack of boxes and yanked on the knob, but it was locked. "Get the key," he told the barista. He just hoped it wasn't a closet, or they were screwed.

The barista ran to the desk while Parker hurled the boxes aside. The kid tossed him the key, and Parker unlocked the door. *Not a closet.* Relief spiraling through him, he turned to the barista again. "Come on."

"Wh-what?" The kid's eyes nearly bugged from his face.

"I said, come on. Through here." He waved his gun, and the terrified barista rushed to comply. Parker followed Brynn through the door and secured it from the other side.

Knowing he'd only bought seconds, he scanned the unlit room. Dust covered the floor. The air smelled stale from disuse. Stray pieces of furniture hulked in the shadows, like ships in a mothball fleet.

"Upstairs," Brynn urged and took off running.

"You stay here," Parker told the barista. "Just sit tight and you won't get hurt. And whatever you do, don't call the police."

Hoping the kid would obey him, he bounded after Brynn up a flight of stairs. When they reached the top, he paused again. Faint light slanted through the filthy windows, revealing dust motes hanging in the air.

"There's a balcony next door," Brynn said, peering out the rear window. "Part of the old fire escape. It might be another way out." She pulled on the window frame, but it didn't budge.

Parker hurried to help her. A car door slammed near the building. In the distance a siren wailed, and nerves coiled deep in his gut. Their time had nearly run out.

"Stand back." He positioned himself under the window. Putting all his force behind it, he heaved on the warped wooden frame. He grunted and strained, sweat beading on his face, until it finally gave way and slid up. They both looked out.

Police cars blocked the ends of the alley. If they hoped to get away, they had to move *now,* before the SWAT team arrived on the scene. But the only thing under their window was a narrow, metal platform leading to nowhere. The neighbor's balcony was yards away.

Parker's hopes tanked along with their options. They were trapped, all right. He just wished to hell he could figure out *why.*

"Look." Brynn pointed to a delivery van parked beneath the neighboring balcony. "If we can get on top of that truck, we can sneak over to the Dumpster and climb over the wall."

Parker sliced his gaze from the truck in question to the Dumpster bordering the alley's cement wall. It offered a way to escape, all right—assuming they could reach the truck.

"We can't jump that far." They'd break their legs or worse.

"We don't have to. Part of the fire escape's still there." She pointed to the half dozen metal steps dangling off the neighbor's balcony. But the steps still ended an ungodly distance from the truck. And even to get to the balcony, they'd have to jump several treacherous yards through the empty air.

Shouts came from the unit beside them. The cops had entered the building. In minutes, they'd breach the door. Parker tensed, unwilling to risk Brynn's safety, but he couldn't see another choice.

Not waiting for an answer, Brynn hiked her knapsack onto her shoulder and scrambled over the sill. She paused for a moment on the platform, then leaped through the air like a flying squirrel, aiming for the neighbor's balcony.

She missed.

Parker's heart stopped dead. Powerless to help her, he watched in absolute terror as she tumbled toward the ground. But at the last second, she caught the edge of the balcony's railing one-handed and miraculously held on, not quite muffling her shriek of pain.

His pulse wild, Parker followed her out the window and jumped. He grabbed hold of the railing as Brynn worked her way around the balcony to the steps. She climbed down the truncated ladder and dangled off the end, agony racking her face. Then she let go, landing on the truck with a solid thud.

Parker didn't hesitate. The police were only seconds behind them. The SWAT team would soon arrive. He hurried down the ladder and dropped onto the truck beside her, the impact jolting his legs.

By the time he regained his feet, Brynn had already leaped off the truck and raced to the Dumpster. As he followed suit, she scurried up the metal container and disappeared over the wall. Admiring her speed and courage, he rushed to follow suit.

"Stop, police!" an officer shouted as Parker made it to the top of the wall. His energy surging, he dove over the edge just as a shot rang out.

"Hurry," Brynn called, and he jumped up, another burst of adrenaline powering his steps. Then he sprinted after her through the alley and across a parking lot. They ran through a park, exiting on a side street, and raced down another block. Still in the lead, Brynn forged a course through the city, covering the distance with surprising speed. And with every passing block, his respect for her increased. She was fast, determined, smart. She refused to let her injury slow her down, even though her shoulder had to ache. No wonder she'd eluded the authorities for years.

Thirty minutes later, when the café was miles behind them, she finally slowed to a walk. Then she leaned against the side of a building, gasping and heaving for breath.

"You okay?" he asked, his own lungs fiery from the frenzied flight.

Wincing, she pushed her tangled hair from her flushed face. "My shoulder hurts."

Still panting, Parker scowled, the heart-stopping image of her near miss emblazoned in his mind. "You're lucky to be alive."

Her chin came up. "It was the only way out."

She was right. But knowing that did nothing to calm his nerves. The sight of her plummeting from that balcony had aged him twenty years.

But he couldn't think of that now. They still had the cops on their heels. He glanced around to get his bearings, then pushed away from the wall. "Come on. I know a hotel near here where we can rest. And we'll get some ice for your arm."

"All right." Clutching her injured shoulder, she started to walk again.

But as they headed down the street, the enormity of their predicament began to sink in. Hoffman was after him. But why? Parker didn't believe that drug-selling rumor for a minute. He'd spent too many years acting like a choir boy for Hoffman to believe that crap.

Was this about Brynn? But Parker had told his boss he'd found her. So why hadn't he waited for him to bring her in? Didn't the Colonel trust him?

Or was something more sinister going on?

He didn't know. But he couldn't stop the terrible sense of betrayal congealing his heart. All his life, he'd dreamed of becoming a cop. He'd worked his butt off to make it happen. He'd worn his badge with pride. Even his father's corruption scandal hadn't diminished his confidence in the integrity of the force.

But now… He couldn't trust his fellow officers. He doubted everything he'd once believed. Because suddenly, this case had nothing to do with justice, nothing to do with the C.I.D. chief wanting to help his troubled stepdaughter. Something bigger was going on here. Something deadly. Something he had to figure out fast.

But whoever their enemies were, they'd just made a major mistake. They'd made this war personal.

And Parker would fight to win.

Brynn peeked out the curtain of their hotel room an hour later, still too wired to relax. Her stepfather had tracked her down. He'd set the police on their trail. Thanks to Parker's quick thinking, they'd escaped— this time. But what if their luck didn't hold?

She rubbed her throbbing shoulder, decades of self-preservation clamoring at her to flee. She had money. She could fly to Europe or Asia, hide out on a distant island, change her identity one more time.

But this had gone too far. Innocent people were dying because of her. She couldn't run anymore. She had to stay and fight back.

Nerves still jangling from their narrow escape, she let go of the drapery and turned to Parker. He sat at the corner desk, connecting her laptop to the hotel's WiFi. She skimmed the rigid cast of his profile, the angry jut of his chiseled jaw, and more guilt stacked up inside. She'd dragged him into this mess. He'd only wanted to find his brother's killer, and now he was in danger, too. But how could she get him out?

Struggling to find a solution, she perched on the edge of the king-size bed. Pain sizzled down her badly wrenched shoulder, and she bit down hard on a moan.

Parker swung his head around. "Does your arm still hurt?"

"It's fine." Actually it ached like hell, but that was the least of her concerns right now.

"Did you take the ibuprofen?"

She nodded. "I tripled the dose."

"You need more ice." He rose and strode to the bathroom, returning a second later with the ice pack he'd fashioned from a plastic bag. He sat on the mattress beside her, then arranged the pack on her wounded shoulder, holding it in place with his hand.

Deciding it was futile to argue, she tried to relax. But with his hard thigh resting against hers and his wide shoulders cradling her back, she found it difficult to concentrate. "So what's next?" she asked, determined to focus on what mattered—staying alive.

He blew out a heavy breath. "Right now we have a bunch of loose ends that don't seem to match up. We need to look at this thing logically and figure out how they connect."

That sounded reasonable. "So where do we start?"

"With that photo. It's the only concrete evidence we have right now. We know the guy with the killer in the warehouse was Dustin Alexander, a City of the Dead gang member. He died a couple years after you took that shot. We can't see the executioner, so we don't know anything about him. But about ten years ago the City of the Dead survivors merged with the Ridgewood gang.

"The Ridgewood gang killed Jamie," he continued. "We don't know who made the hit—one of their hardcore members or someone lower on the chain. But the decision to kill her probably came from the top."

She processed that. "So you think the executioner survived and is a member of the Ridgewood gang?"

"It's possible. And he'd be high enough in the organization by now to order a hit like that."

That made sense—so far. "So when my picture appeared in the newspaper, the killer recognized me. He traced me to my agent to find out where I was. Somehow he found me and followed me to Jamie. Then he killed her, maybe to keep her from tipping us off."

"Or he had someone do it for him. That could be why Markus Jenkins got released from jail."

"It still doesn't make sense. How exactly did he find me? And what about that necklace? What does it have to do with this?"

"Let's not worry about the missing pieces yet. Let's just start by laying out the facts."

"All right." But there were an awful lot of holes to plug. "So we need to find out who was behind that pillar. And since those photos disappeared, there's a chance that he's a cop."

"It explains why they're after us now." Parker's gaze connected with hers, the desolate look in his eyes making her chest contract.

She understood how he felt. A cop might have killed his brother. A fellow officer had deceived him, violating their sacred bond of trust. And she knew better than most exactly how devastating that was, how deep a betrayal like that would cut. "It's not easy when someone you trust betrays you," she whispered.

Parker didn't answer, but the flash of anguish in his eyes gutted her heart. And suddenly, she needed to reach him, to show him he wasn't alone. Words bubbled up, crowding her throat, reckless words she'd never spoken before—about her relationship with her stepfather, how the despicable man had abused her, how even her mother had failed to protect her, refusing to believe the sordid truth.

But the words stayed trapped in her throat, the startling intimacy she felt toward Parker shocking her into silence again. She couldn't afford to reveal the truth. Not yet. No matter how much she wanted to trust him, Parker was still a cop, a man wedded to his badge. And for all she knew, he'd side with her stepfather, no matter how disillusioned he felt right now.

Needing space to regain her perspective, she grabbed the ice pack and rose, then took the seat he'd vacated at the desk. "So what's next?"

"We need to find out who worked in Homicide when Tommy died. The only ones I remember are Hoffman and Vern Collins. Collins was the lead investigator in Tommy's case." He hesitated. "Do you have a cell phone I can use? The hotel's too easy to trace."

"A disposable one."

"Even better."

"Sure, go ahead." She handed him her phone, then watched as he placed the call. "Who are you calling?"

"The admin secretary in Homicide. She might not know they're after me, depending on who's involved. Hey, Alice," he said into the phone. "Parker McCall here. I need you to do me a favor." He rose and walked to the window, then nudged the curtain aside and peered out. "I need to find out who worked in Homicide fifteen years ago. Could you email me the roster?" He paused, his brow wrinkled as he listened to what she said. "I'm not coming in today. You'd better use my private address. Do you have a pen?"

While he chatted with the secretary, Brynn decided to do her part by searching her stepfather's background online on the off chance that he had a connection to that gang, an angle she'd never had reason to consider before. She pulled up several bios, then skimmed through information she already knew—about his suburban childhood, the glory of his football years, how he'd worked his way up the ranks of the Baltimore Police Department, earning accolades and respect. He'd constructed an impressive public persona, she had to admit.

Too bad it was based on a lie.

Parker ended his call and returned her phone. "I looked up Hoffman's bio," she told him. "There's nothing in it about belonging to a gang, but he probably wouldn't publicize it if he did."

"You never know. Senator Riggs belonged to a gang when he was young. He's turned it into an asset. It's one of the reasons he's big on community outreach. He's trying to keep kids from dying on the streets."

She couldn't argue that. But as badly as she wanted to crucify her stepfather, she couldn't see him belonging to a gang. Preying on defenseless children was more his style.

"If you don't need your computer," he continued, "I'll access my work account and check out Hoffman's schedule, see what he was doing the night Erin Walker died. I left my computer in my truck at the café. They've probably towed it by now."

"Go ahead. I'll look through those photos from the camp again in case we missed anything." Scooting past Parker, she headed into the bathroom and deposited the ice pack in the sink. Then she took her camera from her backpack and settled on the bed again.

But while she tried to focus on checking the date stamps, her mind kept returning to the disillusionment she'd seen in Parker's eyes. And like it or not, she realized last night had changed something fundamental between them. No matter how hard she tried, she couldn't think of him as just a cop anymore. She cared about Parker McCall. He mattered to her now. And despite the potential danger, she couldn't stay detached from this complex man.

Even more disturbed by that thought, she frowned at the photographs. Several minutes later, she released a sigh. "I can't find anything new. Hoffman was at the camp on July 14, two days before Erin died. That doesn't mean he wasn't there on the sixteenth, just that no one caught him on film."

Parker nodded, his gaze still on the computer. "According to his schedule, he attended a gang conference at the Baltimore Convention Center on the sixteenth. Later that night he went to a reception in D.C. hosted by Senator Riggs."

"What time was the reception?"

"It started at eight."

Her hopes plummeted. "So that rules him out in Erin's death." And she'd been so sure…

"Not necessarily. He still could have made it to the camp, depending on when he left the reception."

"How can we find that out?"

"Pay the senator a visit and ask."

She blinked. "Don't tell me you know him?"

"No, but if I tell him I'm investigating Hoffman…"

She stared at him in disbelief, stunned by the risk he was willing to take. Parker wasn't the type to defy the rules. He had absolute faith in the law. For him to gamble his career, going against everything he believed in…

"He'll never buy it," she argued. "He'll call Hoffman and check."

"You have a better idea?"

Her heart made a sudden zigzag. She rose and went

to the window, wondering if she had enough nerve. But she'd sucked Parker into this mess, and she owed him at least that much.

Inhaling sharply, she turned around. "I do, actually. *I'll* call the senator. I'll tell him I'm B. K. Elliot, and that I want to meet with him this afternoon about a partnership helping runaway teens. He won't turn me down. The publicity will boost his career."

A frown etched Parker's brow. "How will that help us? We need information about Hoffman's schedule."

"It'll get us through the door. Once we're inside, you can ask him whatever you want. Even if he's suspicious, he won't be able to call Hoffman until we leave. That'll give us time to get away."

Parker got to his feet. He paced to the door and back, one hand gripping his neck. She knew he was weighing the pros and cons, probing the flaws in her plan. But it would work. It had to. It was the only real option they had.

"I won't tell the senator you're with me," she added. "Not until we get there. He doesn't know the police are after me, so I doubt he'll lay a trap."

Parker stopped beside her again. "But he'll learn who you are. Your identity will come out. You're sure you want to take that risk?"

Of course she didn't want to risk it. But she knew what she had to do. "It's going to come out regardless. Now that the newspaper has run my picture…"

"It still might take them a while to find you. You should wait until we've arrested the killer at least."

"We don't have time. That gang's already attacked us once. Now the police are after us, too. Our luck won't hold for long."

Parker hesitated, then shook his head. "There must be another way."

"I don't see one. Besides, I want to do this." She was the one they were after. Only she could stop the slaughter—no matter how terrifying the thought.

"What about your friends?" he asked. "I thought you had to protect them."

"I'll call Haley and warn her. Nadine's in South America, so she's safe enough for now."

"I still don't like it. Too much can go wrong."

Knowing she had to convince him, she feigned courage she didn't feel. "It's going to work. I'm sure I can get us in."

But would they get back out?

She met his worried eyes, his concern for her touching her heart. And all of a sudden, she was certain of something else. They might not survive this ordeal. They might never see each other again if they did. But she knew with dead-on certainty that she wanted to make love to Parker one more time.

She dropped her gaze to his mouth. Memories tumbled through her mind—of how he'd tasted and looked and smelled. And she desperately needed to feel him, to experience that delirium again.

Because the truth was, she didn't care if he was a cop. She didn't care if she'd get hurt when they parted ways. Even if it was just an illusion, she longed to relive the feelings he'd evoked—of being sheltered, cherished, *loved*.

She swallowed hard. Parker didn't know it, but he'd given her a precious gift last night. For the first time in her life, she'd had a taste of how real love might feel, the security of being safe in a strong man's arms. And

God help her, even if this all ended badly, she wanted to experience that one last time.

She reached up and stroked his jaw. Surprise flared in his hypnotic eyes. "Kiss me, Parker," she whispered, stepping so close she was cradled between his thighs.

His eyes went hot. The muscles worked in his whiskered throat. He curled one hand around her neck, the sensual touch scrambling her thoughts. "Are you sure? Your arm—"

"Forget my arm," she whispered. "Just put your hands on me before I go insane."

He growled then, a deep, feral sound that sent thrills shuddering down her spine. Then he pulled her hard against him and lowered his mouth to hers. And she didn't think again for a long, long time.

Chapter 12

"You're sure you want to do this?" Parker asked Brynn again as they exited the staircase just off the atrium in the Hart Senate Office Building and turned down a light-filled hall.

"I'm sure."

"We can wait for the senator to come back." As it turned out, Senator Riggs was out of town. But several phone calls and various staffers later, they'd managed to get an appointment with Gwendolyn Shaffer, the senator's chief of staff.

"I'll be all right, Parker."

It didn't feel all right. It felt like a huge mistake—another potential screwup he was going to regret. He'd already messed up by making love to Brynn again. He'd had no business touching her, no matter how blinding the sex. But instead of whisking her to safety, instead of doing his sworn duty and shielding a vulnerable civilian from harm, he was exposing her to a situation he feared could go lethally wrong.

But they had to take the initiative. They couldn't stay on the defensive, waiting for an attack—especially with the police involved. Still, he wished they were meeting somewhere neutral, somewhere public, somewhere he could plan for a quick escape. But Shaffer had flat-out refused.

"Anyhow, it's better this way," Brynn scooted over to let several people wearing suits and carrying briefcases hurry by. "The senator won't know the details, like who attended what event. Junior people handle stuff like that. And they're usually more willing to talk."

"Maybe." But Gwendolyn Shaffer was hardly a flunky, according to the online bios he'd read. Despite an impoverished childhood, she'd worked her way through law school, then embarked on a meteoric career—clerking for a federal judge, serving as a city commissioner and sitting on various boards. Her current duties included everything from advising the senator on domestic and foreign policy to managing his reelection campaign.

Still, Brynn was right. The senator's chief of staff was their only hope right now—and Brynn was their ticket in. He just hoped they'd escape unscathed.

Still battling his reservations, Parker accompanied her down the gleaming corridor to the office and followed her inside. After giving their names to the secretary, he prowled around the reception area while they waited for the chief of staff. He glanced at the usual political photos decorating the walls—the senator with the president, the senator hosting a conference with leaders from the Muslim community, the senator with the ambassador of Jaziirastan in front of the embassy.

Brynn came up beside him, and he shifted his gaze to her. And once again her beauty bulldozed through him—her soft, downy skin, her glorious, auburn hair, the perfect contours of her creamy lips. And a fierce feeling of possessiveness stole through him, the need to claim and protect this woman in the most fundamental of ways.

He shook his head, appalled at how thoroughly she'd captivated him, obliterating any impartiality he'd once had. But this wasn't the time to examine his feelings. He had to focus on keeping her safe.

"That must be Erin Walker's father," Brynn said, peering at a photo.

Still struggling to subdue his emotions, Parker shifted his gaze to the shot. According to the caption, Senator Riggs had brokered a weapons deal between Walker Avionics and the government of Jaziirastan, a small country bordering Afghanistan. The deal had brought his state hundreds of jobs.

"That figures. The senator gets Walker business in exchange for campaign contributions and touts it as creating jobs." No wonder Hoffman had warned him off. There were billions of dollars involved.

And speaking of power... Parker scowled at his watch. The chief of staff was taking her time. Five more minutes and they were out of here. He wasn't risking Brynn's safety longer than that.

His uneasiness mounting, he trailed Brynn past another row of publicity shots—the senator touring a housing project, the senator christening a shelter for victims of domestic violence, the senator playing golf at a fund-raiser for disadvantaged kids.

Brynn abruptly came to a stop. "I know that man."

Parker looked at the shot. The senator and another man stood laughing beside a golf cart, waiting to tee off. "Who is it?"

She shot a quick glance back at the receptionist, then lowered her voice. "Oliver Burroughs—he's Haley's father. He's a criminal defense attorney in Baltimore. A real big shot. I've never met him, but Haley showed me his picture once. And I don't usually forget a face."

"Criminal defense, huh?" Parker studied the photo with interest now. So Senator Riggs golfed with a prominent Baltimore defense attorney. That didn't mean much; politicians networked all the time. But if there was a chance that attorney defended gang members...

He switched his gaze to Brynn. "Can we visit your friend?"

"Haley?"

"I'd like to ask her some questions about her father, whether he had a connection to Markus Jenkins, that gang leader who was released from jail."

"You think her father got him released?"

"I don't know. It doesn't seem like it. From what I've heard, it was some sort of paperwork glitch. I'd still like to talk to your friend, though, and find out what she knows."

Her eyes thoughtful, Brynn gave him a nod. "Sure. We can go there as soon as we leave here."

A woman strode into the reception area just then, and they both turned around. The senator's chief of staff was in her early forties, average height, and slightly plump. She wore a gray plaid suit, low-heeled shoes and an old-fashioned strand of pearls. She had chin-length, mouse-brown hair peppered with streaks of gray. Yet despite her unremarkable appearance, her steps were brisk and her gaze steady as she crossed the room. She radiated poise and power.

"Good afternoon. I'm Gwendolyn Shaffer," she said to Brynn. "Senator Riggs's chief of staff."

"Brynn Elliot." Parker watched the exchange, noting the sharp curiosity in the woman's eyes as they shook hands.

"This is Detective McCall," Brynn said. "From the Baltimore Police Department."

The chief of staff's smile didn't falter, nothing in her expression indicating any surprise. *This woman wasn't a novice,* Parker realized, his respect for her rising a degree. He'd have a tough time shaking her composure enough to glean anything of note.

She ushered them into her office and offered drinks, which they refused. As they took their seats by the bookcase, Parker ran his gaze around the room, taking in the huge window overlooking the atrium, the plush carpet and leather chairs. *No trace of her hardscrabble roots in here.*

"I'm quite a fan of your work," Shaffer told Brynn, taking a seat in an armchair across from them. The chit-chat dwindled a moment later, and Shaffer sat back, an expectant look in her eyes.

Parker cleared his throat, drawing her attention to him. "I'm afraid we came here under false pretenses." For the first time Shaffer blinked. "I need information about an event the senator hosted in July. I didn't want to go through the usual channels because the investigation is sensitive. I don't want word getting out just yet."

"I see." A cautious note crept into her voice. "How can I help you?"

He shifted in his chair. "The senator hosted a reception for the ambassador of Jaziirastan at the Willard InterContinental Hotel on July 16. I'm interested in one of the attendees, Hugh Hoffman, the chief of the Baltimore Police Department's Criminal Investigation Division."

Shaffer pursed her lips, her expression giving nothing away. "So this is official police business? You're investigating Colonel Hoffman?"

Smart question, one he'd expect a lawyer to ask. "No, it's not official yet. I'm only gathering information right now."

"Exactly what do you need to know?"

"Whether he attended the reception and what time he left. I'd also like a copy of the guest list, if that's possible."

Shaffer steepled her hands. He could almost see her mind spinning, weighing the repercussions for the senator, her boss. Then she rose and went to her desk.

He traded a glance with Brynn, caught the worry in her eyes over how Shaffer would react. But Shaffer picked up the telephone receiver and punched a key. "Nancy, I need you to bring me the guest list from the Jaziirastan reception on July 16 and the schedule of events. Right away. Thanks."

She replaced the receiver in its cradle, then turned to face them again. "Colonel Hoffman was at the reception, but I don't know what time he left. He was there for the senator's speech, which I believe was around nine-thirty. I didn't see him again after that."

Parker frowned. "You're sure he was there?"

"He stood beside me during the speech."

"And the event took place at the Willard?"

"That's right."

So if Hoffman had left by ten, he'd had enough time to get to the camp in western Maryland, which was just over an hour away. And while that information didn't necessarily convict him, neither did it rule him out.

A soft knock came from the door. "Come in," Shaffer called.

The secretary entered the room and handed several papers to the chief of staff. "Just as I thought," Shaffer said when the secretary left. "The senator gave his remarks at nine-thirty. He usually speaks for fifteen or twenty minutes. There was nothing scheduled after that. As I said, I don't remember seeing Colonel Hoffman later, so I really don't know when he left."

She walked over and handed the other sheet to him. "This is the list of guests."

"I appreciate it."

Her gaze was cool. "I'm happy to cooperate. If you have further questions, don't hesitate to call and ask."

In other words, go through the proper channels. Parker rose, recognizing a dismissal when he heard it, no matter how polite her tone of voice. "Thanks for your time."

"Of course." She cast a quick glance back at the phone. And suddenly Parker knew with absolute certainty that she was going to contact Hoffman the instant they left the room.

Which meant he had to get Brynn to safety at once.

Shaffer walked them to the door and turned to Brynn. "If you'd still like to speak with the senator, I'm sure we can set something up."

Parker waited, his impatience mounting, as Brynn took her card and murmured a polite reply. Then he hurried her away from the office and back down the corridor, an urgent feeling quickening his steps.

"Walk faster." He steered her to the nearest stairwell.

Brynn shot him a glance. "You think she's going to report us to Hoffman?"

"She's probably on the phone right now. We need to get out of here before he tells her to alert the guards."

They reached the stairwell a moment later and raced to the bottom floor. Then they walked as fast as they dared through the lobby toward the tall glass doors.

A guard stepped into their path. Several more guards appeared out of nowhere, fanning across the room. His heart thundering, Parker grabbed Brynn's arm and steered her into a crowd of businessmen converging on the door. Then he shuffled with her through the exit, hoping the guards wouldn't notice them amid the men.

What a disaster. He hadn't proven Hoffman's guilt. He hadn't unearthed a single detail that would help them save their skins. Instead, he'd tipped off the chief of staff—who was now putting the D.C. cops on their trail—endangering Brynn even more.

They reached the sidewalk a second later, and the businessmen began to disperse. A sudden shout came from behind them. "Go!" he urged.

They broke into a run.

Brynn's pulse still hadn't returned to normal as they exited the Metro several blocks from Haley's shelter and headed up the street. Thankfully, it appeared they'd escaped the police. The last thing she wanted was to bring more danger to Haley or her pregnant teens. But their luck couldn't last, not with both the Baltimore and D.C. cops now on their trail—not to mention that deadly gang.

Still skittish, she shot another glance behind her, then surveyed the quiet street. Haley's shelter was in a transitional section of D.C. Newly refurbished row houses were interspersed with derelict buildings still bearing the call signs of local gangs.

"So tell me about your friend," Parker said.

She lifted her gaze to his. "What do you want to know?"

"Where you met, where she's from, what her father's like."

Brynn hesitated, the instinct to protect Haley's identity ingrained after years on the run. But it was ridiculous to doubt Parker given their current plight.

"We met on the streets in Baltimore," she said. "That's where she's from. Her family comes from money. Old money. They live in Guilford, have a summer home at Saint Michaels—the whole nine yards."

"High society."

"The highest. They're even listed in the Blue Book." The Baltimore Society Visiting List, better known as the Blue Book, was an elite social registry that dated back nearly a century, listing Baltimore's upper crust.

"Interesting profile for a runaway," Parker said.

"Not really. You'd be surprised at what goes on behind closed doors, even in *respectable* families." She couldn't keep the bitterness from her voice.

"I'm a cop, Brynn. I've seen some pretty bad stuff."

Not the horror she'd endured.

She frowned at the cracked sidewalk, wondering how he'd react if he knew her past. Would he recoil in disgust? Blame her for the abuse? Most men would race for the exits if she even hinted at the revolting truth.

She slipped him a sideways glance, surprised that she even cared. But his opinion mattered to her. Somehow in the past few days Parker had penetrated the decades-old buffer she'd built around her heart. And once again, she was so incredibly tempted to tell him the details, to reveal her nightmarish past.

But this wasn't the time. They had too much else on their minds. And what if he didn't believe her? Could she survive that humiliation again?

Pushing aside that disturbing thought, she skirted a pile of construction debris, then glanced at a carpenter working in a weed-filled yard, sawing a pile of boards. She raised her voice above the noise. "Anyhow, Haley got pregnant and ran away."

"And now she runs a shelter for runaway pregnant girls."

Brynn's mouth ticked up, pride welling for her best friend. "She's always been a rescuer—stray cats, stray dogs, stray people." A woman with a nurturing heart. "In any case, I can't imagine her father belonging to a gang. He's more the country-club type."

"Like you said, you never know. He might use drugs or have some other connection to them."

True enough. She just hoped they found out *some-thing* on this visit that would incriminate her stepfather and end the danger before more innocent people got hurt.

Several houses later, they reached the shelter, a tidy, Federal-style row house with freshly painted black shutters and yellow bricks. Brynn climbed the steps and pushed the bell. A small bronze plaque bearing the inscription "Always Home" decorated the wooden door.

A pregnant girl let them inside a minute later. Brynn crossed the threshold, then paused, experiencing her usual shiver of pride. Sunlight streamed over the hardwood floor. Flowers brimmed from vases, adding bursts of color to the cheerful room. Oversize, sagging armchairs formed an arc around the fireplace, inviting a weary runaway to put up her feet and relax. The mouthwatering scent of baking cookies filled the air.

Haley's shelter was a sanctuary, the kind of place they'd both yearned for as runaway teens—a safe, comfortable home where they could escape the danger, where there was a nonjudgmental shoulder to cry on, where they could curl up beside the fireplace and figure out how to mend their shattered lives.

Haley emerged from the kitchen, wiping her hands on a towel. Concern filled her eyes when she saw her old friend.

"Brynn! I've been so worried! Are you all right?" Her cheeks were flushed from baking, her thick, chestnut hair slipping from a haphazard knot atop her head. But she still managed to look poised, despite her flour-dusted T-shirt and jeans—a legacy from her former life as a debutante.

"I'm fine. I brought someone to see you. This is Parker McCall."

Haley's gaze whipped to Parker, sudden caution stealing into her eyes. Brynn knew she'd pegged him as a cop. Despite her gentle appearance, Haley was as street savvy as Brynn. She'd had to be to survive. And Parker was the epitome of danger with his dark, gunslinger eyes, his tall, muscular build, the lethal masculinity oozing from every pore.

"He's Tommy's brother," she added.

Surprise replaced the wariness in Haley's eyes. She tilted her head, studying him anew. "You look like him."

Parker gave her a nod. Brynn realized it had to be odd for him to meet people who'd known his brother back then. And she could tell by the tension rippling his rough-hewn jaw that it affected him more than he cared to let on.

"Can we talk?" she asked Haley. She glanced at the teenager watching from the kitchen doorway. "Somewhere private?"

"Let's go in my office." She turned to the pregnant teen. "Jessica, can you take out the cookies when the timer rings? Then turn the oven off. It's the last batch."

"Okay." Smiling shyly, the teen disappeared into the kitchen.

"She looks young," Brynn said, trailing Haley into her office down the hall.

"Sixteen. About the same age I was when I ran away. It seems incredible now."

It was a lifetime ago. They'd both changed and become much stronger—strength they needed now if they hoped to defeat their ghosts for good.

Haley ushered them inside and shut the door. Brynn plopped down beside Parker on the faded couch and sighed. Haley's office was the opposite of Gwendolyn Shaffer's with its threadbare sofa and mismatched chairs, ironic given Haley's privileged childhood. But it was the type of place a kid could unburden her heart— which was exactly Haley's intent.

"So what's going on?"

"We're trying to identify the man who shot Tommy," Brynn said. She summarized the recent events, including the possible link to the Ridgewood gang. "It's complicated, but we were wondering about your father and how he knows Senator Riggs."

Haley pursed her lips. "They go way back. They were classmates at Georgetown Law. He came to a lot of parties at our house when I lived at home. He's friends with my mother, too."

Parker leaned forward. "Your father's a criminal defense attorney, right?"

"That's right. He's the senior partner at the firm, so he mostly takes the high profile cases. And he hardly ever loses. He's a real SOB in court."

And at home, according to the stories she'd told Brynn.

"Any chance he defended Markus Jenkins?" Parker asked. "He's the leader of the Ridgewood gang."

"I don't know. I don't follow his cases now."

But if Haley's father *had* defended Markus Jenkins, it made for an interesting twist. Haley's father golfed with the senator, his former classmate. Now Hoffman was the senator's protégé—linking the three men. And Markus Jenkins led the gang that was trying to kill her, possibly at Hoffman's behest.

"I wish I could help," Haley added. "But I haven't had contact with him in years."

Parker seemed to process that. He asked a few more questions about her father's practice, but while it was possible he defended gang members, Haley couldn't confirm it. "I'm sorry," she said. "I know that's not much help."

"It was worth a try."

"No one's bothered you, have they?" Brynn asked. "You haven't seen anyone hanging around?"

"No. Everything's peaceful here—or as much as it can be with pregnant girls."

"Good." She prayed it stayed that way.

"You mind if I use your computer for a minute?" Parker asked Haley. "I'd like to check my email."

"Go ahead. I need to see about those cookies. Jessica tends to get distracted and forget." She rose and caught Brynn's eye. "Come on. I'll bag up some cookies for you to take with you."

Resigned to the inevitable grilling, Brynn followed her into the kitchen. Haley had begun renovating her shelter years ago, and only had the kitchen left. It desperately needed updating with its gold linoleum floor, cheap particle board cupboards and the ugliest avocado-green countertop Brynn had ever seen. But French doors opened onto a pretty patio. A farmhouse table lined one wall, more flowers sprawling over the top. Chocolate chip cookies cooled in racks on the counters, the sugary scent making her stomach growl.

"So what gives?" Haley demanded as soon as they were inside.

"I told you. We're investigating—"

"I mean with Tommy's brother."

"Nothing."

Haley snorted. "Nothing? The way he looks at you?"

Brynn's face warmed, a kaleidoscope of erotic images flashing through her mind. And she knew she'd never fool Haley. Her friend knew her too well. "Okay, fine. I'll admit it. We're having a…a thing. But it's not serious."

Haley raised a brow.

"It's not. It's just…I don't know, a fling."

"You're not the type for a fling."

"Well, I'm not the type for fairy-tale endings, either, so don't you dare start in with that."

Haley's eyes instantly softened. "Of course you are. You just haven't met the right guy yet."

"Right. Well, maybe in my next life." Shaking her head, Brynn snatched a cookie from the rack and took a bite. The argument wasn't new. They'd been debating this for years. Brynn was a die-hard realist. She knew her limitations and never indulged in dreams. Whereas Haley was an eternal optimist who clung to the misguided belief that true love awaited her someday no matter how much evidence proved her wrong.

"Great cookie," she mumbled, hoping her friend would take the hint.

But Haley wasn't easily deterred. "Tommy was a good guy, you know."

"So?"

"So maybe his brother's like him."

Brynn released a sigh. "Maybe he is. In fact, I know he is. But that still doesn't make him right for me."

"You're sure about that?"

Brynn rolled her eyes. "I'm sure. Now can we please let this go?"

Haley raised her hands as if to ward her off. "Fine. If you want to reject a man like that, it's up to you." She took a paper bag from a drawer and piled some cookies inside, then handed it to Brynn. "But guys like that don't come around twice. Don't mess this up because you're scared."

Scared? Stung, Brynn gaped at her closest friend. "How can you say that? I'm not scared."

"Not of the big stuff, no. But sometimes I think…"

"What?"

Haley leaned back against the counter, then sighed. "Don't get me wrong. I really admire your work. It's brilliant. *You're* brilliant. And you know I love you. You're the best friend I have. I wouldn't even be here without your help. But sometimes I wonder if maybe you aren't hiding behind your work, using it as a way to keep people out."

Brynn's jaw dropped. She stared at her friend in shock. She didn't hide behind her work. She used her photos to expose the evil in the world, to show the unvarnished reality of homeless life—not as a crutch.

"Maybe I'm wrong," Haley added quickly. "I hope I am. All I'm saying is…you had a terrible past. You had every right to retreat. What you suffered…no one should have to go through that. But don't let the evil you've suffered rob you of a happy life."

"I won't. I'm not."

"Good." Haley gave her another hug. "Now go give that man those cookies while I clean up."

Still reeling from the accusation, Brynn left Haley to her cookies and went back down the hall. Sure, she was cautious around people. Why shouldn't she be? She had killers tracking her down, her stepfather trying to do her in. She'd be foolish *not* to fear for her life.

But as for her relationship with Parker…Haley was wrong. She simply wasn't the happily-ever-after type. And it had nothing to do with fear.

Parker looked up as she entered the office. His somber eyes stopped her cold. "What happened?"

"I got the list."

The officers who'd worked in Homicide when Tommy

had died. Her pulse quickening, she set the bag of cookies on the end table and sank onto the sagging couch. "Any surprises?"

"A couple." His eyes turning even grimmer, he worked his bristled jaw. "It turns out my supervisor, Enrique Delgado, was there."

Brynn's heart tripped. "The guy who worked in the gang unit? The guy you were talking to when the police showed up?"

"Yeah."

She turned that over in her mind. "You're saying he might know Markus Jenkins?"

"It's possible."

"You think Delgado got him out of prison?" But that would mean her stepfather wasn't involved.

"It wouldn't have been too hard. He could get a court order to have Jenkins released into his custody, claim he needed his help with a case. But I'm not so sure it was him." He rose from the desk and joined her on the couch, then handed her the list.

"I knew Hoffman was there," he said as she skimmed the names. "And Vern Collins, the detective who investigated Tommy's case. But I'd forgotten Collins was Hoffman's partner."

She tore her gaze from the list. "Does that matter?"

"It might." Parker's mouth turned flat. "Collins left the force a few months after they shelved Tommy's case. He got caught up in a sexual harassment charge. I don't remember the details, but a complaint like that kills your career. He probably knew he'd never get promoted, so he left."

Brynn waited, her eyes glued to Parker's face. From

the intensity of his expression, whatever he'd learned was big.

"I did a little research," he said. "And guess where Collins works now? The Roxbury Correctional Institution in Hagerstown, Maryland."

Her heart swooped. "You mean… Wasn't that the prison where Markus Jenkins was jailed?"

"Yeah. So it looks like Hoffman got him out."

And sent the gang leader after them.

Chapter 13

His boss was trying to kill him.

Feeling oddly hollow, Parker struggled to process what he'd learned. *Hoffman*. The man he'd always respected. The man who'd mentored his career. The man who'd taken him under his wing, helping restore his faith in the integrity of the police force after his father's corruption sting. Hoffman had lied to him, manipulated him. He'd tried to do him in.

But why? And why now when they'd worked together for years? Because he was investigating Erin Walker's death? Because he'd delayed in turning in Brynn? Or was it because he was finally closing in on Tommy's killer after all this time?

"You think Hoffman got that gang leader out of jail," Brynn repeated, sounding just as stunned.

"It wouldn't be hard. He'd call up his old partner at

the prison, tell him he wants Jenkins released. Collins switches up the paperwork and gets him out."

And then Hoffman feigns outrage when the media howls about the mistake.

"And once he's out, Jenkins attacks my agent. He kills Jamie, then tries to murder us."

"Yeah." After Hoffman fed Parker a story about wanting to get Brynn help.

He inhaled again, not wanting to believe it. Another man he'd looked up to had betrayed his trust. But he couldn't dwell on that right now. He had to think, plan, figure out how to bring Hoffman down. Because if the Colonel thought he was going to win this fight, he was wrong. Dead wrong. Parker might have been slow to make the connection, but he'd be damned if he'd give up now.

He rose and stalked to the window, then braced his forearm on the glass and scowled out. The hell of it was, he couldn't prove Hoffman's involvement. There was no incriminating evidence, nothing to tie him to the gang leader's release—let alone the attempt on their lives. Even his old partner's involvement was circumstantial; Collins could claim he'd simply made a mistake.

Brynn joined him at the window a moment later. Her face was drawn, her eyes troubled, reflecting her doubts. "What about your supervisor? Where does he fit into this?"

"Damned if I know. Delgado's not much older than I am. So he'd just started working in Homicide back then. He was there for a couple of years, then went over to the gang unit."

"And that's where he met Markus Jenkins."

"Maybe." It certainly looked suspicious. Delgado had

tracked Parker's movements. He could have fed Hoffman the story about the drugs. So was Delgado directing Hoffman, or the reverse?

Not knowing what to think, he blew out a frustrated breath. Both Hoffman and Delgado could have known the gang leader. Either could have arranged his release. And either one could have set the cops on Parker's trail.

But only one was Tommy's killer. Only one had a motive to want them dead.

The question was—*which one?*

The office door swung open, and Brynn's friend Haley came in. "You got a fax," Parker told her, his mind still on the case. His instincts urged him to focus on Hoffman, given his possible involvement in the Walker girl's death and his relationship to Brynn. But Parker couldn't afford to discount Delgado—because if he made a mistake and guessed wrongly, Brynn would pay the price.

"Did you find out anything about my father?" Haley asked, walking over to the fax machine.

"Not yet." But if he *had* defended Markus Jenkins, it provided yet another link in this twisted chain. "I doubt he had anything to do with his release, though." Collins was a better bet.

But that still left both Hoffman and Delgado as potential suspects. And until he figured out who the killer was, he couldn't trust either one.

"Oh, no," Haley groaned, looking at her fax.

"Bad news?" Brynn asked.

"It never stops." Haley walked over and handed the paper to Brynn. "This girl went missing last night. Any chance you've seen her around?"

Brynn took the page from Haley. Her gasp caused his heart to skip. "What is it?"

Her hand trembling, she turned the paper his way. On it was a picture of a preteen girl. A girl with a long, black ponytail. "It's the girl from High Rock Camp." The girl who'd been sitting beside Hoffman at the campfire.

And she wore that now-familiar necklace around her neck.

Her stepfather had attacked another child.

Brynn stared at the photo of the girl, her head light, the room weaving in and out of focus as the realization sank in. Hoffman had struck again. Another child was suffering the hell that she'd been through. She'd failed to stop him in time.

"Are you all right?" Parker asked, his voice sounding far away.

"Yes, I…"

"Come on. You need to sit down. You look like you're going to faint." He led her to the couch, and she slumped down on the threadbare cushions, jarring her injured arm.

"Here. Drink some water," Haley thrust a bottle into her hands.

Brynn obediently took a sip, then shuddered hard, fighting down an onrush of bile. Hoffman was on the hunt. He'd harmed another innocent child. That necklace *had* to be the proof.

"Hoffman took her," she whispered, feeling sick. "We didn't stop him in time."

Parker lowered himself to the couch beside her, his

eyes dark with concern—and something else. Fear. Determination. Guilt?

Shaking away that wild thought, she motioned toward the fax. "The necklace she's wearing," she asked Haley. "Have you seen it before? We think that symbol might mean something."

Haley studied the picture again. "No, but I can ask the girls."

Parker climbed to his feet. "I'll go with you. I want to hear what they have to say."

But Haley shook her head. "You'd better stay here. They won't talk to a cop." Taking the paper with her, she rushed away.

Parker returned to the couch. His gaze traveled over her face. "You're sure you're okay?"

"Just scared." She pressed her fingers to her lips. Her worst fear had just been realized. Another innocent child was at the mercy of that sadistic man. "We have to find her, Parker."

"We will."

"But Hoffman—"

"You don't know for sure that he has her."

"Of course he has her. You can't possibly think this is a coincidence. Not when she has that necklace on."

"It looks bad," he agreed. "But we still need evidence. I can't get a warrant based on a hunch."

"You saw that picture. He sat next to her at the campfire."

"Which he had every right to do. For God's sake, Brynn, he's friends with a powerful senator. He's the head of the Criminal Investigation Division. No one's going to go against him without proof."

"Not even to save that child?"

He rose and paced to the window. He spun on his heel and came back. "Listen. I want to stop him as much as you do. Probably more if he had anything to do with Tommy's death. But I need something else to go on— facts, evidence. Suspicions aren't enough this time. If I try to have him suspended, it's going to look personal, like I'm retaliating for his charge about drugs. I need something to back me up."

She stared at him, slack-jawed. "I don't believe this. He tried to arrest you. He tried to *kill* you. And you're still protecting him?"

"I'm *not* protecting him."

"Of course you are! He's a cop, so of course you're going to take his side."

"It's not that. It's just…a charge like this…they'll suspend him. Someone will leak it to the press. Word will get out that he's a pedophile, and he'll never recover from that. Even if he's found innocent later, his reputation is ruined. And no matter what I *think* he's done, I can't destroy him without proof."

Brynn shook her head, desperation knotting her insides. Somehow she had to convince him. They had to find Hoffman and stop him fast. But then the office door swung open, and Haley came back in. "One of the girls recognized the symbol," she said, sounding breathless.

Brynn's belly tensed. "What is it?"

"It sounds really sick, but it's something pedophiles use. She says it's like an insider symbol, a member of the club type of thing."

So she was right. She shot Parker a pointed look. "I told you."

But he only shook his head. "It's still not enough. We don't know that he gave it to her. And what if he did? He could claim he didn't know what it meant. He can explain all this away."

Too frustrated to sit still anymore, Brynn rose and walked to the window, then stared out at the gathering dusk. That child was in terrible danger. And she *knew* that Hoffman had her. She knew her stepfather, knew how he operated, knew the kind of child he preferred.

But she didn't have proof. She turned to Parker again, determined to find a way. "What kind of evidence do you need?"

"Photos. Emails or phone calls. A credible victim would do."

A credible victim. She went stone-still. Her heart made a frantic skip. She'd been Hoffman's victim. But would Parker believe her if she told him the truth? No one else ever had.

She closed her eyes, her belly pitching, the thought of revealing those horrific details making her want to wretch. But she had to rescue that girl—no matter what the personal cost.

And Haley was right. Parker was a good guy. He'd saved her from the drive-by shooting. He'd helped her flee the cops. In the end he might not believe her, but she knew that he'd hear her out.

Assuming she had the nerve to reveal the truth.

Another wave of dizziness barreled through her, and she placed her hand on the glass. She didn't want to relive the past. But she had to do this. She had to reach deep inside her and find the courage to admit the truth—before another innocent victim died.

She turned to her best friend. Haley held her gaze for a moment, then nodded her approval, understanding what she intended to do. She left the office and closed the door, leaving Brynn and Parker alone.

"All right," Brynn said, knowing she couldn't turn back now. "If you need a victim, I'll give you one. *Me.*"

Needing a moment to compose herself, she turned toward the window again and stared out at the small backyard. Bare branches clawed the sky. Withered bushes bowed in the fitful breeze. Dusk crept inexorably over the patio, turning the landscape an ominous, tombstone gray.

Knowing she couldn't postpone this, that every passing second mattered to that missing girl, she inhaled and turned around. Parker leaned against the back of the sofa, his arms folded across his broad chest, his eyes inscrutable as he waited for her to speak.

"I told you my stepfather was a cop," she began. "What I didn't tell you is that he's Hugh Hoffman, the C.I.D. chief. He sexually abused me when I was young. That's why I ran away from home."

Parker's eyes flickered, but his face remained impassive, making her wonder if he already knew. But that was silly. How could he have figured it out? She'd been so careful not to let it slip.

Deciding she'd imagined his reaction, she forged ahead. "My dad died when I was five. Hoffman started dating my mother a year later, when I was six. At first I thought he was nice. He talked to me, paid attention to me. He took me places—swimming, fishing, roller-skating. He gave me candy and little gifts."

She hugged her arms, ignoring the twinge of pain. "My dad and I…we were really close. I adored him. And when he died I fell apart. It was a really bad time. Then

Hoffman came along. He played me perfectly. He saw that I needed attention and filled the void."

She flattened her lips. "It was typical grooming behavior. First he established a bond. Then as soon as he married my mother, he graduated to the next stage. He started finding excuses to touch me. He hugged me, tickled me, kissed me. He had me sit on his lap while we watched TV. He always wanted to wrestle and horse around, especially if I was in my nightgown. He even came into the bathroom when I was taking a bath and insisted on drying me off. And then he started showing me pictures...."

"Stop." Parker's jaw turned to iron. He pushed away from the couch and strode to her side. "You don't have to do this."

"You need to know how he works."

"Not if it's too painful." His eyes blazed into hers. "I mean it, Brynn. You don't have to tell me this."

She searched his eyes, tempted to take the easy way out. But if there was some clue she could reveal, some way to help that missing girl...

Taking another deep breath, she forced herself to go on. "I knew something was wrong. He seemed creepy. He was always watching me, touching me... But my mother loved him. She kept saying how great he was."

She made a derisive sound. "And he *was* great. He drove me places. He took the time to play with me. He even volunteered at my school. And my mother fell for the act. He was her savior. We didn't have much money after my dad died. She went back to work as a waitress, but we were just scraping by. Then Hoffman came along and supported her so she didn't have to work so hard. So whenever I tried to tell her what he was doing, she just got mad. She accused me of making things up.

"And then he began to abuse me." She closed her eyes, trembling wildly, her mind caught up in the dreadful past. "I won't go into the details." Bad enough that she'd suffered through it. She couldn't inflict that horror on him. "But he…he likes violence. The more he hurt me, the more excited he got."

"Brynn…" Parker's voice broke, but she had to go on. She had to tell him the rest before she lost her nerve.

"He gave me gifts afterward. The worse the attack, the bigger the gift. That's why when I saw the necklace…"

Parker clenched his hands. Fury and indignation burned in his eyes. "You reported this, right?"

She gave him a bitter smile. "Yeah, I reported it. But no one believed me. He claimed I'd misunderstood, or that I'd exaggerated or lied. That I was acting out against him because he'd taken my father's place. And everyone believed him because he was so nice. All the teachers liked him. He coached my soccer team. And he was a cop. You know what his reputation is like. Of course they believed him over me. Even my mother bought the story. She thought he could do no wrong.

"And the worst part was that he was right. I *did* lie. I was so angry, so desperate to stop him that I accused him of all sorts of things. And when those turned out to be lies…"

"They didn't believe the rest."

She managed a nod. "He was smart. He made sure everyone thought I was unbalanced, while he was the caring stepfather who was only trying to help. So when

I accused him of abuse, he came across as the victim of a vindictive child."

"You never saw a doctor?"

She shook her head. "I wouldn't let anyone near me. My mother tried, but I was so angry and ashamed…. But that only convinced them even more that I'd lied."

Parker closed the distance between them. He cradled her jaw with his strong, warm hands, his dark gaze drawing her in. "I believe you."

A flurry of warmth billowed through her. Tears of relief sprang to her eyes. His words were so simple, so ordinary, but they meant the world to her. "Parker…"

He pulled her head to his chest. A swarm of emotions thickened her throat. She closed her eyes, relishing his heat, his strength, the dependable beat of his heart.

A good guy, Haley had told her. She was right.

"I'm sorry," he murmured into her hair. He stroked gentle circles on her back. "I wish I could have been there to help you."

She lifted her head, so touched she could hardly speak. "I'm okay now. I saw a therapist for a long time. I did a lot of reading, talked with other survivors of sexual abuse. It wasn't easy. I had nightmares for years. And I couldn't…date for the longest time. But I've put it behind me now."

"This doesn't define you," he said, his voice suddenly fierce. "This isn't who you are."

He was wrong. It *did* define her. "I can't escape my past, Parker, no matter how terrible it was. It shaped my life, my career. It made me who I am."

"It made you stronger." His gaze held hers. "You're the strongest person I know." The frank words hung between them. His blatant admiration nearly did her in. Her throat closed up. Moisture sprang to her eyes again. Her emotions on overload, she looked away. His acceptance and belief in her innocence meant more than she could say.

Parker stepped back and released her, as if sensing she needed space. "Is that why he's trying to kill you? To keep you from testifying against him?"

Grateful for his understanding, she shook her head. "I don't think so. He's convinced everyone I'm unstable. No one would believe me, even now. And you know how powerful he is."

"Then why come after you? You think he's the one who killed Tommy?"

"Maybe. But I know something else about him, something that could bring him down. He likes porn, really despicable stuff. He used to make me watch. And I...I'm pretty sure he took videos. I think that's what he's afraid of, that I might find them. If it's just my word against his, he's in the clear. But if I can find those videos..."

Parker's eyes turned hard. His steel jaw bunched, a sudden blast of fury vibrating right out of his muscled frame. "We'll find them. And we'll find that girl." He raised his hands and cupped her face, his gaze locked on hers. "I promise you, Brynn, we'll bring him down, no matter what it takes."

Her heart tumbled hard. She bit her lips, battling the reckless words that nearly spilled out. Because Parker had just given her the most precious gift of her life, something far more valuable than trust. He'd given her *hope*.

And despite what she'd said to Haley, she feared she was fast falling in love with this amazing man.

* * *

For the first time in his life, Parker didn't care about breaking the rules. Nothing mattered more than stopping Hoffman from harming that missing girl.

He grabbed Brynn's cell phone from the dashboard of their borrowed car and punched in Guerrero's number again. The call instantly cut to voice mail, and he swore. Where the hell was his coworker? Why didn't he answer his phone?

They didn't have time to waste. They needed to issue an Amber alert. They needed to interview the missing kid's parents and examine her computer for clues. They needed to mobilize their forces, using every available resource to capture Hoffman.

But Parker couldn't make those calls, not with every police force in the area trying to bring him in. No one would believe him. He'd end up tipping off Hoffman, giving him a chance to destroy the evidence they needed to put him away for good.

He couldn't do this alone. He needed help.

Hissing his frustration, he tossed the phone into the cup holder beneath the console and glanced at Brynn. She stared out the windshield, her knuckles white on the steering wheel. His thoughts veered back to what she'd told him about the abuse, and his heart made a sudden lurch. He couldn't think about that right now. He couldn't dwell on the pain she'd endured. It made him too crazed, made him want to hit something, smash something, pound Hoffman to a bloody stump. And he had to hold it together until they rescued that missing kid.

Brynn exited Interstate 270 at Frederick, the town where she'd grown up. Parker turned his gaze to the windshield, his tension rising as they headed toward her childhood home.

"You're sure he still lives here?" Brynn asked.

"He lists this address on the roster." He'd checked before they'd left. But whether Hoffman would be here was another question—or if he'd have the girl with him if he was. The camp was a better bet. But since this was on their way, better to rule it out before they spent the night tramping uselessly through the woods.

A minute later Brynn turned down a quiet side street, a residential neighborhood filled with 1960s era ranch-style homes. She slowed partway down the block, then stopped at a one-story brick rancher with its porch light on. Huge trees towered over the house. A garbage can sat at the curb. Overgrown hydrangea bushes swallowed the front windows, making it impossible to see inside. A dog yapped in the house next door.

"Is that his car?" she asked, motioning toward a small sedan in the carport.

"No. He drives an SUV. Your mother must be home alone." He paused. "How do you suggest we get inside? I want to check his office for clues."

"We don't need to go inside. He uses the woodshed in the backyard as his office. He ran wires out there and even had plumbing installed."

Her voice sounded strained, and suddenly Parker understood what she hadn't said. Hoffman had taken her to that shed. And there was no way he could make her revisit the place she'd been abused. "Wait here. I'll go check it out."

"I'll go with you."

"Forget it. I'm going in alone."

She reached out and touched his hand. "I have to do this, Parker. I can't keep avoiding the past."

His heart rolled, a maelstrom of emotions tumbling through him as he gazed at her in the dark. She was the most courageous woman he'd ever met.

And he realized something else. This wasn't just about the runaway girl anymore. Naturally, he wanted to save her, but he also wanted justice for Brynn. No one had ever believed her. No one ever helped her. She'd been abandoned by every adult who should have cared.

For once in her life, she deserved a man who wouldn't betray her, a man who'd face down her enemies, a man who'd fight to keep her safe.

And God help him, but he wanted to be that man.

No matter how many rules he had to break to get it done.

Brynn had lied. She didn't want to go anywhere near that dreadful shed.

She stood rooted in the shadows behind Parker, her gaze on the wooden structure as he jimmied the lock on the door. Her pulse was going berserk. A cold sweat moistened her skin in spite of the chilly air. The last thing she wanted to do was enter the place where she'd experienced such terror and pain.

But Hoffman wasn't here. No one could hurt her now. And they needed clues. They had to find evidence that would lead them to that missing girl.

The neighbor's dog continued to bark. The wind gusted again, sending shivers down her neck and spine. Brynn hugged herself, the pain of her injured shoulder hardly registering as Parker opened the creaking door.

Then he stepped inside the shed, his footsteps heavy on the wooden floor. "Where's the light?"

"The switch is on the right. But we'd better close the door first." Judging by the glow in the family room window, her mother was immersed in her TV game shows, but there was no point taking a chance.

Trembling even more now, she stepped over the threshold into the shed. The door thudded shut behind her with the finality of a coffin lid. "All right."

Parker flipped on the overhead light. Brynn blinked in the brightness. The shed was empty. Completely empty. Every trace of Hoffman's presence was gone.

"Looks like he moved his stuff," Parker said, echoing her thoughts.

Still unable to believe it, Brynn turned on her heels, taking in the filthy, scuffed-up floorboards, the sound-absorbent panels covering the walls, the now-empty cupboard, its door hanging ajar. Only that same, off-balance ceiling fan wobbled overhead, its fluted globes black with dust.

"He must have taken his stuff to the camp," she said. "There used to be a desk over here with his computer, a bed on the other side." With a locker underneath containing his "toys."

Bile rose in her throat. She pressed her hands to her mouth, not wanting to relive the past. But the walls began to weave. That paddle fan twirled overhead, making the same relentless tick. Screams echoed in her ears, the frantic, high-pitched cries of a helpless child.

"Come on," Parker said. "Let's get out of here. The way that dog is barking, someone has probably called the cops."

Fighting off her panic, she wheezed in a strangled

breath. "Good idea." She couldn't wait to leave this awful place.

He flipped off the light. Her back drenched with sweat now, Brynn shoved the door open and stumbled into the yard. Even empty, the shed gave her the creeps, as if the pain she'd suffered during all those years had forever permeated the walls.

Instead of just destroying her soul.

Chapter 14

Taking the wheel this time, Parker sped toward the mountains of western Maryland, every passing minute like the countdown on a ticking bomb. They never should have stopped at Hoffman's house. Not only had they squandered valuable minutes, making it harder to find that girl, but it had forced Brynn to confront her past, witnessing that shed where she'd been abused.

He thinned his lips, wanting to get his hands on Hoffman so badly he'd started to shake. But the cold truth was that he needed help. Even if he hunted down Hoffman, he couldn't bring him in alone. He was out of his jurisdiction. He had no authority here—assuming he still had his badge. And with a hostage involved, Parker couldn't afford to make a mistake. He needed to call in the FBI, get a hostage rescue team on scene to liberate that girl.

But Guerrero still hadn't answered his calls.

Hissing in frustration, Parker stomped on the gas pedal and flew past a semi crawling up the hill. By rights he should contact his supervisor and follow the chain of command. But since he couldn't trust Delgado, he'd have to bypass the chain completely and go straight to the one person he knew he could trust.

Terry "The Terror" Lewis. The woman who'd brought down his father. The woman who was out to get him.

Wishing he had another option, he exited the interstate, then barreled down the two-lane highway toward the mountains at breakneck speed. But as much as he disliked the older woman, he knew he had no choice. Lieutenant Lewis was a straight shooter. She didn't play office politics, didn't care who she offended in her pursuit of the truth. He could depend on her to do her duty, regardless of Hoffman's rank. It galled him to have to ask her—he'd be confirming every bad suspicion about him she'd had—but she was their only hope.

"I need you to look up a number for me," he told Brynn, handing her the phone. "Terry Lewis. She lives in Baltimore. But you'll have to hurry. We're going to lose our signal in a few more miles."

She shot him a worried glance. "Who is she?"

"A cop. We go way back." And not in a happy way. "I think we can trust her to help."

He hoped. Because if he'd guessed wrongly, the mistake could cost them their lives.

Half an hour later, they bumped down the dirt road leading to the farmhouse at the edge of High Rock Camp. The dense woods crowded around them. Low-hanging branches grabbed at the car, blotting out the star-filled sky. Reduced to a crawl, they jolted through ruts and potholes, the ominous scrapes as the car hit bottom adding to Parker's nerves.

Lieutenant Lewis had agreed to help them. But she'd needed time to contact the local and federal authorities and get teams into place at the camp. She'd instructed Parker to head to the farmhouse, then wait for help to arrive. Under no circumstances was he to act alone.

The car crunched over branches and pinecones. Parker jerked the wheel to avoid a pothole, wincing when the tailpipe dragged. "You see any tire tracks?"

Brynn braced her hands on the dashboard and leaned closer to the windshield to see. "No, not yet. There's too much brush."

"I know." It didn't look as if a car had come this way in years. But Hoffman had to be here. He wouldn't have used the main office. There wasn't enough privacy there. And the cabins were too close together, not offering enough seclusion when the camp was filled with kids. He needed an isolated place where he could come and go without being observed. But he also needed electricity to run his computer. And since Erin Walker had died at the lookout tower, the farmhouse was the likely choice.

They bounced crazily through another pothole, barely clearing a jagged rock. Then suddenly, the headlights stalled on a fallen tree blocking the road. He hit the brakes and swore. The pine tree was enormous, at least several feet in diameter, far too big to budge. And brush grew over the trunk, indicating it had lain undisturbed for years.

There was no way Hoffman could have driven down this road. They were heading on a senseless wild-goose chase, wasting precious time. But Hoffman *had* to be here. Erin Walker had died at the lookout tower with that necklace on. Where else could he have gone?

"We'll have to go the rest of the way on foot," he decided, cutting the engine. "Any chance there's a flashlight in the glove compartment?"

Brynn opened it, then shook her head. "Check the trunk. Haley doesn't go anywhere without emergency supplies."

He popped the trunk and climbed out, then waded through the knee-high weeds around the car. As Brynn had predicted, there was a cardboard box inside containing survival supplies—a first-aid kit and blanket, a flashlight and boxes of food. An innate sense of caution or a legacy from life on the run?

Regardless, he appreciated her foresight. He grabbed the flashlight and flicked it on, then propped it against the box. He pulled out his sidearm and checked the rounds, then slid it back into his holster, making sure nothing would impede his draw.

Brynn joined him at the trunk, shivering hard in the frigid air. But it was the worry in her eyes that made his heart contract. This wasn't a game. Hoffman was armed and dangerous. If he felt threatened, he'd kill them both.

"We're not going near him," he warned her. "We're just going to find out where he is, then wait. When the hostage team gets here, they'll rescue the girl and bring him down."

"I know."

"I mean it, Brynn. We can't risk doing anything to harm that girl. You have to stay out of the way."

"I said I would."

Right. Like when she'd thrown that bottle at the gang

member. Determined to convince her, he strode to her side. He gently gripped her shoulders, intending to read her the riot act. But the soft feel of her rocked his senses. Her alluring scent went straight to his head. And instead of arguing his point, a jumble of emotions muddled his thoughts—panic over her safety, guilt over his deception, fury over the torture she'd endured.

Unable to resist, he pulled her into his arms. Suddenly needing to kiss her, he slid his lips over hers, relishing her warmth, her taste, giving vent to a deluge of emotions he couldn't express—fear, tenderness, love.

He loved her. He ended the kiss and pulled back, poleaxed at the thought. But it was true. He didn't know when it had happened, but he had fallen head over heels in love with this amazing woman.

And his timing couldn't be any worse.

"We'd better go," she said.

"Yeah." Swearing at his predicament, he picked up the flashlight and closed the trunk. He helped her over the fallen tree trunk, then led the way down the overgrown trail, trying to stifle his unruly thoughts. Right now he had to concentrate on Hoffman. He'd worry about his future with Brynn later, once they'd rescued that runaway girl.

The flashlight bobbed over the ground. Dried leaves crackled under their feet as they hiked along. The road turned even wilder, more downed trees and branches sprawling across their path, more proof that a car hadn't driven this way in years.

A few minutes later, the farmhouse loomed into view, and his hopes tanked even more. The house was completely dark. The roof had partially caved in. Even the chimney had collapsed, littering stones across the ground. A huge tree grew through the sagging porch.

Still, he circled the perimeter, crawling through the bushes and weeds. Finally he shone the flashlight through a broken window, but there was no sign anyone had used it in decades, aside from squirrels and mice.

"He can't be here," Brynn murmured.

"I know." So where had he gone? "Give me a minute. I'll go inside and make sure."

He climbed the rickety porch steps, the boards protesting under his weight, and worked his way to the door. He checked the rooms on the bottom floor, then climbed the narrow staircase and flashed his light around. But every room had the same peeling wallpaper, moldy, water-stained ceilings and piles of trash.

A minute later, he rejoined Brynn outside. "You're sure he wouldn't have used the cabins near the office?" Puffs of frost accompanied his words.

"I'm sure. He needs somewhere private where no one will hear the noise."

His belly tensed, that unhinged feeling threatening to overwhelm him at the thought of the torture she'd endured. But he couldn't go there yet. He had to stay in control until he had Hoffman in his sights.

And then he'd make sure that bastard paid.

"Let's try the lookout tower." He knew he was grasping at straws. The detectives who'd investigated Erin Walker's death would have searched the area, taking note of anything odd. Still, Erin had gone there for a reason. And what other option did they have?

Aware that time was dwindling quickly, he took the lead, trying to envision the camp's layout in his mind. Hoffman couldn't have gone to the lake. That campsite was too far away, without an easy way in. They'd already discounted the office, cabins and farmhouse. So where had he taken that girl?

Dodging a decaying tree stump, he tried to reason this out. The night Erin Walker had died, Hoffman had attended a reception in D.C. He'd been present for the senator's speech, which had ended by ten o'clock. The camp was an hour and a quarter from the hotel, maybe more, so Hoffman couldn't have arrived before eleven. And since the autopsy put Erin's death around midnight, that gave Hoffman less than an hour to do his work.

So Erin couldn't have run very far. Hoffman must have a private place, not far from the lookout tower. But where?

An owl hooted in the night. The cold wind blew, making the pine boughs moan. Parker glanced back at Brynn, glad she was keeping up. They were quickly running out of time.

They reached a clearing a moment later, and the old fire lookout tower loomed into view. Parker came to a halt and studied the wooden structure; the full moon cast it in an eerie glow.

"I'll climb up," Brynn whispered from beside him.

"Not with your bad arm. You wait here, and I'll go."

He handed her the flashlight, then jogged across the clearing to the tower and started up. But as he scaled the steep, wooden steps—the same five flights Erin Walker had climbed that fateful night—his doubts about the case increased. Why had she climbed this tower? Had it been a result of the drugs? Meth users sometimes experienced delusions of superhuman power, causing them to risk their lives. Or had she been fleeing Hoffman in terror, so desperate to escape him that she'd decided to risk the tower—and then jumped or plunged to her death?

He reached the top of the stairs. His breathing labored, he strode across the platform and peered inside the room. *Empty.* And with every passing moment, their hopes of finding that girl unharmed dwindled even more.

He strode back onto the platform, then scowled at the inky woods. Moonlight dusted the treetops. Stars glittered across the sky, their beauty lost to his mounting fear. He couldn't fail that child. He couldn't fail Brynn. Because this was it. If he didn't prove Hoffman's guilt tonight, he wouldn't get another chance. Hoffman would destroy any evidence. Terry Lewis would turn Parker over to Hoffman, leaving Brynn unprotected. And she'd pay the ultimate price.

Knowing there *had* to be a clue he'd missed, he shoved his hand through his hair. Erin Walker had left her cabin. She'd run to this lookout tower, crossing the river somewhere—proven by her wet shoes. But why? He still couldn't see a child that age making a trek like that through the woods at night.

Unless she *hadn't* walked all the way. Maybe Hoffman had picked her up. Then he'd driven her to a closer point, somewhere not too far from the tower. With the surveillance cameras down, no one would have seen them leave the cabin. But where had he taken the child?

Frowning, he pictured the map with the river running east to west. But there'd been another creek on that map, a tiny thread running north to south where the rafts and canoes were stored.

His heart thudding, he turned to the north and stared into the dark. And suddenly he saw a flash of light. He blinked, certain he'd imagined it, then looked again. It was gone.

His pulse began to race. He looked away, letting his eyes drift over the woods, then jerked his gaze north again. There it was. A faint light flickering behind the swaying trees, a half a mile or more due north.

His hopes leaping, he rushed down the steps and rejoined Brynn. "Come on, I saw a light. About half a mile from here. We need to run."

He set out at a jog, crashing through the undergrowth, not worrying about making noise. They had to hurry. They'd already delayed too long. And backup was still minutes away.

He zigzagged through the trees, ducking under branches, then hurtled over logs and vines. Brynn kept pace, her breath rasping as they rushed along, despite her wounded arm.

Suddenly, the sound of rushing water increased. Parker slowed and shone his flashlight ahead. They'd reached the creek. He stopped on the bank, then studied the water rushing by. It was a dozen feet wide, probably a few feet deep.

"Up there," Brynn said, pointing upstream. "We can go across those rocks."

"I'll go first, then help you across." He jumped across the stones to the opposite shore. Brynn followed a moment later, gasping when he took hold of her injured arm. "You okay?" he asked.

"It's just my shoulder."

"We'll get it looked at later."

Her eyes met his in the moonlight, and he could guess what she was thinking, that they might not survive the night. "Don't worry. We're going to get him."

"I know. But we'd better hurry."

Returning his mind to Hoffman, he started jogging again. A few yards later they reached a trail. It wasn't much bigger than a deer path, narrow and bumpy with tree roots, but it was the first sign of civilization they'd seen.

His heart began to drum. The trail widened and turned. And then he glimpsed a light through the trees.

He came to stop, throwing his arm out to keep Brynn back. "Quiet," he warned her. He turned off the flashlight, then crept to the edge of a clearing. In the center was Hoffman's car. So there *had* been another road in. It just hadn't appeared on the map.

He ducked behind a tree, thinking hard. Brynn stood close behind him, her breath rasping in his ear. There were two log cabins and a toolshed, similar to the one at Hoffman's house. The lights were on in both.

He checked his watch. Within minutes Terry Lewis would be arriving at the farmhouse. But there'd been no way to leave a note, no way to tell her where they'd gone. For now they were on their own.

He tucked the flashlight into his pocket and pulled out his sidearm. "Stay behind me," he murmured. Then he led the way toward the nearest cabin, the faint glow flickering through the window guiding the way. He ducked below the window, waited for Brynn to join him, then rose and peeked inside. He scanned the bunk beds along the wall, the dresser and corner desk. The computer on top of the desk was on, its soft glow illuminating the room. But Hoffman was nowhere in sight.

"Wait here." His nerves stretched tight, he climbed the steps to the door. Then he nudged it open and stepped inside. No one was there. He went to the desk and searched the drawers, unearthing a pedophile's treasure trove—computer disks, photos of naked children, magazines. In the bottom desk drawer was a cache of necklaces, all bearing that hand-engraved heart design.

They'd found their proof—enough to put Hoffman away for good. But they had to find him first.

He forced in a calming breath, the need to exact vengeance riding him hard. Then he hurried through the door and rounded the building.

But Brynn was gone.

Chapter 15

Parker stood stock-still in the cabin's shadows, shutting down every thought but one. Hoffman had taken Brynn hostage.

He had to save the woman he loved.

He shifted deeper into the shadows, careful not to make any sound. Then he stopped behind a tree and listened intently, struggling to hear above the stark fear bludgeoning his skull. Tree branches creaked overhead. A night creature cried in the distance, the wild sound scraping his nerves. The frigid wind gusted, howling through a crack in the wooden shed, while bushes frothed in the pulsing night.

It was too quiet. Too tense. Locking his gaze on the second cabin, Parker battled the need billowing inside him to burst through that door in a frenzy and rescue Brynn. But he couldn't afford to make a mistake. He had to stay cool and think this through—or Brynn would pay with her life.

He melted farther into the darkness, every sense attuned to the slightest sounds. He skirted a rotting woodpile, crept to the small shed standing between the cabins and peered inside. Empty, just as he'd expected.

Only one place left.

He merged back into the forest, taking a circuitous path through the trees. Twigs crackled underfoot. The brisk wind blew again, raising goose bumps along his spine while ice congealed in his heart. Something had tipped Hoffman off. Did he have a scanner inside the cabin? Had his wife somehow seen them at the house and contacted him? Was he aware that even now police were converging on the camp, preparing to bring him down?

If so, he'd be desperate, even more dangerous, which didn't bode well for Brynn.

Dread making his heart thud, Parker neared the cabin and stopped. He took a deep pull of air, struggling to think through the overload of adrenaline blurring his mind, and snuck a peek at his watch. The police should have reached the farmhouse by now. Local law enforcement would take the lead, coordinating the SWAT and HRT teams as they searched the camp. Given Hoffman's rank, Lieutenant Lewis would be on scene, along with various department bigwigs—the deputy commissioner, a PR representative, the head of internal affairs.

But none of that was going to help Parker. No one knew about these old cabins. No one knew where he'd gone.

But he couldn't do this alone. He needed a hostage negotiator to make contact with Hoffman. He needed an expert to convince him to surrender without harming Brynn or that runaway kid. At the very least he needed their stun grenades to get inside that cabin. The blinding light and noise would disorient Hoffman, incapacitating him long enough to free the captives and bring him in.

A whimper cut through the night. Parker's heart stuttered hard, then took off in a rush. *Brynn.* He clenched his hands, shaking with the need to save her, to forget every bit of training he'd ever had and barge through that cabin door.

But he had to resist. Too much could go lethally wrong. And it could be a ploy, a trick to lure him into a trap. He had to keep his head, sit tight and hope to God those teams figured out where he'd gone—and arrived in time.

Then another wild cry split the night.

To hell with it. Trap or not, he couldn't stand by and let Hoffman torture Brynn. By the time the hostage rescue team discovered their whereabouts, she could be dead.

He darted across the clearing to the cabin, then crouched beneath the bushes beside the door. The windows were boarded up. A sliver of light peeked through the cracks, but he couldn't see inside.

He drew in a breath, trying to think this through. No matter how desperately he wanted to save her, he couldn't rush in blind. He had to locate everyone's position in the cabin first.

Figuring Hoffman would monitor the door and windows, Parker worked his way around the perimeter of the cabin, searching for another way in. Then a piece of wooden lattice covering the crawl space caught his eye. He ripped it off and set it aside, then shimmied through the opening. Turning on his flashlight, he belly-crawled through the dirt and weeds, hoping he'd get lucky and the cabin would have a trapdoor to drain the pipes. He finally spotted it several feet away, draped with spiderwebs.

Positioning himself beneath it, he waited a beat, but no sounds came through the floor. Why was it so quiet? What was Hoffman doing in there?

Not wanting to imagine the answer, he tested the door, but it didn't budge. Putting more force behind it, he pushed again. *Locked.* Hoffman had secured it from the other side.

Swearing, he crawled back out. Aware that time was fading quickly, he ran through his options again. He could discharge his weapon to alert the cops. That would bring them to the area fast. But it could also cause Hoffman to panic and kill his captives—a disaster he had to avoid. Parker could surrender to Hoffman in order to get inside, then hope to fight it out. But he'd save that as a last resort.

Deciding to try the windows, he crept to the back of the cabin again, tugging on the plywood for signs of give. He finally came across a loose board and pried it up, far enough to peek inside.

It led to the back bedroom. He made out a dresser and chair and in the corner a narrow bed—with a small figure huddled on top. His heart missed a beat. *The runaway girl.* That put Hoffman and Brynn in the living room.

His mind racing, he lowered the board. Hoffman needed this child for leverage. If Parker snuck inside and released her, he took away Hoffman's bargaining chip.

He would also remove Hoffman's only reason to use

restraint. Once he realized he couldn't escape, Hoffman could decide to retaliate—on Brynn.

But Parker couldn't leave that child inside. The risks were far too high. He had to free her while he had the chance—and then try to neutralize Hoffman before he could murder Brynn.

His heart beating even faster, he pulled on the plywood again. It creaked, and Parker cringed, hoping Hoffman hadn't heard the noise. But he was committed now.

Working quickly, he yanked the final nail loose and tossed the board aside. Then he braced his hands on the sill and heaved himself over the ledge. The girl whimpered and shrank back against the wall.

"Shh. I'm a cop. I'm here to help you." He strode across the room, but the sight of her small hands tied to the bed frame nearly razed his self-control. Not wanting to spook her, he knelt on the floor beside the bed. "I'm going to untie your hands, okay? And then I'm going to lower you out the window. I want you to run into the woods—not too far—and hide until the police get here. Do you understand?"

Her eyes were huge, but she managed to nod, and his admiration rose. Even badly traumatized, she was a fighter.

Like Brynn.

He shut down that thought fast, needing to focus on freeing this child. "Okay, I'm going to untie your hands now. Don't be afraid." She flinched as he reached for the rope, but didn't make another sound. He quickly worked the knots loose, mentally cursing when he saw her wrists. The bastard had tied her so tightly that her skin was raw.

Suddenly footsteps sounded in the other room. Tensing, Parker reached for his gun, his gaze locked on the bedroom door. But then the footsteps retreated, and he eased out his breath.

With no time to waste now, he undid the final knot and rose. He started to help her stand but stopped when she jerked away. Instead, he stripped off his leather jacket and held it out. "Here, put this on. It's cold out there.

"I'm going to lower you out the window," he continued as she shrugged his jacket on.

"Okay," she whispered, still trembling.

He crossed the room to the window and held out his hands. "Ready?"

She grabbed his hands, and more respect for her swelled inside. He could only imagine how much it cost her to trust a man right now. He lifted her over the sill, releasing her when she reached the ground. She stumbled, but regained her balance and darted into the woods.

One down.

Drawing his weapon, he turned around. But the wind gusted again, blowing through the open window and knocking papers off the dresser beside the door. Parker lunged forward to grab them, but something plastic clattered to the floor.

Oh, hell. He leaped toward the wall, intending to hide behind the door. But the door crashed open and the overhead light flicked on. Hoffman stood in the doorway, holding Brynn in front of him like a shield, his gun wedged under her jaw.

Parker's world spun away at the sight of the gun pressed to her fragile throat. He took in her terror-glazed eyes, the dark bruise puffing her cheek. She was trembling so violently he could detect it from across the room.

A frantic feeling took hold inside him. He met his boss's glittering eyes—the eyes of a man teetering on the edge of control—and his hopes plummeted even more.

His worst fear had just come true.

Hoffman knew that the kid was gone. He knew that he'd been exposed. He had no chance to escape arrest, no reason to stay alive.

In seconds they'd all be dead.

"Put down your gun," Hoffman ordered.

"Don't do it," Brynn cried. "Don't—" She gasped, her body stiffening as the gun dug into her neck.

"Right now," Hoffman said.

Parker's palms turned slick. He lowered the gun slightly, struggling to think. Brynn knew how to fight. She'd nearly bested him in the alley the night they'd met. And Hoffman was older, fatter, slower. If Parker could give her an opening, she could break free.

But he had to be careful. Hoffman barely had a grip on his nerves. If Parker blundered, he'd snap.

"All right," Parker said. "I'll put it down. But you owe me some answers first."

"Answers?" Hoffman scoffed. "About what?"

"Tommy. How you killed him."

Hoffman blinked. "I didn't kill him."

"The hell you didn't. You executed that guy in the warehouse. You went after Brynn, then killed Tommy when he got in your way. You were there with that gang, the City of the Dead."

Incredulity crossed Hoffman's face. "You're nuts. I wasn't there. I had nothing to do with that."

Parker frowned, doubts worming through his anger, but he shook them off. The evidence pointed to his boss. "And when those photos showed up in Homicide, you destroyed them to cover your tracks."

"You're crazy. I've never killed anyone in my life."

Until now.

The unspoken words hung between them. Parker's gaze connected with Brynn's, the desperation in her eyes wrenching his heart. And it took every ounce of willpower he possessed not to rush over and grab her away. But he'd never make it. She'd be dead before he went two feet.

"You killed Erin Walker," he pointed out.

"Erin?" Hoffman's indignation rose. "I did not. I wasn't anywhere near her when she died."

"You brought her here that night. You gave her drugs."

"She wanted to come. But then she went berserk. It had nothing to do with me."

"You abused her."

"That's a lie. I never hurt her. We were friends. She liked what I did."

Parker realized that he believed that. In his sick, twisted mind he hadn't harmed that child.

But what about Tommy? Was Hoffman telling the truth about that? He definitely molested children. There was enough evidence in these cabins to convict him, even if that girl didn't testify. But had he killed Tommy? Or was Delgado responsible for that?

Parker shook away the thought. He'd sort that out later. Right now he had to save Brynn.

But Hoffman tightened his grip on her throat, causing her to wheeze for breath.

And Parker knew with a sinking feeling that he'd run out of time.

"Put down your gun," Hoffman said. "Right now, or she's dead."

Not seeing an option, Parker bent over and set his gun on the wooden floor.

"Kick it over here."

Parker sent it skidding across the floor. It came to a stop several feet from Brynn. She rolled her eyes sideways, and he knew she was calculating the distance, trying to figure out a way to get that gun. But she needed him to create a diversion first.

"That's better." A triumphant smile slashed Hoffman's face. "You always did obey orders."

Like a fool. "I trusted you. I thought you were an honest man. But you used me for your own sick ends."

"I only wanted you to bring her in. That's all. I tried to warn you about her. I said she'd manipulate you. But you didn't listen…and now I don't have a choice."

Brynn went still. Her gaze snapped to his, the shock over his betrayal edging out her fear. Parker's stomach took a sudden dive. "It's not what you think," he told her.

"You lied to me." The pain in her voice ripped through his heart.

He couldn't deny it. Any attempt to justify his behavior would only seem like a lame excuse. But he *had* intended to tell her; he'd just wanted to do it at a better time, when he could explain how his opinion of her had changed, how he admired her, cared for her.

How he loved her.

But he'd waited too long. And now that she'd learned the truth from Hoffman, she'd never believe him again.

Their eyes remained locked. And suddenly he knew what he had to do. He had to prove that he hadn't betrayed her. He had to give her a chance to survive.

He lunged toward his boss. Hoffman swiveled his gun his way.

And fired.

Brynn screamed. She stared at Parker aghast as he staggered another step forward, then stopped and slumped to the floor. He'd just forfeited his life to save her. He was giving her a chance to get free. But she refused to leave him at this madman's mercy, no matter how much his betrayal stung.

Jerking herself into action, she shoved away from Hoffman and whipped around. Then she slammed her foot behind his knee, causing him to fall down.

But he wouldn't stay down for long.

She dove for Parker's gun, managing to wrap her hands around it just as another shot rang out, the earsplitting bang reverberating through her skull. She rolled over and swung around, feeling as if time had slowed to a standstill, and squeezed off a shot. Hoffman dove behind a chair.

Scrambling to her feet, she glanced at Parker. He lay facedown on the floor, blood pooling around him, groaning with pain. Desperation drummed inside her. She had to help him. She had to stanch the bleeding and rush him to the hospital before he died.

But she had to stop Hoffman first. She had to get him away from this bedroom before he finished Parker off.

Banking that Hoffman would try to stop her, she

bolted through the doorway into the next room, skidding on the wooden floor. His footsteps pounded behind her. His gun barked out, and she flinched, but the shot went wild.

She whirled around and fired back. Her aim was off, but it made him dive into the kitchen, giving her time to scramble behind the couch. *Dumb,* she realized, gasping for breath. A bullet would go straight through the sofa. She had to get to the door.

"Stop," her stepfather called out. "I'm not trying to hurt you."

Hysteria burbled inside her. He'd kidnapped her at gunpoint. He'd knocked her out, slamming his fist into her face when she'd tried to escape. He'd just shot Parker and was trying to murder her. "You expect me to believe that?"

"I never wanted to hurt you," he said. "I loved you."

Love? She shuddered, totally repulsed. "Torture isn't love."

"You liked my games. You know you did. You begged me to play with you."

Her face turned hot. Her vision hazed. Fury scorched through her veins, nearly incinerating what remained of her self-restraint. But this wasn't the time to lose control, not when Parker needed her help. Struggling to harness her temper, she gauged the distance to the door, but she knew she'd never get that far.

"I did everything for you," he continued. "You were my little angel, the one I loved. But then you ruined everything." Rage hardened his voice. "You told lies. You ran away. I loved you, and you lied about me."

Revolted, she thinned her lips. This man had raped her. He'd robbed her of her innocence in the most despicable of ways. But she couldn't let him distract her. Parker was dying in the other room. She had to lure Hoffman away from Parker and summon aid.

"I didn't want to hurt you," Hoffman said. "But you ruined everything. You didn't give me a choice. I had to get Parker to bring you in."

His voice was getting nearer. He was crawling across the room. Panic morphed into a frenzy inside her. She had to get out now!

Summoning her courage, she lifted her head. She spotted him creeping toward the sofa and fired. He wheeled back, clutching his arm, and howled. Her palms so slick she could hardly grip the gun, she squeezed off another round.

She missed.

Knowing he'd recover at any second, she leaped toward the cabin's door. She flung it open and lunged outside but missed the step and fell. Landing on her injured shoulder she let out a strangled cry. Then she stumbled upright in a surge of adrenaline and whirled around.

Hoffman slumped against the door frame. Trembling wildly, she raised her weapon and squeezed the trigger—but there was an empty click. She'd run out of ammunition.

And she didn't have any more rounds.

Hoffman smiled, a maniacal look filling his eyes. He lifted his gun and took aim. She turned and fled just as the shot went rocketing past. She tripped over a tree root and sprawled facedown again.

Oh, God. He was going to catch her. He lurched down the porch steps. Frantic, she jumped up and raced into the woods, running for her life—just like Erin Walker had.

And just like Erin, Brynn needed to reach the lookout tower. The cops would be waiting there. If she could just hold on long enough to find them, she could alert them to the danger and make sure Parker survived.

Trees rose up in her path, and she swerved around them. Low-hanging branches tore at her face and hair. She plunged through stands of brush, stumbling over logs and rocks, trying desperately to escape. But which way was the lookout tower? Without any light to guide her, she was running blind.

Then suddenly something darted into her path. Unable to turn in time, she collided with it headlong. *A child.* Thrown off balance, Brynn fell into a pile of brush, her head smacking against a rock. Pain scorched through her scalp, and she cried out.

The child flailed and kicked beneath her, finally breaking free. They both scrambled to their feet, and Brynn recognized the missing girl.

A crashing noise rose behind them. Hoffman was only steps away.

"I'm a friend. I'll help you. Follow me!" Brynn urged and took off running again. The girl sprinted behind her, keeping up despite her smaller size. Seconds later, Brynn reached the creek and plowed across, the frigid water icing her feet. She slipped on a rock and nearly fell, then clawed her way up the opposite bank, pure panic driving her on.

"Help!" the girl called out.

Brynn stopped and whirled around, her breath sawing loudly in the air. Moonlight seeped through the trees, enabling her to see. The child was on her hands and knees in the rushing stream, struggling to rise. Hoffman burst through the trees and stopped.

He raised his gun, aiming at the fallen girl, and Brynn gaped at him in shock. He wasn't human. Even a gunshot wound hadn't brought him down. But she'd die before she let him harm that child.

Her fury exploding, she picked up a rock and hurled it with all her might, ignoring the sharp pain searing her arm. The rock glanced off his shoulder, not hard enough to stop him, but enough to make him jerk back. The bullet thudded into a tree.

The girl made it to her feet. She stumbled out of the creek and ran toward Brynn just as Hoffman took aim again. Brynn shoved the girl behind her, but she knew that she'd reached the end. She couldn't escape death this time.

His weapon jammed.

A stunned look crossed his face. He looked down in disbelief, then let loose with a torrent of obscenities as he fumbled to clear the jam. The magazine dropped out, spilling rounds on the forest floor. Brynn spun on her heels, nearly weeping with relief, and ran.

Careful to keep the child with her, she angled through the woods toward the lookout tower, desperate to reach the police. She shoved through a patch of brambles, nearly collided with a boulder and tripped over logs and vines.

Her lungs burned. She could hardly wheeze in a fiery breath. Then she staggered into the clearing by the lookout tower, the absolute mayhem catching her off guard. Red-and-blue lights flashed in the darkness. Emergency vehicles and squad cars surrounded the tower. Cops swarmed the area in bulletproof vests and SWAT gear, shouting orders. Their radios squawked and blared.

"Help!" she cried, stumbling to a halt. She pulled

the girl close to protect her and whipped around. "He's coming! He's got a gun!" Several officers rushed to their side.

Then Hoffman burst through the trees.

"Watch out!" she screamed, and the officers drew their guns.

But Hoffman was no longer armed. He raised his hands, causing the cops to hold their fire. He swayed for a moment, the colored lights illuminating his face, then sank to the ground. Dozens of officers raced over, shouting for medical help.

Brynn's knees wobbled, threatening to collapse. "Are you all right, ma'am?" an officer asked her.

"I'm fine, but—"

"This woman's bleeding!" the man shouted over the noise. "We need an EMT here!"

"No, I'm fine. But Parker…" The memory of his betrayal sliced through her, but she shoved it aside. "He's at the cabin. That way." She motioned toward the woods. "You have to hurry. He's been shot!"

"We'll find him."

More radios crackled. Sirens rose in the night. Several officers took off running through the woods while others piled into cars. As Brynn watched in a daze, medical personnel loaded Hoffman onto a gurney, and started wheeling him her way.

But a woman in a uniform stepped into their path, causing them to stop. She was tall, middle-aged, so thin she was almost gaunt. Lieutenant Lewis, Brynn guessed, judging by the authority in her stance. The woman Parker had called for help.

"Colonel Hoffman," she said, her voice sharp. "You're under arrest."

Hoffman raised his head from the gurney. His eyes met the lieutenant's and filled with fear. He let out an anguished moan.

So he realized he wasn't going to escape. It was about time he suffered for his crimes.

"Where are you taking him?" Lieutenant Lewis asked an EMT.

"Meritus Hospital in Washington County. They'll probably fly him to Shock Trauma in Baltimore from there."

"Fine." She turned to another cop. "Read him his rights on the way."

She turned her attention to Brynn, who was still hugging the terrified girl. "Are you all right?"

Brynn managed a nod, but the pain pulsing through her shoulder halted her breath. "Parker—"

"Don't worry. We'll get him." Lieutenant Lewis signaled to the EMT. "Take these two to the hospital." Pulling out her radio, she strode away.

Several officers surrounded the gurney, along with the ambulance personnel. Hoffman rolled his head as they pushed him past, and, without warning, his eyes met hers. And for a moment, time ground to a halt. She stared into the eyes of the man who'd abused her, a hollowed-out feeling inside. This man had terrorized her for decades. He'd stolen her innocence, done despicable, evil things to her that no child should have to endure. He'd forced her into a life on the run, a precarious existence of desperation, violence and fear—all because of his perverted needs.

Defeated, he looked away. The men closed around him, then loaded him into the waiting ambulance.

Brynn eased out her breath as they put on the siren and drove away.

His reign of terror had come to an end.

And she was finally free.

Chapter 16

Exhausted, Brynn slumped in a padded armchair inside Parker's room at the Shock Trauma Center in Baltimore the following afternoon. She could hardly keep her eyes open after the grueling night she'd had. After her rescue, she'd spent hours giving statements to both the Washington County and Baltimore police, relating her story about Hoffman and his history of abuse. She'd also relayed Parker's suspicions about Delgado, who seemed to have disappeared. Thankfully, the police had believed her. Lieutenant Lewis had agreed to bring Delgado in for questioning, assuming they could find him first.

Brynn stifled a yawn, the movement causing her injured shoulder to throb inside its sling. She'd escaped their ordeal without major injuries. Aside from gashing her scalp, she'd partially torn the tendons and inflamed the bursa around her rotator cuff—thus the sling. After a few weeks of painkillers, anti-inflammatory medication and rest, her shoulder would heal just fine.

Too bad she couldn't say the same about her heart.

Sighing, she gazed at Parker as he slept in the hospital bed. His thick black hair was mussed, his unshaven jaw coated with stubble, his eyelashes dark against his too-pale skin. He had an IV taped to one arm, his shoulder heavily bandaged where he'd been shot. His breath rasped in the quiet air.

Both Parker and Hoffman had been flown to Baltimore during the night. They'd both undergone surgery, and both were expected to survive. Hoffman was down the hall, under arrest in a guarded room, while Parker recovered in his.

She picked up his heavy hand, taking in the warmth of his skin, the rough calluses on his palms, the sinews and tendons standing out on his muscled arms. Her gaze traveled from the stark white bandages on his shoulder to the alluring hollow at the base of his throat, and her heart made a sudden lurch. How he could manage to look sexy in a hospital gown, she didn't know. But instead of appearing weak and vulnerable, he looked even more virile, like everything she'd ever wanted in a man.

If only he hadn't lied.

Her emotions suddenly chaotic, she placed his hand on the starched white sheet. Then she leaned back in her seat and gazed at his face, lingering on his slashing black brows, his sensual mouth, his rough-hewn features now slack with sleep. He'd lied, all right—a detail she'd avoided thinking about until now. But she couldn't put it off anymore.

A heavyset nurse in blue-flowered scrubs entered the

room just then, her sneakers squeaking on the linoleum floor. Brynn exhaled at the timely reprieve.

"Good afternoon," the nurse said with a pleasant smile. "How's our patient?"

"Still asleep."

Making a noncommittal sound, she set her laptop on a high, roller-wheeled table and plugged it in. Then she frowned at Parker's chart.

Brynn waited for several heartbeats, her anxiety mounting when the nurse didn't say anything. She studied the crease puckering the nurse's brow, the way she worried her plump bottom lip with her upper teeth. Her chubby fingers tapped on the keyboard, the soft clicks adding to Brynn's strained nerves.

"Is everything all right?" she finally asked, unable to bear the suspense.

The nurse tore her gaze from the computer, and her eyes crinkled into a smile. "He's fine. You don't need to worry about him. He's young and strong. He's going to recover in no time."

Brynn inched out her pent-up breath. "How long will he be in the hospital?"

"You'll have to ask the doctor, but probably a week. He'll have to wear a sling for a couple of months after that. And he'll need physical therapy down the road. But barring complications, he'll be just fine."

Brynn leaned back in her chair, relieved. No matter how complicated their relationship, she couldn't stand the thought of him suffering—or worse.

The nurse checked his vital signs and changed the bag on his IV. Then she picked up her laptop and turned to go. "There's coffee at the nurses' station if you'd like some," she offered with another smile.

Brynn thanked her, and she left the room, her shoes squeaking as she retreated down the hall. Alone now, Brynn turned her gaze to the monitors beside the bed. Numbers flashed across one screen. Lines zigzagged across another, recording Parker's heartbeat, rhythmic and steady and strong. And she realized the time had come. She couldn't avoid the topic she'd danced around for hours—Parker's deception—no matter how much it hurt. She had to confront the truth.

Parker had been working for Hoffman. Hoffman had asked him to bring her in. She didn't want to believe it. Even now, the betrayal flayed her, slashing through the illusions she'd built about this man.

But the reality was that he'd deceived her. Badly. Maybe he hadn't lied outright, but neither had he revealed the truth. He'd told her about his father's corruption. He'd confessed his feelings of failure and the pain he'd suffered at Tommy's death. And he'd made love to her, touching her in ways no one else ever had.

But he'd concealed the one thing that really mattered, his relationship to her stepfather, even after she'd told him about the abuse.

No, he'd done worse than that. He'd intentionally misled her. He'd known she was Hoffman's stepdaughter from the start. She'd ignored the signs, but now that she thought back, she didn't have any doubt. He'd kept their connection secret, despite multiple opportunities to reveal the truth.

Closing her eyes, she massaged the ache between her brows. In some ways, she didn't blame him. Hoffman put on a convincing act. He'd fooled Brynn's mother. He'd fooled her elementary school teachers and the various social workers who'd filed through her life. He'd even fooled the people he worked with, impressing Senator Riggs so much that the senator was backing his political career. And Parker respected authority. He believed in following the rules. Of course he'd trust his boss.

She opened her eyes and gazed at Parker, a tumult of emotions crowding her throat. She couldn't forget that he'd saved her life. He'd battled the gang members in that drive-by shooting. He'd saved her from the police. And now he'd taken a bullet for her, nearly dying on her behalf.

Even more disturbed now, she rose and went into the hall. A grim-faced doctor hurried past. People crowded around the nurses' station down the hall. A voice came over the PA system, calling for a doctor *stat*.

Hoping a walk would clear her mind, she headed in the opposite direction to the bank of elevators, then waited for one to arrive. A woman and her young daughter joined her, reminding her of the traumatized girl.

Brynn had last seen the girl at the Washington County hospital. Her horrified family had met her there, sticking close beside her even when the doctors wheeled her away for tests. She had a long road of recovery ahead, years of nightmares and distrust to overcome— a journey Brynn knew well. But she seemed strong. With her family's support, she might make it through.

A soft *ding* announced the elevator's arrival. Brynn stepped inside, then leaned against the handrail as it traveled to the bottom floor. She watched the floor numbers decrease, her mind returning to Parker McCall. She wanted to trust him. He'd saved her life. He'd risked everything to help her, putting himself on the line. Except for that one glaring omission, he'd acted honorably at every step. Should she forgive him? *Could* she forgive a lie of that magnitude?

Not able to come up with an answer, she exited the elevator on the first floor. Following the signs to the Courtyard Café, she walked down a hallway, past a pizza place and sandwich shop to a bright, airy room bustling with people and noise. Various scents filled the air—coffee, French fries, pizza—and her stomach growled. She couldn't remember her last meal.

Deciding she needed an infusion of caffeine more urgently than she needed food, she ordered a large coffee from the nearest stall. Working one-handed, she loaded it with sweetener and cream, then downed several much-needed gulps. Already feeling better, she turned and scanned the room, searching for a quiet corner where she could think.

Her gaze landed on a woman sitting by the window, her face angled toward the street outside, and everything inside her froze. *Her mother.* The woman who'd refused to believe her. The woman who'd failed to protect her. The woman who'd turned her back on her, ignoring her desperate cries for help, leaving her at the mercy of a brutal man.

She'd come to visit her husband at the hospital, no doubt.

Brynn couldn't move. She stood locked in place, anger erupting inside her, decades of bottled resentment threatening to explode. But the change in her mother's appearance penetrated her fury, giving her pause. She'd put on weight since Brynn had seen her last. Her face was sallow and lined. Her hair was lanky and gray. She wore sloppy knit pants and a rumpled sweatshirt, her once-meticulous appearance now so slovenly that Brynn wondered if she'd been ill.

Did it matter? Did she care about her mother after all she'd put her through? Why should she? Her mother had enabled Hoffman's abuse.

But surely her mother realized the truth about him now. Even she couldn't deny the proof they'd recovered from that cabin—the photos, the necklaces, the videos in which he'd starred. Maybe she was sorry. Maybe she'd want to repair the past. Maybe she'd want to apologize for having been so blind.

Her mother lumbered to her feet. She threw her trash in a nearby receptacle, then headed down the corridor toward the exit sign.

Making a quick decision, Brynn took several more swallows of coffee, then dumped her cup in the trash. Keeping one eye on her mother, she dodged the people crowding the food court and hurried to catch up.

She reached her a minute later. "Mom, wait!" she called.

Her mother came to a stop. She turned, causing people to swerve around them, her gaze connecting with Brynn's. Her face paled. Her eyes turned tortured, filled with something that looked a lot like remorse. "Brynn…"

Brynn didn't trust herself to answer. Her belly churning, she stood in the busy corridor, facing the woman who'd had the power to save her—and failed.

"It…it's true, then?" her mother asked.

"Yes, it's true."

Her mouth twisted. Pain racked her bloated face, her expression turning even more stricken now. "I thought I knew him. That he was a good, generous man. I couldn't imagine him doing those despicable things to you. I didn't think he would ever hurt a child."

"I tried to tell you. You didn't believe me."

"I thought… He was so good with kids. So generous. I didn't know."

"You should have. You should have believed me instead of him."

"But you liked him at first. It wasn't until later, after we were married…"

"When he started abusing me."

Her mother blanched. And Brynn took a long, hard look at the woman who'd raised her, knowing her world was crumpling apart. She'd based her life on a lie.

Brynn turned away. Then she headed down the corridor, past the pizza store, past a gift shop, hardly caring where she went. Her mother now knew the truth. She had to face the reality of her actions and suffer the guilt. She'd enabled an evil man to prey on defenseless kids.

Her own feelings in turmoil, Brynn wove her way through the crowd. Should she forgive her mother? Did she even want to see her again? Everything inside her rebelled against the thought. The pain was too deep, the betrayal too horrific, the shock of seeing her again too fresh. Maybe someday…or maybe not. Right now she didn't know.

And what about Parker? Should she forgive his deceit? She had every right to be mad at him. He'd lied to her about her stepfather—a betrayal that truly hurt.

But people made mistakes. He'd had good cause to suspect her at first. And she knew deep down she could trust him. He'd proven it time and again.

Yet did she *want* to forgive him? She resumed walking, that thought disquieting her even more. Because frankly, she felt safer holding on to her anger, that righteous indignation that had sustained her for all these years. It felt familiar, secure. If she let it go, if she stopped thinking of herself as a victim and forgave Parker, she lost the barrier protecting her heart.

And that made her vulnerable, the feeling she dreaded most. Because once she dropped that emotional shield, Parker would see the woman inside—with all her flaws. And he might not like who he found.

She reached the elevators and pushed the button, her thoughts swirling from Parker and her mother to the accusation Haley had hurled at her. But as much as it wounded her pride to admit it, her friend was right. She was hiding behind her work. Her photos weren't only about the runaways; they were about her. They'd always been about her—her fear, her vulnerability, her shame. Not that what she did wasn't important; she thoroughly believed in her cause. But she'd hidden behind those photos, taking refuge in her anonymity, afraid to need, afraid to trust, afraid to subject herself to betrayal again.

The elevator arrived. She stepped inside, then watched the numbers flash as it climbed to Parker's floor. So now she had to decide—to cling to the anger or stop blaming Parker and make herself vulnerable by taking a risk on love.

The elevator bounced to a stop. The doors slid open, and she headed to Parker's hall. She rounded the corner, the sudden commotion bringing her to a standstill. Police officers swarmed the corridor. Doctors ran past, barking orders and talking on phones. Nurses huddled in groups in doorways and near their stations, their eyes startled, their hands covering their mouths. The PA blared overhead.

"Watch out!" a doctor said, knocking into her as he hurried past.

Clutching her sling, Brynn flattened herself to the wall, still trying to process the hectic scene. What on earth was going on? *Has something happened to Parker?* Fear jolting through her, she started toward his room to find out.

"Get out of the way," someone shouted behind her. "Let the police by."

She ducked into a doorway to let them pass. Then, eyeing an opening, she darted across the hall to a group of nurses clustered behind their desk.

"What happened?" she asked.

One of the nurses turned her way. "You can't be here. You need to leave."

"But what happened?"

"A man died. One of the cops they just brought in."

Brynn's belly flipped. A dizzy feeling roared through her head. *Not Parker. Please, not Parker.* Her knees threatening to buckle, she struggled to breathe. "Which one?"

"The older one, the guy they had under arrest. Now you need to go."

Brynn staggered to the nearest wall, the relief sweeping through her nearly causing her to collapse. Trembling badly, she closed her eyes, knowing she should probably feel pity or compassion—or even guilt since she'd inflicted the wound that had caused her stepfather's death. But she couldn't summon any regret. Hoffman's death was a blessing. The world was rid of a dangerous predator. He'd never harm an innocent child again.

She opened her eyes, but the urgency swirling around

her still didn't make any sense. Nurses were huddling behind their stations. Police were racing down the hallway, going in and out of rooms. Why this sudden commotion? Why the urgency? As unfortunate as it was, people died in hospitals all the time.

Just then an officer ran up, his expression grim. "You need to leave, ma'am. We're clearing the hall."

"Why?"

"This is a crime scene. Several men have been murdered. And the killer's still on the loose."

Several men? And they'd been murdered? Shock rendered her speechless. Hoffman hadn't died from his injuries. Someone had come here and killed him? But who...

Delgado. The man who'd killed Parker's brother. The man who'd executed that prisoner in the warehouse. The man who'd sent the gang leader after her. He'd finished off Hoffman—and apparently, his guards. Now he was going to kill Parker, too.

And Brynn had left him alone.

"Find Lieutenant Lewis," she told the officer. "She's in charge of this case. She knows all the details. Tell her it's urgent, that Delgado is here."

Praying that he'd listen, she took off for Parker's room at a run.

Chapter 17

Parker drifted into consciousness, loud voices and the thunder of footsteps dragging him from sleep. He opened his eyes a slit, disoriented by the sudden brightness, and battled the urge to succumb to oblivion again. He scanned the white sheet covering his legs, the IV attached to his arm, the monitors beside the bed. To one side was a skinny table bearing a cup filled with chips of ice and a remote control unit attached by a cord to the bed. He was in a hospital—but where?

He frowned, trying to clear the fog muddling his brain and remember exactly what had put him here. Images sprang to his mind—Brynn being held at gunpoint. His desperation as he tried to save her. The shock of betrayal in her eyes. Crawling under the cabin. Lowering the kidnapped girl from the window. The terrible panic that overtook him when he'd realized Brynn was gone.

Where was she? Had she survived? He sat bolt upright, his heart in a frantic race. He had to get out of here and find her fast.

Then another memory slashed through the turmoil—Brynn standing beside him, her face ashen, as they'd wheeled him into the hospital. He slumped back against his pillow in relief. *She's alive.* He was sure of that.

The remainder of the night clicked into place—Lieutenant Lewis barking out orders. Riding in the helicopter to Shock Trauma. The *whomp* of the rotor blades. Learning that the police had captured Hoffman, that both Brynn and the child were safe.

But would Brynn forgive his deception? He'd seen the hurt in her eyes when Hoffman had revealed that Parker worked for him. Dread taking up a drumbeat inside him, he struggled to sit up again. He couldn't let it end like this. He had to find her and beg her forgiveness. He had to explain about Hoffman and make her give him another chance.

Shouts in the corridor caught his attention. More footsteps raced past his room. He frowned at the door, unable to ignore the ruckus in the hall. Something was going on. Some kind of emergency, judging by the noise.

He tossed the blanket aside, but a sudden wave of dizziness plowed through him, and he closed his eyes. *Damn.* His entire body trembled as if he'd just run a marathon. He didn't even have the strength to stand.

Another shout came from the hall. He wrenched himself into motion, knowing he had to investigate—no matter how weak he felt. He gauged the distance to the door, then eyed the IV connected to a pole. He'd have to haul it along.

He pushed aside the railing. The nurse call button's cord got in the way, and he looped it over the side. Then he swung his legs over the edge of the bed and waited for another bout of light-headedness to subside. Air hit his naked back, and chills prickled his skin. *Great*. Not only was he unarmed, but he was bare-assed, wearing one of those ridiculous hospital gowns.

Suddenly the door flew open and crashed against the wall, making him start. *Brynn*. He took in her flushed face and panicked eyes, her red hair wild around her face. A dark bruise stood out on her cheek.

But his surge of relief instantly faltered. Brynn wasn't prone to panic. Something was terribly wrong. His stomach took a precipitous dive. "What is it?"

"Delgado. He's here. We need to leave."

"What?"

She raced to his side, her bum arm wrapped in a sling. "He just murdered Hoffman. And the guards. I don't know how. It just happened, down the hall. Now he's on the loose. He's going to come after you next. We need to go somewhere safe."

Parker gave his head a swift shake, trying to make sense of her disjointed words. But Hoffman's claim of innocence winged into his mind. *So he was telling the truth. He really didn't kill Tommy.* But Delgado had—and now he was after them.

His thoughts raced as he struggled to rise. "Lieutenant Lewis. We need to tell her what's going on."

"She already knows. I told her about him last night. She's got people looking for him."

"But then…" Parker paused, suddenly confused. Delgado wasn't dumb. He would be monitoring police communications, and he'd know they were after him.

"Why would he come here? Why would he risk getting caught?" He should be miles away, trying to stay incognito, not waltzing into the hospital where his co-workers could recognize him. "And why would he kill Hoffman? It doesn't make any sense."

Brynn shook her head, her frantic eyes pleading with his. "I don't know. Does it matter? *Hurry.* We need to hide somewhere fast."

The panic in her voice convinced him. He grabbed the IV pole and pushed himself upright, the floor tiles cold against his bare feet. But his head began to swim. His vision hazed, and he swayed, his knees threatening to collapse. Brynn lunged over and caught him, her soft, slight body propping him up. He leaned against her, black spots dancing before his eyes. "Damn."

"Sit down," she said.

"But—"

"I can't hold you. Not with one arm. Just sit down for a second, and we'll try again."

He perched on the edge of his bed, disgusted at how wobbly he felt. He must have lost a lot of blood. "Sorry. Just give me a minute."

But more shouts rose in the hall. The door abruptly slammed open, and his heart sprinted into overdrive. He reached for his gun out of habit—but it wasn't there. A spasm of fear put on a lock on his lungs.

But Lieutenant Lewis appeared in the doorway. She strode into the room, accompanied by another cop, and Parker released his breath in a rush. *Thank God it's her.* If that had been Delgado, they'd both be dead.

She took a quick look around, then turned to the other cop, a detective Parker didn't recognize. "Everything's fine in here. I'll stay inside. You stand guard in the hall." He left with a nod, and she closed the door. Then she strode to the bed and stopped.

He'd never seen her look worse. Her short, gray hair was disheveled. Her usually crisp uniform was wrinkled, as if she'd been sleeping in it for days. She carried a leather satchel, her white-knuckled grip revealing her nerves. The harsh overhead light emphasized the lines in her narrow face, aging her several years.

He didn't blame her for feeling stressed, considering the public relations nightmare she faced. Parker had been shot by a fellow officer. Colonel Hoffman—a prominent member of the community and the protégé of Senator Riggs—had turned out to be a child molester who'd used his camp to torture girls. Sergeant Delgado was a former gang member, a murderer who'd killed Tommy and Allen Chambers in that warehouse years ago. And now Delgado had brazenly murdered Hoffman, along with the police guards protecting him. No wonder she looked ready to explode.

"What's going on?" he asked her.

"Colonel Hoffman's dead."

So he'd heard. "What happened?"

She opened her mouth to answer, but a *thump* came from the door. She whirled around, one hand going for her gun in its holster. But after several seconds, when nothing more happened, she turned to face them again.

"Move over there," she told Brynn, motioning to the side of the bed farthest from the door. "Stand near the wall and behind the bed."

Brynn shot him a questioning look, and Parker nodded for her to comply. Lieutenant Lewis was taking precautions, getting a civilian out of the line of fire in case shots broke out. But it also made it harder for Brynn to escape.

An unsettled feeling took root inside him, a sliver of alarm clamoring hard. Something about this situation felt off. Something besides the obvious. "Why would Delgado kill Hoffman?" he asked Lieutenant Lewis.

She held up her hand. "Hold on." She went back to the door and peeked outside, her voice low as she consulted with the guard.

The feeling of wrongness hit him again.

He rubbed his unshaven jaw, trying to clear his mind. He knew he was missing something important, a detail wavering just beyond his reach. Cursing the painkillers turning his brain to sludge, he struggled to figure out what.

Delgado had murdered his brother. Both Delgado and Colonel Hoffman had worked in Homicide at the time. One of them, presumably Delgado, had intercepted Brynn's photos, destroying crucial evidence that could have convicted him of the crime.

Vern Collins had been Hoffman's partner. He'd investigated Tommy's case. He'd eventually left the force and taken a job at the Hagerstown prison, where that gang member had been released. Hoffman had probably asked him to do it, hoping to hide his pedophile activities by killing Brynn.

All that seemed to make sense. But why would Delgado kill Colonel Hoffman? Had the colonel found out about the murders? Was Delgado trying to keep him from revealing the truth? But why kill him *now,* after Lieutenant Lewis had caught on to his activities—when it wouldn't do any good?

Blowing out his breath in frustration, Parker ran

through the facts again. Vern Collins was Hoffman's partner. Collins had left the force after Tommy's case was closed, due to a sexual harassment charge...which in itself was rather odd. There hadn't been that many women on the force back then. And sexual harassment had been a hot topic, mandating sensitivity training and workshops. Even the most bullheaded officers had understood that any insinuation of harassment could ruin their careers.

Parker's gaze went to Brynn. She stood beside the bed, a frown creasing her face, that bruise standing out in sharp relief on her pale cheek. He shifted his gaze to Lieutenant Lewis, who was walking back across the room.

A memory floated at the edge of his awareness, something he couldn't quite grasp. Something about Lieutenant Lewis... She stopped beside the bed and met his eyes. And, suddenly, it clicked into place. "You were there, too—in Homicide, back when Tommy died."

Surprise rippled across her face. She whipped open her leather bag and pulled out a gun—with a suppressor screwed on the end. "Don't move." The gun swerved between Brynn and him.

He stared at her aghast, the realization sinking in they were trapped in the room with a killer.

Why hadn't he figured it out before?

He stole a glance at Brynn. Her eyes were dark with shock.

"That's right," Lieutenant Lewis confirmed. "I'd been detailed there."

On temporary duty—which explained why she wasn't on the list. There would have been a personnel order floating around back then assigning her to the unit, but until she was posted there permanently, they wouldn't have entered her name in the books. "And they didn't pick you up."

The lieutenant's eyes flashed. "I didn't want to stay there. I wanted something bigger than homicide. Intelligence was a better choice."

Of course. And an EEOC victim—the victim of an Equal Employment Opportunity Commission violation—had power. The commissioner would have bent over backward to avoid adverse publicity, giving her any job she desired.

Then another realization sank in. "You invented the charge."

Her mouth formed a little smirk. "Collins was a fool, like most men are. It was easy to set him up."

And it began to make sense. The person behind the pillar in the warehouse had been a woman—a tall, thin woman—not a man. "You were the gang leader, the one who ran the City of the Dead."

"No, I wasn't. I never belonged to the gang. I don't approve of that type of thing."

"But you killed Allen Chambers."

"I had to. My cousin Dustin got in over his head. He didn't understand what being in a gang really meant. And when they ordered him to execute that man, he chickened out."

"The other gang member was your cousin?" Hell, no wonder he'd looked familiar. He'd resembled Terry Lewis, a woman Parker had known for years. They had the same oddly narrow face.

She shook her head. "I told you, I wasn't a gang member. But I had to bail Dustin out. The gang would have killed him if he didn't come through. And I'd practically raised him. He was my only family. I couldn't let him die."

"So you shot Allen Chambers," Brynn said, her voice trembling. "And then you killed Tommy."

The lieutenant curled her lips. "Allen Chambers was a heroin addict, a useless piece of humanity. And Tommy…" She shrugged. "He got in the way."

Parker worked his jaw, struggling to control his own rage now. "He was my brother."

The lieutenant spared him a look of disdain. "He would have died sooner or later. You know what the mortality rate is for drug addicts. I did him a favor, just like Chambers. I saved them both from an overdose."

Parker stared at her in shock, her complete lack of remorse robbing him of words. He'd worked side by side with this woman for years. He'd respected her. He'd admired her moral rectitude. And she'd murdered his brother without a flicker of guilt.

"And then you tried to kill me," Brynn cut in, sounding just as numb. "You tried to kill my friends."

"That was your own fault. You never should have been there that day. And you took those photos."

"Which you destroyed," Parker said, drawing her attention back to him.

Terry Lewis sighed. "I told you. I didn't have any choice. I had to protect Dustin. And there was no way I was going to prison for killing an addict. He was worthless. No one cared if he died. I did the world a favor by getting him off the streets."

"A favor?" he scoffed. "Is that what you just did for Hoffman and those guards?"

"They had to go." Her eyes burned. She leveled the gun, and his heart leaped into his throat. They didn't stand a chance. The instant they moved, she was going to fire. And the noise wouldn't alert the guards, not with a suppressor on the gun. He couldn't even sacrifice himself to save Brynn.

"Don't move," she warned, as if guessing his thoughts.

He swallowed hard, knowing the only solution was to overpower her before she could murder Brynn. But she'd positioned them perfectly, making it impossible for him to move in time.

He met Brynn's eyes. Her gaze flicked to the bed, then back. He frowned, not sure what she was signaling, but then he understood. *The nurse call button.* He'd draped it over the railing. She couldn't reach it, but maybe he could.

Trying not to draw the lieutenant's notice, he slid a glance at the cord. The control was dangling off the bed, out of her line of sight. But could he reach it without tipping her off?

"So why did you kill Hoffman?" he asked again, needing to distract her. "What was the colonel's role in this?" Praying she wouldn't notice, he inched his hand toward the edge of the bed.

"Hoffman." She grimaced. "Talk about a waste of humanity. He was a sleazy little pervert who didn't deserve to live."

"So you knew what he was like?" He reached the cord and tugged.

She nodded. "I found some photos he kept in his desk. Really nasty stuff. And after that…"

"You blackmailed him."

"We had an agreement. I kept quiet about his twisted hobby, and he did favors for me. But he screwed up in the end. He needed to get rid of Brynn, but he was too squeamish to do it himself. He put Markus Jenkins on her trail, but you found her first. And when it seemed you'd joined forces and weren't going to bring her in, we decided you both had to go. But Markus Jenkins failed to kill you, too. And now it's up to me."

"But why kill us?" Brynn asked, the desperation in her voice gutting his heart. "Why not let us go? We didn't know you were involved. We never would have connected it to you."

"Parker would have." She waved the gun at him, and he froze, thinking she'd seen him move. But she continued speaking, and he seized the remote control. "Once he joined up with you, I knew he'd figure it out."

"Still—"

"Look." Her voice hardened. "It doesn't matter. I have my orders to kill you. I'm not the only one who wants you dead."

Parker blinked, her revelation making him pause. Someone else wanted to kill them? "Like who?"

But Lieutenant Lewis only shook her head. "I can't tell you that. This thing is huge. It goes way up the chain. Powerful people are involved, more than you'll ever guess. You have no idea how big this is."

She cocked the hammer on her gun.

Parker's pulse raced. Knowing he only had seconds, he ran his finger over the buttons, trying to decide which one to push. He didn't dare hit them all and risk tipping Lieutenant Lewis off.

Sweat popped out on his brow. He tried to envision the remote control, but he'd hardly glanced at it as he'd shoved it aside. He slid his finger to the button in the center, then paused.

Brynn cleared her throat. He spared her a glance,

and she raised her chin in a barely perceptible nod. His heart warming, he sent her a mental thanks, then jabbed the button to call the nurse.

A signal trilled down the hall. The red light beside the bed turned on. Parker silently swore, hoping Lieutenant Lewis wouldn't attribute it to him.

But then a shout rang out. Footsteps pounded in the hall. Lieutenant Lewis glanced at the light, and fury blazed through her eyes. She jerked her gun toward Brynn. "Don't move or she's dead," she warned, freezing Parker in place.

The door swung open behind her, and Enrique Delgado appeared in the room, flanked by several cops. They all had their weapons drawn.

"Drop your weapon," Delgado ordered.

The lieutenant stilled. Fear flashed through her gaze, every shred of color fading from her face. But her gun never veered from Brynn.

Parker sat frozen in horror, understanding how this would end. The lieutenant knew she couldn't escape. She wouldn't leave here alive. But if she was going to die today, she intended to take someone down with her—*Brynn*.

The lieutenant's hand began to shake. Sweat glistened on her waxy face. Then her expression changed, her eyes filling with resignation. And Parker knew in that instant she was going to shoot.

Desperation screamed through his skull. He had to do something. He had to stop her somehow. But the slightest move, and Brynn would die.

Her trigger finger moved. Knowing it was hopeless, Parker dove off the bed toward Brynn, flinging himself toward her with all his strength. But she was too far away.

The gun went off, the suppressor silencing all but a quiet pop. Brynn cried out. Her eyes flew to his, her shock turning to pain. Blood welled through her shirt. She clutched her chest with her free hand and staggered toward him, then sank to the tiled floor.

Gunfire broke out, the officers mowing down Terry Lewis where she stood.

But he'd arrived too late to save Brynn.

Chapter 18

The rules be damned.

Flanked by half a dozen guards, Parker strode down the hallway to Brynn's hospital room the following afternoon, determined to get inside. He was still pushing his IV pole, still wearing the ridiculous, open-backed hospital gown, but he'd added a robe and socks. Police swarmed the hall. Access to the floor was tightly restricted, the security extreme. In the twenty-four hours since that shooting, he hadn't spent a single moment alone.

Outside the hospital was even worse. This was the biggest story to hit Baltimore in decades. It was a complete media circus with news vans and reporters everywhere. And every law enforcement agency in the region had flooded the hospital—state and city police, the ATF and FBI.

A nurse trotted up beside him. "Excuse me, sir. You need to get back into bed. You're not authorized to get up yet."

"Try to stop me," he muttered, striding past her. He'd twiddled his thumbs long enough. He wasn't going to wait another second to see the woman he loved—no matter what the regulations said.

He neared Brynn's room—obvious by the armed guards blocking the door—the desperate need to see her hardening his resolve. Watching Lieutenant Lewis shoot Brynn had been the worst moment of his life—worse than seeing Hoffman hold her at gunpoint, worse than hearing about her abuse, worse even than learning about Tommy's death. He'd never recover from that heart-stopping moment when he'd thought that she was dead.

And he'd been frantic ever since—during the hours she'd spent in surgery, during the night as she'd lain in the ICU, hovering between life and death. Now they'd finally moved her to a recovery room under heavy police protection, refusing to let him near.

But enough was enough. Nothing was going to stop him from reaching her side. He had to see for himself that she'd survived.

A second later, he reached her room. He recognized several police officers, including the one blocking the door. "Martinez," he said with a nod.

"Hey, McCall. Love the dress," Martinez quipped. "You here to give us a fashion show?"

His mouth quirking up, Parker flipped him a rude hand signal, and everyone around them laughed.

But then the guard's expression sobered. "Sorry,

man, but she can't have visitors yet. Nobody's supposed to go inside."

"I'm not here. You didn't see me."

"Hell, McCall. You know I can't let you inside."

Parker leveled him a gaze.

The guards exchanged glances. Martinez heaved out a sigh. "Fine, you're not here. I didn't see you come by. But you owe me for this." He moved aside to let him pass.

Still wheeling the IV pole, Parker opened the door and stepped inside. His gaze arrowed straight to the bed, and his heart made a crazy loop, fear and love tangling up inside. Brynn looked so small, so defenseless, so pale. But she was alive.

Her eyes fluttered open. Her gaze connected with his, and he struggled to breathe. Dark circles underscored her eyes. The bruise stood out on her cheek. Her hair was a messy splash of color against her white pillow. She still had her arm in the sling. But now bandages covered her chest. Cords ran across the bed like wires at an electrical substation, connecting her to a bank of machines. Black stitches marched across her scalp, trailing a smear of brown antiseptic over one temple. She looked like an alley cat who'd barely survived a brawl with a Rottweiler.

She was the most beautiful woman he'd ever seen.

"Hi," she whispered,

His throat suddenly thick, emotions somersaulting inside him, he went to her side. For an endless moment he simply gazed into her eyes, too overcome to speak. There was so much he needed to tell her, so much he had to explain.

He managed to clear his throat. "How are you feeling?"

The corner of her mouth slid up. "Like I've been shot. But I'm not in any pain. The drugs are doing their job."

"Good." He couldn't bear the thought of her suffering. He wanted to scoop her up and hold her close, to run away with her to someplace safe.

Like he should have done from the start.

His legs unsteady, he pulled up a chair and sat, cursing his weakened state. He could only imagine how she must feel, despite her insistence that she was fine.

Needing a moment to compose himself, he glanced around the room. "Who sent flowers?"

"My agent. She phoned a while ago."

"So she's all right?"

Brynn nodded. "She's at home now. But she still has the bodyguard. She found out who took that photo, by the way, the one that appeared in the newspaper."

The photo that had started it all. "Who was it?"

"A reporter. He'd been following her for months, watching everything she did. He saw me meet with her a couple of times and figured it out."

"I'm sorry."

"I'm not. At least Hoffman is dead now. And we found out who killed Tommy."

Unable to resist, Parker reached out and took her hand, the soft, silky warmth of her skin, the fragile feel of her slender wrist reminding him of how perilously close she'd come to death. He gazed into her eyes, struggling for the words to say, his heart kickboxing in his chest. "God, Brynn. I thought for sure I'd lost you."

"Yeah." Her voice sounded rough. She squeezed his

hand, her luminous eyes on his. He battled back a rush of memories, not wanting to relive the terror of hearing that deadly pop, of seeing her fall to the floor.

"I was scared," she admitted. "When she pulled out that gun…I didn't see how we were going to survive."

They nearly hadn't. *She* nearly hadn't. And it was all his fault.

"I'm so sorry," he said, his voice raw. "I should have figured it out sooner."

She tightened her grip on his hand. "You couldn't have known she was involved."

"I knew something was off when you told me Hoffman was dead. It didn't make any sense." But he'd been too slow, his mind too foggy to figure it out. And as a result, Brynn had nearly died.

"What happened to her?" she asked.

"You don't know?"

She shook her head. "No one's told me anything yet."

"She's dead. Suicide by cop. She knew she couldn't escape, so she decided to die instead. That's why she shot you. She knew that as soon as she fired at you, they'd take her down."

Brynn squeezed his hand, a myriad of emotions passing through her eyes—relief, understanding, sympathy. "I'm sorry, Parker."

He ran his thumb over her knuckles, his chest suddenly tight. He knew what she meant. She wasn't sorry that Lieutenant Lewis had died. She was sorry that another officer had betrayed him. She understood how deep this cut, undermining everything he'd once believed.

But had he acted any better toward her? He'd lied

about his relationship with her stepfather, destroying her trust—just when she'd needed him most.

He had to plead for forgiveness. He needed to tell her he loved her and ask for another chance. "Brynn," he began. He swallowed hard, regrets piling up inside. "I'm sorry. I never meant to deceive you. I mean, at first I did. I didn't know you. I thought you had something to do with Tommy's death. And Hoffman showed me your file."

"It's pretty convincing."

He nodded, his throat dust-dry. "I didn't know who to believe. But I realized pretty fast that something was off. Those reports didn't match what I saw about you, the woman I was getting to know. And when I finally figured it out, I didn't want to hurt you. You'd already suffered too much. I was trying to find a good time to tell to you. But I really did plan to tell you the truth."

"I believe you."

A rush of relief spiraled through him. Declarations crowded his throat—his hopes for their future, his need to stay with her forever, *his love*.

But a sharp knock came from the door. Then Sergeant Delgado strolled in, accompanied by several guards. Delgado's gaze met his, and his mouth kicked into a smile. "I figured I'd find you here."

Parker frowned and released Brynn's hand. Of all the people to show up now… He gave him a reluctant nod. "Have you met Brynn?"

"Not officially."

"This is Sergeant Delgado," Parker told her.

The sergeant swaggered over to Brynn, an interested gleam in his eyes, and clasped her hand. Parker's eyes narrowed, his face heating when Delgado didn't let go. But the sergeant was in Don Juan mode, puffing out his chest, flashing her the smile reputed to make women swoon.

Two seconds, Parker decided, working his jaw. And then he'd wipe that smirk off his playboy face.

Brynn extracted her hand, then shot Parker a questioning look. "He's been working undercover," he explained, wishing to hell he'd back off.

But Delgado cocked one hip and folded his arms across his chest—to better display his biceps, Parker guessed. "One of our informants gave us a tip," Delgado told Brynn. "He said there were rumors that a senior officer was involved with child pornography, but he didn't know who it was. The trail seemed to lead to Colonel Hoffman, but we didn't have any proof. So internal affairs sent me to the cold case squad, thinking I could monitor him better from there."

So Delgado hadn't gotten his position through brownnosing. Parker's faith in the police force rose. "What the lieutenant said—that something big was going on—any chance that's true?"

Delgado switched his gaze to him. "Yeah, we think so, but we don't have any leads yet. We were trying to bring her in alive, to interrogate her." He shrugged. "About the only thing we know right now is that whoever this mastermind is, he has power."

Power? "You mean like another cop?"

"Maybe, but our sources are all tight-lipped. Whoever this guy is, he's got them running scared." Delgado turned to Brynn again. "And until we catch him, you're in danger. As soon as the hospital discharges you, we want to put you in protective custody."

A startled look entered Brynn's eyes. "You mean a safe house?"

Delgado gave her a nod. "Probably some place out West. Wyoming, maybe. Just until we figure out what's going on."

"But why would he want to kill me? My stepfather's gone. Lieutenant Lewis and her cousin are dead—and they're the ones I saw in the warehouse. I thought I was safe."

To Delgado's credit, sympathy filled his eyes. "I wish you were. But someone ordered Lewis to kill you. Both of you. And this mastermind appears to have a lot of influence, even within the police department. Until we bring him in, we need to put you somewhere safe."

But Brynn's mouth turned flat. A stubborn look entered her eyes. "I'm not hiding out again."

"I know it sounds drastic," Delgado said. "But—"

"No, absolutely not. I'm not going into hiding again."

Parker caught his eye. "Listen, Sergeant. Give her some time to think about it, okay? She just got out of surgery."

"Fine. We'll talk about it later." He looked at Brynn again. "We need another statement from you, too, but that can wait until you're ready." He gave Parker a nod and left the room.

For a minute, neither spoke. Parker finally broke the silence with a sigh. "As much as I hate to agree with Delgado, he's right. This isn't a joke. They don't put people into protective custody unless there's a good reason."

"I don't need to think about it. I'm not going."

"Brynn—"

"Listen, Parker. I know you think I'm being unreasonable. But I've spent most of my life on the run. Ever since I left home I've been hiding, always looking over my shoulder, always worrying that Hoffman would catch up to me. And when Tommy got shot it was even worse. I had to keep moving all the time. When you showed up, it was the first time I'd allowed myself to do anything even remotely permanent—to own a house, to have a garden, to have even a hint of a normal life. And I can't go back to hiding out again. I'm not going to keep living in fear."

"It's only until they track this guy down." He shifted forward, taking hold of her hand again. "For God's sake, Brynn. I couldn't stand it if something happened to you. That moment when Lieutenant Lewis shot you…" His voice broke. A huge lump blocked his throat.

Her eyes softened, all trace of her temper gone. "I know," she whispered. "I felt the same way in the cabin when Hoffman shot you."

"Then you can see why…"

"I can't do it, Parker. It would kill me to hide again." Her gaze held his. "Are you going to do it?"

"I can't. I need to stay here and help track him down."

"Then you're not quitting your job?"

"I thought about it," he admitted. "First Hoffman, then Lieutenant Lewis…"

She squeezed his hand. "I know how much that hurts."

"Yeah." Their betrayal hurt all right. Even after his father's arrest, he'd believed in the integrity of the force—an idealism he'd now lost for good. He'd become more realistic over the past few days, more jaded. The blinders he'd worn were gone.

"I might switch to internal affairs, though. There seems to be a need for that."

Her eyes warmed. "You make a wonderful knight in shining armor, Parker McCall."

"Hardly." He'd nearly failed her. "But the bad guys are still in the minority. Most cops are good."

"Like Delgado."

"Yeah." He shook his head. Delgado had turned out to be one of the good guys, even if he was still obnoxious as hell. "But the main thing is that I can't give up. You taught me that."

"*I* did?" She looked surprised.

"Yeah. Your courage... You never gave up."

"How can you say that? All I've ever done is run."

"You survived. There's a difference. And you stopped running when people needed you. You risked everything to help them, even when no one believed you. You're the most courageous person I know."

Her face turned pink. Her gaze dropped to their joined hands. "You took risks, too. You didn't hand me over to Hoffman, even when you thought I'd caused Tommy's death."

The corner of his mouth edged up. "Yeah. I've been breaking the rules since I met you." But he no longer cared. He didn't need the regulations to guide him. He knew who he was inside.

And he knew who he needed. *Brynn.*

His heart drummed hard. His throat turned parched,

nerves stampeding around in his chest. *Now or never.* "I love you, Brynn."

Shock flickered through her eyes. Then she covered her face with her hand, her sudden silence damning, as if she couldn't bear to look at him.

His heart plummeted. He'd waited too long. She wasn't going to forgive him. He'd destroyed any chance he'd had at love.

Desperation clawed through his gut. He had to convince her. He couldn't stand a lifetime without Brynn. "I need you," he said. "I love you so much."

She opened her eyes, and the joy in them crashed through his heart. "I love you, too. I didn't want to. I was scared. I've spent my entire life trying to keep people out. But you snuck through all that. I couldn't keep you out of my heart. And I fell in love with you."

Happiness swelled in his chest. Lightness flooded through him, demolishing years of loneliness. "I know this isn't romantic. The hospital. These machines. I don't even have a ring. But I promise I'll ask you again, someplace better. With flowers, champagne, whatever you want. But I have to know... Will you marry me?"

Her lush mouth trembled, her eyes shining with tears. "I don't want champagne. I just want you."

His heart went berserk. "Is that a yes?"

"Parker..." Tears brimmed in her eyes. "You gave me hope. You taught me to dream again. Do you have any idea how precious that is? Of course I'll marry you."

He surged to his feet. Hardly able to contain himself, he perched on the edge of her bed, careful not to tangle her cords. Then he cradled her jaw and stared into her gorgeous eyes. "I'll keep you safe. I promise, Brynn.

No one will hurt you again. If you won't go into protective custody, then you can stay with me."

"Forever?"

"I promise."

She lifted her hand to his face. He slanted his mouth over hers, ignoring the bandages and bruises and pains. Focusing on her taste, her incredible feel, the miracle of the woman he would love for all time. The woman his brother had brought to him. The woman who'd healed his heart.

And knew he was exactly where he wanted to stay.

* * * * *

Don't miss Haley's story, A KISS TO DIE FOR, the next thrilling chapter of BURIED SECRETS, *Gail Barrett's exciting new miniseries for Harlequin Romantic Suspense! On sale August 2013, wherever Harlequin books are sold.*

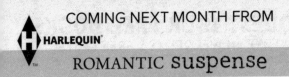

REQUEST YOUR FREE BOOKS!
2 FREE NOVELS PLUS 2 FREE GIFTS!

ROMANTIC suspense

Sparked by danger, fueled by passion

YES! Please send me 2 FREE Harlequin® Romantic Suspense novels and my 2 FREE gifts (gifts are worth about $10). After receiving them, if I don't wish to receive any more books, I can return the shipping statement marked "cancel." If I don't cancel, I will receive 4 brand-new novels every month and be billed just $4.74 per book in the U.S. or $5.24 per book in Canada. That's a savings of at least 14% off the cover price! It's quite a bargain! Shipping and handling is just 50¢ per book in the U.S. and 75¢ per book in Canada.* I understand that accepting the 2 free books and gifts places me under no obligation to buy anything. I can always return a shipment and cancel at any time. Even if I never buy another book, the two free books and gifts are mine to keep forever.

240/340 HDN F45N

Name	(PLEASE PRINT)
Address	Apt. #
City	State/Prov.	Zip/Postal Code

Signature (if under 18, a parent or guardian must sign)

Mail to the **Harlequin®** Reader Service:
IN U.S.A.: P.O. Box 1867, Buffalo, NY 14240-1867
IN CANADA: P.O. Box 609, Fort Erie, Ontario L2A 5X3

Want to try two free books from another line?
Call 1-800-873-8635 or visit www.ReaderService.com.

* Terms and prices subject to change without notice. Prices do not include applicable taxes. Sales tax applicable in N.Y. Canadian residents will be charged applicable taxes. Offer not valid in Quebec. This offer is limited to one order per household. Not valid for current subscribers to Harlequin Romantic Suspense books. All orders subject to credit approval. Credit or debit balances in a customer's account(s) may be offset by any other outstanding balance owed by or to the customer. Please allow 4 to 6 weeks for delivery. Offer available while quantities last.

Your Privacy—The Harlequin® Reader Service is committed to protecting your privacy. Our Privacy Policy is available online at www.ReaderService.com or upon request from the Harlequin Reader Service.

We make a portion of our mailing list available to reputable third parties that offer products we believe may interest you. If you prefer that we not exchange your name with third parties, or if you wish to clarify or modify your communication preferences, please visit us at www.ReaderService.com/consumerchoice or write to us at Harlequin Reader Service Preference Service, P.O. Box 9062, Buffalo, NY 14269. Include your complete name and address.

HRS13R

Turning his back on Gabby, Trevor strode out of the living room.

The moment he did, Gabby immediately followed him.
Since the area was still crowded with people, she only managed
to catch up to him just at the front door.

Trevor spared her a look that would have frosted most people's
toes. "Where do you think you're going?" he asked.

He sounded so angry, she thought. Not that she blamed him,
but she still wished he wouldn't glare at her like that. She hadn't
put Avery in harm's way on purpose. It was a horrible accident.

"With you," she answered.

"Oh no, you're not," he cried. "You're staying here," he ordered, waving his hand around the foyer, as if a little bit of
magic was all that was needed to transform the situation.

Stubbornly, Gabby held her ground, surprising Trevor even

though he gave no indication. "You're going to need help," she insisted.

Not if it meant taking help from her, he thought.

"No, I am not," he replied tersely, being just as stubborn as she was. "I've got to find my daughter. I don't have time to babysit you."

"Nobody's asking you to. I can be a help. I *can,*" she insisted when he looked at her unconvinced. "Where are you going?" she wanted to know.

"To the rodeo."

That didn't make any sense. Unless— "You have a lead?" she asked, lowering her voice.

"I'm going to see Dylan and tell him his mother's dead," he informed her. "That's not a lead, that's a death sentence for his soul. You still want to come along?" he asked mockingly. Trevor was rather certain that his self-appointed task would make her back off.

Trevor was too direct and someone needed to soften the blow a little. Gabby figured she was elected. "Yes, I do," she replied firmly, managing to take the man completely by surprise.

**Don't miss
THE COLTON RANSOM
by Marie Ferrarella**

**Available July 2013 from
Harlequin Romantic Suspense
wherever books are sold.**

All Arizona Ivy needs is one good story to
get her career kick-started. Investigating
weapons smuggling, she gets mixed up with
sexy military weapons engineer Braden McCrae.
While one lead after another brings them closer
to exposing the arms dealer who appears to
have kidnapped his sister, Braden begins to
realize he and Arizona have more in common
than a thirst for adventure. She's found her
story—but she might have lost her heart.

Look for **FRONT PAGE AFFAIR**
next month by Jennifer Morey.

Available wherever books and ebooks are sold.

Heart-racing romance, high-stakes suspense!

HRS27831

HARLEQUIN®

ROMANTIC suspense

Security genius Campbell Steele goes undercover to out the internal threat sabotaging Abby McBane's company. But when Abby becomes the target, Campbell sees a greater threat to his heart.

Look for *THE PARIS ASSIGNMENT*
next month by new
Harlequin® Romantic Suspense®
author Addison Fox.

Available wherever books and ebooks are sold.

Heart-racing romance, high-stakes suspense!

HRS27832

Love the Harlequin book you just read?

Your opinion matters.

Review this book on your favorite
book site, review site, blog or your own
social media properties and share
your opinion with other readers!

HARLEQUIN®

A Romance FOR EVERY MOOD™

Stay up-to-date on all your
romance-reading news with the
Harlequin Shopping Guide,
featuring bestselling authors, exciting new
miniseries, books to watch and more!

The newest issue will be delivered right to you
with our compliments! There are 4 each year.

Signing up is easy.

EMAIL

ShoppingGuide@Harlequin.ca

WRITE TO US

HARLEQUIN BOOKS
Attention: Customer Service Department
P.O. Box 9057, Buffalo, NY 14269-9057

OR PHONE

1-800-873-8635 in the United States
1-888-343-9777 in Canada

Please allow 4-6 weeks for delivery of the first issue by mail.